Let's Go
if
You're Going

Let's Go
if
You're Going

STEPHEN PATTERSON

LET'S GO IF YOU'RE GOING

iUniverse books may be ordered through booksellers or by contacting:

iUniverse
1663 Liberty Drive
Bloomington, IN 47403
www.iuniverse.com
844-349-9409

ISBN: 978-1-6632-3872-6 (sc)
ISBN: 978-1-6632-3871-9 (e)

Library of Congress Control Number: 2022907394

Print information available on the last page.

iUniverse rev. date: 04/26/2022

Special Thank You

I would like to thank all of my friends
and family who help live and
inspire the book and story. Those who helped make Sanford
Central High School and the Lee County Fair so special.

"A special thank you to Joan Kareiva. Joan expertise,
input and professionalism served as a valuable
resource in bringing the book to life."

Also, a special thank you, to McGill Management, Winston
Salem North Carolina for insight support and direction.

Let's Go if You're Going

Robert Brent Kirby, known by his friends as Brick, had lived in the town of Sanford, North Carolina, for his entire life. The nickname, "Brick", was given to him by a younger cousin, who one day mistakenly called him Brick rather than Brent, and the rest is history. Brent liked his nickname. It was unique and helped separate him from the usual; for Brick, unusual was always better.

It was the fall of 1969 when Brick would soon be embarking on a new chapter in his life; it was a chapter that would take him out of his beloved Sanford. In a few days, he would be leaving for Elon College— about an hour away from home. He was excited about all the adventures ahead of him but being excited failed to keep him from feeling a little anxious and fearful of what his college life would bring.

The end of summer also marked the time of year for something Brick had always enjoyed; he loved the annual Lee County fair. Almost everything about the fair, from the special foods to the unorthodox sideshows, fascinated Brick. When the time came for its arrival, Brick would spend countless hours on his grandmother's front porch in hopes of catching a glimpse of the cars and trucks bringing the fair to town. Every year, you could rely on an array of colorful vehicles parading through town, announcing the arrival of that year's fair. A year's worth of excitement crammed into one week was exactly that. Once Brick spotted the caravan, his anticipation for the week rose with each passing vehicle. Many in Brick's hometown shared his enthusiasm and anxiously awaited the fair's arrival.

The summer of 1969 was a summer to remember. It had been filled with tension, adventure, and accomplishments. A series of events took place, making it a memorable time for nearly everyone. One such event was Neil Armstrong's walk on the moon where he proclaimed, "That's one small step for man, one giant leap for mankind."

Although Armstrong's walk on the moon had created tremendous national pride, it did little to ease the country's unrest resulting from the civil rights movement and the escalating war in Vietnam. In addition, the younger generation had been captivated by a music festival in Woodstock, New York, where over 400,000 young people came to celebrate peace, love, and rock 'n roll. So much was happening throughout the country. Social unrest as well as political unrest were contributing to a much-needed change in the nation.

Earlier that summer, Brick graduated from Sanford Central High School. It is said that when one door closes, another one opens: for Brick, the next-door would-be college. For him and so many others his age, Bob Dylan's song, "The Times They are A-Changin'," rang true.

Brick was now on the cusp of adulthood. Not only had he finished high school, but he had also registered with Selective Service for the draft. Brick felt the draft was an undesired consequence of turning eighteen; however, upon turning eighteen all males were obligated to register. Once you became draft eligible, you could be called into the service, and that came with the distinct possibility of going off to the war in Vietnam.

Brick knew and understood the duty of serving one's country, but he, like so many others his age, was unsure of the purpose for the war. From what he had learned thus far, it appeared few could explain why the United States was even in the war or what would be accomplished at the endgame.

For Brick, the war and the draft created a fear of the unknown. He had learned from the few people he knew who had returned home from the war that it was horrific. He knew if drafted he would serve and would not consider following the lead of many young people who chose to flee to Canada in hopes of avoiding both the draft and the war. But Brick prayed that would be a decision he would not be forced to make.

Brick's family and those who knew him would have been surprised to learn of his worries; few saw him as anything other than a jokester. It was true that he would be the first to crack a joke at a somber situation, but this carefree attitude failed to prevent him from having concerns over the plight of the country and his future.

Brick himself was conscious of how much turmoil was occurring in the country. Social unrest was contributing to the war in Vietnam, and the civil rights movement was bringing forth its efforts to generate change.

All worries aside, Brick was still happy knowing the county fair would be arriving a few weeks earlier than normal, and for Brick it would give him a much-needed distraction away from the societal turmoil he was feeling. He knew that once the fair was in town, the fairgrounds would come to life with thrills of excitement.

The 1969 county fair would mark the thirty-second year of the community celebration and would run six full days at the end of August. A vigorous advertising campaign led by the local Lions Club announced the fair's arrival and promoted all the attractions that would soon light up the midway.

Brick loved the wide variety of venues that would light up the midway. Games food and shows would add to the local attractions of beauty pageants, livestock shows. This year the talk of the fair had failed to trigger Brick's normal reaction. He had been preoccupied with getting ready for his move to Elon and starting college.

His pending move wasn't the only thing occupying Brick's mind and time. Like most teenage boys of the day, he was also distracted by his on-again, off-again relationship with Emily Dixon. They had dated throughout their senior year and all of the summer. Brick would happily identify Emily as his girlfriend, but he wasn't sure she would do the same. Their relationship was a work-in-progress at best. Brick never one for great self-confidence worried that their courtship would not survive both attending separate colleges in different parts of the state. Such worry did him little good as, he knew if he kept it up, he would turn gray years before his time.

Brick's family got him hooked on the fair. Not only did he attend the fair with his family his grandmother would often enter the cooking and sewing compaction bringing on her share of winning ribbons. As a child he would wait on his grandmother's porch anxious for the fairs schedule to arrive in town. Brick found her front porch swing the ideal spot to await the arrival.

Even with those front-porch swing days behind him, his mind returned to it all when he walked out of Main Street's Lee Drug Store. Maybe it was destiny; when Brick came out of the store, he caught a view of this year's caravan of attractions making its way toward the fairgrounds. It was here!

Brick once again came face to face with the fair's arrival. A convoy of Howard's Amusements' vehicles were once again bringing Lee County's fair to town. As Brick walked toward his car, he smiled as the trucks began to pass. It was as though fate had intervened. The procession of cars, trailers, and trucks transporting a week's worth of fun was now winding down Main Street. Brick understood with each passing vehicle, a transformation would soon begin. A temporary city specializing in fun and amusements would shortly rise from the grounds as the community of Howard's Amusements.

Sunday was moving day for Howard's—the day the attractions would be uprooted from one location and moved to the next. Workers would disassemble it all and recreate it hours later in another locale. Brick knew the arrival meant that the workers would spend most of the day and well into the night assembling the attractions for the coming week's festivities.

The first car he spotted was an aging, dilapidated Chevy Biscayne station wagon suffering from the wear and tear of constant travel. Painted on the front panel was an advertisement for the coming attractions:

Howard's Amusements
(Fun and Thrills for All)
Simpsonville, SC

The rear of the car was weighted down by a trailer in tow. The sight made Brick smile. He realized how fortunate he was to have a front-row seat once again to the arrival of the fair.

Next up was a procession of trucks bringing a wide assortment of entertainment venues, along with vehicles transporting various rides, games, sideshows, and everything in between. The sight of the carnival's caravan brought back Brick's childhood fantasies. For him, it was always a special time when he could see the trucks heading down the highway. Brick knew that in the next few hours a smorgasbord of entertainment would begin rising from the grounds, offering something for everyone to enjoy. Another year of fun was coming to town. Arriving with Howard's Amusements were trucks transporting Hertzog Midway Foods. Hertzog would offer up treats for the coming week—mainly fair favorites, like corndogs and French fries.

Brick leaned back on his car to enjoy the passing of the trucks. He was taken back to the days sitting in his grandmother's swing. Age and adolescent responsibilities may have tempered his excitement, but his accelerating heartbeat at the sight of the trucks gave a different story. A truck with sections of the Ferris wheel soon passed, and then came trailers hauling kiddie rides and more—all needing to be unloaded and assembled.

After a variety of attractions passed, he saw the one truck of which he was hoping to catch a glimpse. It hauled the show that had always stimulated his imagination as well as the imagination of most of the men who attended the fair. The infamous hoochie-coochie show would once again grace the midway. It was the show that enticed and entertained those who dared to attend. A truck pulling a trailer with a crude marquee proclaimed the "All-Girl Nude Revue" was coming to town.

The "All-Girl Nude Revue" would occupy a large tent protected by burlap curtains helping to separate the public from the paying customers. The tent would turn into a fantasy land of hopes and dreams for Brick and his friends—a fantasy land of sexual excitement. Brick, like so many others, could have his sexual desires aroused by the erotic exploits of the women of the revue. Everyone was enthralled with the mysterious women who danced behind the curtains, making imaginations run wild.

The nude show was known by many monikers: "The Female Revue," "The Girly Show," or "The Hoochie-Coochie Show." The name mattered little; what was important was the action on the stage. It was here women would entice and tease every man in attendance with their sultry dances, inviting moves, and most of all, their total lack of clothing.

Brick's earliest memories of the fair occurred when he was a child attending with his parents. He could remember the family walking the midway and at times lingering out in front of the sideshows but never in front of the girly shows. If anything, when they passed a girly show, their pace quickened. At first, Brick failed to understand his parents' need to rush by the tents that were home to the female revues. These shows appeared to be the more popular ones with the largest crowds out front.

On a few occasions, Brick would catch a glimpse of the ladies standing on a small plank stage out front, but he wasn't sure why. Over time, he began to understand more of what the shows were offering. He enjoyed hearing the barker make his colorful introductions of the ladies while encouraging all men to come inside and see the show.

In the days of attending the fair with his parents, even the intros were short-lived as his mother would take quick action and hurry the family along. Years would pass before Brick could finally attend the fair without a parent, and once he did, he could hear the barker's entire sales pitch.

Brick was a young adolescent when he finally learned what took place behind the shows' curtains. Knowledge can be frightening, especially when you're young, and knowing what went on in the tents created many fantasies about the ladies and the shows. It wasn't unusual for Brick to dream about the pleasures one could discover behind the curtains. He and most of his friends longed for the day they could experience the shows firsthand. Everyone wanted to see what the ladies had to reveal.

The girls on the outside stage provided Brick and many of his friends with sexual fantasies. Conversations would often be spiced up with thoughts of the ladies, making the boys' imaginations run wild. All anxiously waited for the day their dreams would become a reality—the day they could finally witness the ladies of the midway entertain and share their unique talents in person.

The largest obstacle for the boys was a "Must be 18" sign that hung at the entrance, and in those days eighteen seemed light years away for them. Fortunately, there was no age restriction on the seductive introductions. Young and old alike would be enticed by the provocative looks and suggestive moves each dancer would make on the outside stage. The barker highlighted the talents of the lovelies and with each introduction hoped to increase everyone's yearning to see the show. The barker would often proclaim the ladies were not only beautiful but had extraordinary gifts, i.e., skills they had learned in their native countries from far and exotic lands. The colorful descriptions just added to the mystery that awaited one behind the curtains.

Brick and his friends would plan their loops around the fair to coincide with the introductions. Although too young for admission, they could always enjoy a glimpse of the dancers on the outdoor stage. Here they could see the women and learn of their talents. According to the barker, these ladies of the midway had talents that could only be found behind the curtains. Such talk fueled the boys' desires to one day gain entrance and see for themselves the mysteries these ladies had to offer.

With the truck passing, Brick began to think about the time a few years back when he and a few friends decided to test fate. Still too young for admission, they came up with a plan to see one of the shows. The boys figured they could walk toward the back of the tent when the lights inside were dimmed, and they would then crawl under the unmanned tent to join the paying customers on the inside.

As one would expect, the plan turned out not to be one of their finer moments. The scheme was lame to begin with, but for young boys, a terrible idea has no limits. Their efforts were stopped before they started. An employee spotted them moving to the rear of the attraction and must have known something was up. He began to follow them as they moved to the back of the tent. Feeling their plan was now detected, the boys aborted the attempt and began to run away from the attraction as fast as they could. They ran as if the law was after them, and in this case, maybe it was. Unaware that the man giving chase had long stopped his pursuit, Brick and his friends continued to run, and they didn't stop until they reached the livestock barns. They started laughing, and their unsuccessful attempt became legendary. Their failed efforts again increased everyone's resolve to one day get behind the curtains.

The boys knew their feeble attempt most likely was being played out in fairs across the Carolinas. And why not? Every teenage boy wanted to experience what the lovely ladies had to offer. But on this night, none of the boys were getting into the tent. Another year would pass without witnessing the magic behind the curtains.

Brick's interest in the shows spiked once his older brother, Gary, gained admission behind the curtains. Gary took great delight in stoking the fires of Brick's curiosity with tales of the dancers and their seductive moves. Gary knew it would be a few years before Brick could experience the ladies for himself. Even though it made little difference if the stories were even true, Brick hung onto Gary's every word. Brick and his friends wanted to hear every celestial detail. Gary had firsthand knowledge of the secrets found behind the curtains. Embellished or not, the talk only added to the mysteries of the ladies of the revue. Brick saw it as the gospel according to Gary.

Brick and his friends considered the girly shows a staple on the midway. They were as much a part of the week's attractions as a ride on the Ferris wheel or throwing darts. Brick knew it was only a matter of time before he could experience the same excitement at the revue as he did when riding the Ferris wheel.

During the fall of Brick's junior year in high school, with age eighteen still in his future, Brick and a group of friends positioned themselves out front of a girly show's tent and as usual were enjoying their view of the ladies on the outside stage. They listened to the colorful introductions thinking—one day!

As they watched, the ladies moved back and forth, making tantalizing gestures and seductive exchanges. Their movement only added to everyone's increased desire to see the show. The dancers stood atop a stage adorned with a large sign painted in gold which read, Erotic Show Girls. The ladies would work the crowd, seeking to make eye contact and seductively lure men into the tent. Everyone enjoyed the barker when he would try to rile the men walking past with dates, shouting: "Come on in; she's not going to mind! Stand up for yourself! Come to see the ladies entertain; your date will be glad you did!"

Although there was always a group of men waiting for a show to begin, the barker took great pride in poking the bear with his taunts. The introduction reminded Brick of the lyrics to an old song by The Coasters, "Little Egypt," who pranced out onto the stage with nothing on but a button and a bow. Such talk only stimulated everyone's imagination.

On this night, while Brick and the others were enjoying the introductions, they moved closer to the curtains, hoping to somehow get into the show. The boys even caught the barker's attention as he asked for all healthy men to come forward and enjoy the show. He would spice up his plea by telling everyone the ladies had received specialized training in Paris, France.

It was almost time for the show to begin, and the crowd of men who had been waiting on the outside began to move to the ticket counter. It was then that one of Brick's friends, Glenn Taylor, decided to try once again to gain admission. Glenn moved to the ticket counter, pulled two dollars from his pocket, and handed it to the barker. To the shock of everyone, the man didn't hesitate to take Glenn's cash—never questioning his age—even telling him to enjoy the show. The barker then looked over at Brick and the others and said, "Let's go if you're going fellows, let's go if you're going." Not only was he letting them in, but he was also issuing an invitation. No one hesitated, and they all began pulling money out their pockets as they made their way to the entrance. The day they only dreamed of had finally arrived. The boys were going to see the lovely ladies of the midway. The curtains no longer prevented them from having a night to remember.

Once the boys came face to face with the dancing ladies, they had to laugh. Although they loved the experience, each was sure if the ladies had received any specialized training, it was in Paris, Texas—not Paris, France. But no one cared. They were now behind the curtains, and the ladies were showing it all. The boys were enthralled with the women as they moved about the stage, making everyone blush with excitement. The mysteries behind the curtains had finally been revealed. It would have been impossible for the show to live up to the boys' imaginations, but they still found the experience exciting and unique. Although no one left disappointed, everyone learned a valuable lesson. Much like the rides at the fair, the girly show was short and left you wanting more.

As they exited the tent, each boy knew they had a story to tell. For many, attending the girly shows represented a rite of passage, crossing from adolescence into adulthood. Being allowed behind the curtains meant life would never be the same.

❧

Patrick Odom

Outside the modest, wood-framed building
on East Main Street was a sign:
The Revival Revolutionary Church
Pastor Patrick Odom
All Welcome

O ver the years, the small structure had been the home of many
businesses, from a funeral home to a dental office. But now it
housed Patrick Odom's dream, The Revival Revolutionary Church,
and it was far from distinctive. No one would have believed the building
was a church if not for the sign out front, and Odom himself would
never be mistaken for a minister—much less a polished one.

Patrick Odom received his call to the ministry late in life. Having
worked his share of odd jobs, he was never able to identify an occupation
that felt right for him. He had always been a dreamer whose desires
outweighed his talents.

Odom had struggled for years as he searched for a path to success.
Unfortunately, his search had remained elusive. His greatest passions
were money and recognition, and he was now hoping the church
would bring him both. Odom had looked to the ministry as a conduit
to a successful life. The church would serve as a vessel to provide
him the notoriety and recognition he always craved. He believed that
by establishing The Revival Revolutionary Church, he had finally
discovered a pathway to obtaining his dream.

Odom's calling to the ministry was less about Jesus and more about
fame and fortune. Although his dream was misplaced and still out of
reach, he found himself settling comfortably into his role as a pastor

of the small church. He held on to his desire to grow the church and remained optimistic it would happen. He would finally realize the success that had eluded him for years.

On this particular Sunday, Odom was energized with a vision; a vision that others would join in and help stimulate the growth of the church. He was now laying the foundation for a movement that would not only grow the church but also raise his status in the community. Unfortunately, those attending today's service were little different from the other Sundays. In attendance was the same group of socially challenged misfits who attended regularly. Odom believed the small gathering failed to do his message justice. According to him, his message was larger than the church, as were his hopes and his dream.

Even before he decided to pursue the ministry, he envied the televangelists who served mega churches. Once he joined the ministry, his ambitions of wanting to create a church that would draw hundreds (if not thousands} of members remained big. This dream, like so many before, was fading. To Odom's credit, he had invested more time and effort in developing his church than all of his previous ventures combined. It had been nearly two years since he set out to create The Revival Revolutionary Church, but regrettably, the church had always struggled. Although he was determined, the golden rings of success remained out of his reach.

During his time as a pastor, Odom had regularly looked for opportunities to grow the church and propel his vision. He had enough insight to realize he would never appeal to mainstream Christians. He knew he needed to look beyond the traditional churches for his flock of followers. Odom lacked a firm grasp of the Bible and was intimidated by those who quoted the scripture as if they were reciting the morning news. He felt if he was going to grow a church to the magnitude he hoped for, he would need to find a niche. He focused his efforts on a fringe group of lost souls who, like him, were in search of something. Odom hoped their search would lead others to his church.

Odom's desire for power and wealth was a far cry from the Christian doctrine, but that failed to alter his lofty goals. If he was going to experience success, the church and the congregation would need to grow. His dream was all about the size of his church. He believed that with a large following, he would be welcomed into the religious community of Sanford, and doors he now found shut would begin to open.

Odom pictured himself as a minister enjoying the finer things in life. Over the years, he had been haunted by personal insecurities and often felt dependent on the opinions of others. He felt by becoming a successful pastor, he could change the perceptions of others. His insecurities would all be behind him if he could make The Revival Revolutionary Church's pastor a religious leader in the community. Odom believed his dream could be realized if he could draw followers to his church like a moth to a flame. Sadly, he was not much of a candle.

One of the few times luck was on Odom's side was when his Uncle James (Osborne), offered him the building he was now using to house The Revival Revolutionary Church. His uncle owned the building, but it had remained vacant for nearly two years. Osborne was looking to do something with the property and felt Odom could use the building while fixing it up, which would be beneficial for both of them. He suggested to Odom that he move to Sanford and use the old farmhouse for next to nothing pricewise. The availability of the building was all Odom needed to convince him this was a sweet deal. He jumped at the chance to relocate once Osborne made the offer, so he and his wife Beverly moved to Sanford rather quickly. He felt the move would give him a clean slate and a fresh start.

James Osborne had retired from the US Army and settled in Sanford years earlier, and he had dabbled in real estate and other businesses since his retirement. He owned several properties, but this particular house in Sanford—known as the old Blue place—had remained vacant and was showing signs of neglect. When Odom's uncle made the offer, he explained that not only could it be used as a church, but there was room enough for him and Beverly to live in the back. The transformation of the property into a church would mean Osborne would no longer have to pay property taxes on the building. It was a win–win situation for everyone.

To his credit, Odom was at least smart enough to take the offer. He, of course, believed it would only be temporary at best. All went well, and The Revival Revolutionary Church was dedicated during the fall Of 1967 in the Jonesboro community on East Main Street in Sanford. It would be in Jonesboro that Odom hoped for once in his life he could cash in on his dream.

For someone with such poor self-worth, he was all in on the church and saw nothing but potential for a bright future. Odom felt it would only be a matter of time before the church's growth would create a need for a larger and more substantial structure. Now, close to two years into his quest, there was no need for more space as the small structure had plenty of room for Odom and his congregation. What Odom felt would be temporary turned into months and then into years, and it was evident the church's struggle was not over. The lack of success was beginning to take a toll on Odom, and he was growing weary. His patience was running thin, and he was becoming more disillusioned with each passing week.

Standing at the pulpit, Odom was hoping this Sunday would be different. He had never been one to find comfort behind the makeshift podium, and it was not unusual for him to move about the pulpit. He felt the movement helped emphasize the seriousness of his sermons, and today he was far too restless to stay in one place for long. Odom held the belief that preaching was as much about showmanship as the message, and today he was doing just that. He was combining his showmanship and his sermon to boost his call for support. With each step, he demonstrated his passion for his message and was hoping this would show the congregation that he was not only sincere but also driven. This display of emotion was self-prescribed.

Odom trusted his actions would create an allure that would be believable and credible. Sadly, he had little going for him when it came to preaching the gospel; he lacked style and knowledge. Many who visited the small church would leave questioning Odom's formal training. Most sensed he was self-educated with little direction, but today that mattered little. He was passionate about the cause, and he was calling on the church to act and make a difference in their community.

Odom began to struggled with his constant movement due to his heavy set build and with his constant movement he began to perspire. It was an unusually hot Sunday and with no air conditioning, the discomfort level in the church was high. Trying vigorously to fend off the heat, the congregation used handheld fans to cool themselves. Only stopping to wipe his brow of the streaming sweat, Odom continued to preach. Today, he felt like a true preacher; he was really feeling it.

His sermon was well prepared, and his words were powerful. If only more people could hear it. He had never preached with such conviction as he did on this Sunday. He believed in his message, and he felt today would be the start of a meaningful and necessary movement. Using an old lace handkerchief to wipe the sweat streaming from his brow, Odom hoped it would help illustrate his passion. He had seen enough television evangelists to understand the need for theater, and the lace handkerchief was a prop for the drama. Whenever he stopped to wipe his forehead, Odom would stare into the small gathering as they fanned from the heat. He wanted all of them to recognize the importance of his message. There would be no denying Odom today!

Raising his voice, Odom preached, "We can wait no longer. Now is the time we must take a stand against the sinful activities threatening our community. We cannot leave it in the hands of others. We need to do the Lord's work with our actions and our voices. Although our numbers are small, our message is powerful. It will not be long before others will hear the call, and once they do, our numbers will grow, and the spirit of the Lord will fill the air. We are being called upon to do away with the sin that is infiltrating our town, our homes, and our families. It is up to each of us in the church, with the Lord's support, to take a stand. We must do away with the roving sin factories preparing to invade our community." Odom was calling on the congregation to rise and take part in protesting against the sin that would be promoted at the Lee County fair.

Although the fair promised family fun, Odom saw it differently. He saw the fair and its attractions as little more than an oasis of sin and temptation, and he called for action to take place now—not next week or next month—but now. No longer could the church sit idly by, allowing the sinful activities that soon would be taking root at the fairgrounds.

Odom continued his sermon, "You must look beyond the facade of family fun and see the truth. Sin and evil are preparing to attack our community. The devil is setting up shop in the games of chance and the sideshows of the midway. Innocent people will be drawn to these attractions, and some will fall under the influence of Satan. We must lead a movement against the evil peddled at this year's fair. Satan will be found behind the curtains of the burlesque shows and in the games of chance, and he must be turned away."

He pleaded with the congregation to take up the banner to defeat Satan as it was the responsibility of every member of the church to do so. He wanted everyone to take a stand and lead the citizens of Sanford in a war against the evil of such sinful attractions. He sought to create an army of protesters to combat the sin arriving in town.

"It is our duty to the Lord that we fight the sin and promiscuity now occupying the grounds of the midway," he shouted. "Let us together show Satan that he is not welcome in our community and that he and his followers will be turned away. There will be so-called girly shows tempting the young and old with their tantalizing dances and public nudity. Good God-fearing men will be pulled into a web of sinful activity. It must be stopped."

Odom painted a picture of men being drawn into a den of immorality few had the strength to resist, which would create family turmoil and unrest.

"The dancers would exploit the weaknesses of men, tempting them with sins of the flesh—sins delivered by women who have gone astray." Taking a deep breath, Odom lowered his voice, "I challenge everyone here today. It is up to us to start a community resistance of no longer sitting idly by, allowing sinful activities to take root and destroy decent people. These shows are helping Satan corrupt the weak and are leading good God-fearing people to sin. We must not permit Satan to set up shop in Sanford. Let us follow God's word and fight Satan at every turn. We must combat the evil by putting an end to such shows once and for all. We need to educate our neighbors that Satan is no longer welcome in our community."

Odom asked the church to join him on Monday at the Lee County fairgrounds to not only take a stand but to send a message to Satan and his followers that their time was up. The Revival Revolutionary Church will no longer be silent, allowing the sins of others to destroy the community. Illustrating how these girly shows were violating Gods law, Odom drew from the Ten Commandments to drive home his message.

"Thou shalt not commit adultery" is our seventh commandment, he said. "These so-called entertainment venues are not only promoting adultery; they are outlets for Satan's work, promoting sexual promiscuity."

"Thou shalt not covet thy neighbor's house" is our tenth commandment, he continued. "These dancers will be desired and lusted for by those in attendance—leading righteous men to sin. The temptations of the dancers must be stopped. Stop the dancers before they have an opportunity to destroy good men as well as our community."

Odom decided not to address personal responsibilities at this time. He chose instead to focus his attention on the shows and the dancers. He seemed to have conveniently forgotten the temptations Jesus endured and yet resisted. To Odom, the temptations being offered by the dancers were too strong for any man to resist. He believed one could attract greater numbers by finding someone or something to blame as opposed to addressing personal weaknesses or shortcomings. This was a numbers game to him, and he needed more followers to reach his goal. He painted a picture of the revue as merely a tool of Satan.

Like so many others, Odom found it easier to play the blame game and say the devil made me do it rather than accept responsibility for bad choices or actions. Protesting the girly shows gave him a platform. Taking a stand against these shows would be a way to grow the church and improve his status in the religious community. In Odom's world, the temptation was the sin; men were only doing what came naturally.

Odom was particularly proud of his sermon. He portrayed the girly shows as the devil and Howard's Amusements as the devil's chariot. The devil was riding into town to disrupt and corrupt the citizens of Lee County.

The small attendance was disappointing to Odom; he saw no new faces. It was especially disheartening after he had invested time and money trying to get the word out about today's sermon. He had taken ads out in the local paper promoting his message and his intentions to lead a protest. In addition to the newspaper, he had contacted all the radio stations and even sent press releases to the stations in Raleigh and Fayetteville.

The sermon was to serve as a catalyst for change, with members of The Revival Revolutionary Church being joined by others, to create a movement that would finally bring down the girly shows. To Odom, the shows and what they represented were nothing more than legalized prostitution, and they needed to be shut down.

In addition to his work contacting the media, Odom constructed a small marquee in front of the church to promote his sermon and the pending protest. Sadly, his efforts had failed. No visitors nor anyone representing the media showed up. He had been dealt a blow, but it would not stop him; he refused to be defeated. He had a mission, and the lack of attendance would not derail his efforts. He knew he was in the right and would soon convince the community to accept good over evil.

Odom felt certain a successful protest would bring other churches to join in his mission, finally gaining him acceptance into the religious community. Once the Christian community recognized him as a church leader, he could then begin growing his church's status and membership.

Even with the small attendance at his last service, he remained optimistic for the coming week. He had faith that the protest would be a success and would be viewed as a turning point for society norms. Odom was confident it would only be a matter of time before the protest would mature into a countywide movement. The protest would put an end to the girly shows and, in the process, elevate him into a religious leader.

Today, Odom was focused. It was time for things to change, and he was taking the first step toward changing his future. Odom may have lacked the charismatic style of other ministers, but on this Sunday, he demonstrated heart and motivation. His message was stronger than the church; he was sharing God's calling. He wanted it known that The Revival Revolutionary Church would not tolerate the exploitation of sin, so he issued a call for everyone to join him in the protest. He wanted his words to be heard throughout the county and state.

❦

The Fair

The fair's arrival would traditionally mark the end of summer. It was a time to celebrate the year's harvest and to welcome fall. The week of activities was designed to give everyone an opportunity to enjoy the fruits of their labor. The Lee County fair drew patrons from all over the Piedmont region of North Carolina. Many of those serving in the military at Fort Bragg and Pope Field were also drawn to attend. The fair was more than rides and games; it was an event that the entire county could enjoy.

Brick was pleased when he learned this year's attractions would be arriving earlier than usual. The dates had been moved up from years past in order not to compete with the N. C. State Fair in Raleigh. This change in the dates would give Brick one more shot at experiencing the fair before going off to college. As the convoy of trucks rolled by, his thoughts returned to his younger years.

Brick had always found a sense of wonderment when it came to the fair. One of the more exciting things for him was the sideshows. His fascination with these attractions may have been the result of his father's lack of interest in them. His dad proclaimed the shows were little more than a low-priced illusion playing on the voyeuristic impulses of the weak. As a young boy, Brick didn't have a clue as to what his dad meant. But then again, most of his dad's rants were generally over Brick's head. He and his brother both agreed it was just another way for their father to say no. But their dad's views failed to dissuade either of the boys from wanting to see the erotic attractions found behind the curtains on the midway. Even if Brick didn't understand his father's reasoning, he was smart enough to know the chance of seeing any of the sideshows was limited.

His father was never one to spend money on such attractions. He once told Brick and Gary that he would rather cram his dime up a wild hog's ass and holler "sooey" than spend money on such things. That was Brick's dad. He was a man of few words (but compelling words just the same). Even their dad's colorful use of the English language failed to prevent the boys from dreaming of one day enjoying all the attractions. What if the shows did exploit the voyeuristic instincts of people? Brick and Gary saw little harm in it. The boys reasoned that the sideshows were only in town once a year, so how much damage could they do?

No matter what one's thoughts were about the shows, each one gave the patrons a chance to see the rare and the not so rare, and when it came to the county fair, you could count on plenty of both. Strippers, freak shows, exotic animals, and even tents of horror had a home on the midway.

Once Brick began working and earning his own money, he was able to see some of the attractions. He gained an appreciation for many of the midway shows. Brick considered the midway a smorgasbord of adventure and thrills; seldom would you leave without a story. It didn't take him long to learn a few of the attractions were pure rip-offs, but even those shows would give you something to talk about. Brick believed it didn't matter what the outcome was, disappointed or amused when the show ended, you would always have a memory to share. One thing you could count on was that the midway offered much more than could be found on the streets of Sanford.

The curiosity Brick held for the fair grew out of his appreciation for all the attractions and amusements. Fair week was indeed memorable. Brick's interest extended beyond the rides and shows; he was interested in the people who brought it all to life. He wanted to know more about the workers, the freaks, and everyone in between.

Early on, Brick had a desire to learn as much as he could about the nomadic lifestyle of those who worked at the fair. He believed the workers had a unique perspective on life, which led them to live such an existence. He wondered where the "Human Blockhead" learned his unusual trade. How does one decide to drive a nine-penny nail into his head? How did Mr. Blockhead spend his free time? Brick hoped it wasn't doing woodwork. This thought made him laugh—talk about bringing your work home!

Another star of the midway that stirred Brick's interest was the "Human Garbage Pail." This guy could eat anything from light bulbs to auto parts. Such a skill causes one to question how Mr. Garbage Pail discovered he had an appetite for such strange objects. Maybe one night he had a hunger he couldn't satisfy and was asking himself what the perfect snack would be. The answer, of course, was a 1957 Dodge carburetor!

Brick spent way too much time thinking about why rather than how, but he was intrigued by these individuals and their many talents. Even the "Bearded Lady" fascinated him—or for that matter, the "Siamese Twins." They all held a special place in Brick's mind.

P. T. Barnum was quoted as saying, "There's a sucker born every minute," and, when it came to Brick and the county fair, he may have been the biggest sucker of all. Sucker or not, he never stopped enjoying the strange and odd folks who brought the shows to life.

Brick was also intrigued with the thought of how the acts may have been discovered. He assumed they didn't answer a want ad or launch their illustrious careers on The Ted Mack Original Amateur Hour.

Brick's mom tried to dissuade him from being fascinated with such acts. In her rational opinion, she believed the stars might have been born with some physical malformation that led them to live the life of a carnival performer. She felt the fair was exploiting these individuals and discouraged anyone from attending such shows. Brick hated her attempts of trying to make him feel guilty for wanting to see the strange talents on display. She was taking all the fun out of the shows.

It was clear that neither of his parents agreed with his love of the shows—one claiming the shows were a waste of money and the other protesting the exploitation of the less fortunate. It's a wonder Brick was attracted to them at all. He was though, and he found it all captivating. Brick, unlike his parents, tried to rationalize that the shows provided work and opportunity for the performers, giving them an outlet for their strange and unique skills. Brick argued that the fair not only gave the entertainers jobs, but it also provided them a means to make money. He didn't see it as exploitation but as a personal choice. To him, the shows and the performers were far more interesting than sad, and he believed they should be supported. After all, there wasn't much demand for a man who could drive nine-penny nails through his head. All the strange and unique talents, coupled with the gypsy lifestyle, only increased Brick's desire to learn more.

During one of his many visits to the fair, Brick learned of the existence of a small village of campers and trailers that made up the workers' living quarters. Once he learned of the village, his interest continued to grow. In Lee County, the living area was little more than a makeshift campsite offering electrical and sewage hookups. In the middle of the living area was a building that resembled a World War II Quonset hut that served as the barracks. Inside were free-standing beds with separate showers and bathrooms. Brick joked that it offered all the comforts of home, depending on what you called home. Nonetheless, it all stirred Brick's curiosity about the lifestyle of living on the road and never staying in one spot for very long. He concluded there probably existed a subculture that the fair workers enjoyed, and it was this subculture Brick wanted to learn.

Brick loved stories of adventure and travel and felt those working at the fair would have hundreds of stories to tell. His love for a good story was handed down from his father. Often on road trips and vacations, his dad would entertain everyone with his stories.

His love for the fair came from his mother. She always enjoyed the rides and the exhibits but not the sideshows. Even though his mom enjoyed the fair, she felt the stories of those working were more tragic than adventurous. Brick, on the other hand, thought they were exciting and daring. To his mom, the fair represented a group of social outcasts struggling to survive. Brick didn't see it that way at all; if anything, he felt she was too negative and could not see the real adventure and excitement one must feel while working and living on the road. To him, the carnie life appeared to be one adventure after another.

While Brick's mind wondered about the people who brought the fair to life, a truck passed with the words "Boy Tarzan Raised by Apes." Although Brick knew many of the shows relied on illusions and lies, he wasn't bothered at all; if anything, he was intrigued by their creativity and imagination. These illusions and lies sold tickets, and each show helped make the fair magical. The rides, the food, the games, and the shows all contributed to the uniqueness of the fair.

Brick wanted to know more about the carnie lifestyle. He wondered what made it desirable. Maybe the workers were running from somebody or something, or possibly it was a family tradition handed down over the years. Perhaps the carnival was a destination for individuals needing to escape the confines of an ordinary world. He speculated the workers knew something many in society failed to understand—the satisfaction found on the road.

Although he may have been naïve, Brick preferred not to look at any dark or tragic side—just the fun and adventure of such an experience. The workers must share a quality that brought them together as they traveled and entertained rural America. He knew it would take a particular kind of person to adapt to the constant travel and endure the rigors of creating a week's worth of entertainment at each stop. Each worker could see America firsthand—one small town after another. Brick's curiosity about human nature may have contributed to his decision to study Psychology in college, but college was still days away, and the fair was in the present. Now, fate was giving him another chance to enjoy the shows and the people.

According to the posters placed in the store windows throughout town, this year's fair would be the best ever. Part of the attractions included a chance to see Batman's car from the hit television series Batman. You could also see a special science exhibit featuring man's trip to the moon and a scaled down Saturn V, the rocket that propelled him there. And as always, there would be a mixture of strange and erotic shows.

One of Brick's favorites, "Tonya, the Gorilla Girl," was returning once again to share her uniqueness. For fifty cents, fairgoers could witness the transformation of a young girl to a gorilla—a show Brick would refer to as a must-see for all fairgoers. Brick had seen the attraction several times over the last few years. The large painting that hung outside Tonya's tent depicted a young girl transforming into an ape. Supposedly, Tonya was captured in the wilds of Africa and brought to the states for her safety. A looped recording invited one and all to see Tonya, who was billed as one of the great mysteries of the world.

Tonya will change before your very eyes from a beautiful girl into a fearless gorilla played loudly for all to hear, an invitation no respectful patron could resist. Warning signs were placed strategically in front of the exhibit, proclaiming the attraction would not be responsible for any injuries that may occur while viewing Tonya and her transformation. One poster indicated medical personnel would be on the grounds in the event of an emergency. Classic advertising was used to lure folks to buy tickets. The tempting signs, all selling the mysterious and fearful, created the perfect atmosphere for a fun show.

Once an individual paid the half-dollar admission and entered Tonya's tent, there would be a dark corridor to walk through before coming to a dimly lit area. In the back of the tent was a stage with a small light illuminating the curtain where she would appear. The light helped produce an image of Tonya's home—a barred, caged enclosure. The cage, constructed to ensure the safety of those attending the show, was a well-orchestrated illusion. When the show would finally begin, the curtain would drop and there on the stage sat Tonya.

She was an average looking young lady seated in a small cage—nothing like the paintings out front. The dropping of the curtain was accompanied with the sounds of an African jungle. As the sound increased, Tonya would begin coming to life. The announcer would encourage her while asking her to change. As she began to move about the cage, he would call for the audience to join in with the chant—"Change Tonya, Change Tonya." She only paraded back and forth at first, but as the chant continued, she became agitated with every step she took.

The cage was loosely constructed and could easily be knocked down, which only added to the entertainment value. As the chant rang throughout the tent— "Change Tonya, Change...." The louder the chant, the more agitated Tonya became. It was great theater! With everyone shouting for Tonya to change, the lights would begin flashing, a siren would sound, the stage would go dark, and smoke would fill the area. When the lights returned, Tonya had transformed into the monster gorilla girl just as advertised.

The fun really began after Tonya's transformation. Her strength now was too much for the cage, and she could no longer be contained.

Tonya, now with the power of a gorilla, could bring down the flimsy structure with little trouble. Once the bars began to fall to the floor, the gorilla girl—now with a menacing look—began staring into the crowd.

The announcer would then begin screaming, "Run, run for your life. Tonya has escaped."

He would tell everyone to save themselves and head for the exits, and those in attendance would do as he said. Not to fear. Tonya had never made it to the midway as the announcer was always able to calm her down. As luck would have it, she would in short order be ready for her next performance. What Barnum said, "There is a sucker born every minute," may be true; however, to the delight of many, it was fun being the sucker—especially at the Lee County fair.

As the truck carrying "Tonya, the Gorilla Girl" passed, Brick decided this year he would not only enjoy the fair, but he would try to learn more about the people who gave it life.

With college over a week away and most of his friends already at school, things had slowed down in Sanford. Brick came up with a plan and felt his friend Ray would join him. He believed the best way to enjoy his final week in Sanford would be to find work at the fair. Brick and his good friend, Ray Hill, had spent the summer painting the county schools, and the job had ended when school returned to session. Both had heard for years that the fair was always in need of some local help and would hire temporary employees. Brick reasoned that if they were hiring, why not apply?

If Brick was going to experience the carnival life, now was the time. He made up his mind he would go to the fairgrounds and ask about work. He also knew it would be more fun if he could convince Ray to join him on this adventure. It would be great if they got a job; if not, at least they tried. Brick drove to Ray's house in hopes he would share his enthusiasm for such a spontaneous adventure.

Odom's Mission

For Odom the call he received from Ralph Hinson the minister of the Free Will Baptist Church in Goldsboro NC could not have come at a better time. Odom patience's were wearing thin in his efforts to grow the church. He was becoming increasingly cynical that his dream would never come to life. It had been nearly two years since he and his wife opened the church, and thus far, The Revival Revolutionary Church had yet developed any traction for growth.

Ralph Hinson asked Odom to join a movement to bring a stop to the girly shows. Leading such an effort excited Odom. He was flattered that Hinson had reached out to him; it was a first for Odom. Since arriving in Sanford, he had never truly felt comfortable—or even accepted—by the community of ministers. Odom wasn't sure many ministers in town were even awhare of his church. The mainstream churches all had a history as well as organizational support, but his church had no national affiliation, leaving Odom with little direction and even less notoriety.

Hinson had no trouble convincing Odom to join the movement, and Odom was eager to accept the offer. He viewed the call as a positive sign for him and the chruch. His religious standing in the community was about to get a boost.

Hinson explained how he planned to establish a statewide movement with a network of churches helping support the protest and finally bring an end to the nude girly shows. Odom knew the shows had been a constant of the county fairs for years, and he quickly agreed with Hinson that it was time to bring an end to such venues. Odom was all in the moment Hinson mentioned the protest, but out of respect for Hinson, he allowed the minister to tell him why he was organizing such a movement. Hinson felt the shows were leading to the downfall of civilization and the damnation of man. Odom hardly heard Hinson's words. He had made up his mind to join the fight and was already thinking of how such a protest could be beneficial for Hinson but for his church as well.

Odom was anxious to accept the leadership role Hinson was offering. He would lead a protest that would resonate throughout the area.

What Odom didn't know was that Hinson had made several calls before reaching out to him. In his other calls to members of the clergy, Hinson had no luck convincing any to join the movement. Most he spoke with were sympathetic to the cause but didn't see a need for a protest. These ministers felt the fair would only be in town for a week and believed the tradition of the shows would be hard to overcome. Some did agree to speak against the sideshows from the pulpits, although none were prepared to lead a protest.

Hinson believed there needed to be more action; he felt a public demonstration would give strength to the movement. His hope was that Odom would take on the fight and lead a community outcry to end the shows. It may have been through the process of elimination that Hinson settled on Odom, but once he did, he found a faithful follower. Unfortunately, Hinson failed to realize Odom had his own agenda regarding the protest.

Odom had tried to bring the church publicity over time with little success. He had worked a homeless food drive, along with the establishment of a food pantry. A tent revival he sponsored ended up costing him more than it brought in. With little attention or publicity, Odom felt it had been one disappointment after another. He hoped today's sermon would serve as a building block for future success. He believed leading a protest now would reenergize his ministry and his dream.

Odom had assured Hinson he was the man for the job. He could count on him leading a successful demonstration that would resonate throughout the state. Hinson had given The Revival Revolutionary Church a new mission. A mission Odom passionately believed in, feeling such a movement would be something the entire community would support. In addition, leading such a protest would help pave the way for Odom's rise in the religious community. He had been anxiously waiting for the day his church would no longer be considered an eyesore.

Eager for the fight, Odom saw the protest as something others would join in and support. Hinson was thrilled with Odom's willingness to spearhead the campaign and asked him to approach the movement as a protest against the evils of legalizing sin.

Hinson could not have known of Odom's ulterior motives. Odom was hoping the rally would deliver greater dividends than merely shutting down the shows. It was clear that each man had his own agenda. Hinson had searched for a leader in Sanford and settled on Odom. Odom was looking for benefits beyond the protest; he needed something to spearhead the growth of his church. Both viewed the arrangement differently.

Unfortunately, Hinson was now dealing with a desperate man. Desperation is never a peaceful motivator as it could create more problems than solutions. Odom assured Hinson he could count on him and The Revival Revolutionary Church. He promised to lead the way in removing the sin and shutting down the shows. Odom proclaimed the citizens of Sanford would proudly support the protest, adding that together they would bring an end to these outlets of sinful activity.

Odom was excited and confident that Hinson's movement would help catapult The Revival Revolutionary Church out of the shadows of mediocrity. He felt sure everyone would soon begin seeing Odom and his church differently. To help with the protest, Hinson told Odom he would send him a packet of information that would explain how to organize and spread the word.

Hinson had been actively leading protests in the eastern part of the state, but he now was relying on others to bring the plight to their neighborhoods. The two men in this partnership may have had their own agenda, but in many ways, it was a natural fit.

As he preached Odom's resolve would not be affected by the small turnout. Maybe it would not happen in the pews, but once the fair opened, things would begin to change. He envisioned the movement attracting new followers into his flock. Odom realized such demonstrations wouldn't generate the passion of the civil rights movement or match the anti-war faction, but he was confident there would be an appetite just the same.

Brick Shares His Plan

B rick was eager to share his thoughts with Ray. He knew Ray would love the possibility of the two working together at the fair. There was little doubt Ray would share his enthusiasm for such an impromptu adventure. They had been friends as long as either could remember. They attended the same church, and their parents had known each other long before Brick and Ray were born. To Brick, working the fair would be the icing on the cake for what had already been an eventful summer. If Ray were game, the two could end the summer experiencing a slice of the life of a carnie.

Brick always felt welcome at Ray's, and it was not unusual for him to drop by. Ray answered the door with his usual question, "What's up?" Smiling from ear to ear, Brick began sharing his thoughts with him. Ray was aware that the fair was arriving as his dad, Russell, was a member of The Lions Club (the principal sponsor of the yearly fair). Russell had left for the fairgrounds earlier that day to help oversee the fair's arrival. After Brick told Ray about seeing the caravan of cars and trucks, Ray started questioning Brick about what he may have seen in the caravan.

Brick answered, "It looks like many of the same attractions—just a new year. And before you ask, I did see a truck pulling the most erotic show on the midway. The girls are back for another year."

He then began telling Ray his thoughts of going to the fairgrounds and trying to find work for the coming week. Brick now smiling with enthusiasm began to explain; "Maybe we could pick up some extra money before going off to school. You and I both know they are always in need of local help." Energetically he raised his hands to the air and said, "We have the time. So, why not?" Ray liked the idea immediately.

Picking up some extra money and learning more about the industry appealed to both.

Before driving out to the fairgrounds, Brick took time to call home and let his mom know he would be late getting in. He told her of his idea; she wasn't thrilled with it but only asked that he be careful. While Brick was on the phone, Ray told his mom of their plan. She too was a little apprehensive and repeated Brick's mom's words, asking them to be careful. Neither mother liked the idea, but there was little either could say; both boys would be off to college in a week.

Leaving Ray's house, the boys began joking about the job prospect—each of them ready for an adventure. Neither of them knowing what to expect made their decision even more exciting. They were about to give Howard's Amusements a try.

Once they arrived at the fairgrounds, there was little doubt Howard's Amusements had arrived. Brick parked in a space near the main gate; in the coming week, the space would be a prime spot for fairgoers. Ray looked around and did not see his father's car and said, "Looks like Russell has come and gone."

They walked toward the midway entrance and began witnessing the transformation taking place. An entertainment plaza was rising from the grounds as rides and tents were now dotting the landscape.

With neither of the boys knowing where to go or who to see, they just started walking. They soon spotted a group of workers, and Brick inquired about finding work. An aging white-haired man replied, "We're always looking for good help. I suggest you go over to the rides near the Shooting Star; it's just past those games." He was pointing toward the back end of the grounds. "Ask for Raeford. He's the one you'll need to talk to. Tell him Grady sent you over." He laughed and said, "Not sure that will help, but hopefully, it won't hurt. If Raeford can't use you, try some of the food vendors; they are usually scrambling to find folks to work."

The boys thanked him and went to find the Shooting Star—a new ride to this year's attractions. It was like a roller coaster; the main thrill was provided by throwing the riders into loops and curves at a high rate of speed. Most of the rides were contained in one area, so they had little trouble locating the Shooting Star. The ride was well lit with shining, illuminated buckets for the riders. The boys walked past several show tents being laid out for assembly. At the ride, they asked a man pulling steel poles from a trailer bed where they could find Raeford. The man pointed to a gentleman wearing an olive-green shirt with a Howard's Amusement's logo. Brick took the lead and said, "Excuse me sir, we were talking with a gentleman named Grady about getting a job, and he suggested we talk to Raeford."

The man looked at them and appeared to be sizing them up before saying, "You're in luck on two counts; I'm Raeford, and we could always use extra help. That is, of course, if you boys are willing to work hard. You interested in working just tonight or the week?"

Without hesitation, Brick and Ray both answered, "The week if possible."

Raeford smiled and responded, "I'll pay you twenty dollars for tonight. After that, the pay will depend on the job. If you show up on time and do good work, you can make a good week's pay."

They both liked what they heard. Raeford stuck out his hand and asked, "You boys ever done this kind of work before?"

Brick spoke up, "Never worked at a fair, but we're willing to learn."

Ray then added, "Never worked a fair but sure do enjoy them."

It appeared Raeford liked the boy's immediately; maybe it was due to their willingness to work. He explained to them, "This work can be fun and at times hard, but I can assure you that it will be something you will always remember. If you are ready, let's get started."

They followed him to a tool shed behind a pickup truck, and there he found them some work gloves. Brick and Ray pulled on the gloves and followed Raeford back to where a large tent was laid out on the ground. Raeford told the men working that he had some help for them and pointed to the boys. The men smiled and said, "Great, can always use some help."

In no time at all, they were helping assemble a tent for one of the many shows at the fair. It would be the temporary home of the "Human Squid." This would also be the first year for this sideshow attraction. Brick felt this thing was a poor man's version of the Creature from the Black Lagoon—a popular movie monster. Quite often, displays were designed to cash in on popular movies or tall tales. Neither boy was about to judge. They were now members of the workforce.

The tent looked to be about twenty-by-twenty feet, fitting behind a drop-down stage from one of the many flatbed trucks lining the midway. Eagerly, they were pulling on the tie lines—smiling ear to ear. Both were happy that they had unexpectedly joined the carnie life.

While assembling the tent, another group of men unloaded a giant vat, placing it on the drop-down stage that would serve as the creature's home for the run of the show. Water would fill the tank, and the reptile man would swim around as patrons watched—at times acting out the role of a monster on the midway. There was a bank of lights that would be hoisted to give the water and the creature a mysterious glow. Ray and Brick were fascinated with how the production would come to life once everything was in place. Brick could not help but believe one of the men unloading the large tank would soon don a costume and become the reptile man.

After the tent was secured, Brick and Ray moved on to help assemble one of the many games of chance that would add to the fun on the midway. When Raeford returned, he showed his gratitude by telling them, "You boys are all right."

The fair gates would not officially open until eleven o'clock the next morning, but for now the midway was turning into an entertainment venue. After about four hours of constructing rides and helping with different attractions, Raeford told Brick and Ray to come with him to the office as he wanted to get their pay for the night and discuss the coming week. They had passed the first test of work.

The time had moved so quickly that neither boy realized how late it was getting. They had enjoyed their first day as a carnie and had given little thought to the money they would get for their work. The process of constructing the rides and securing the tents was fascinating. Brick felt the work resembled a life-size jigsaw puzzle that was slowly completed.

Raeford's office was located in the residential area of the fairgrounds. On the west side of the properties was a group of trailers, one of which served as the office. Ray jokingly asked Raeford where this "Human Squid" lived. With laughter, Raeford replied, "In the water vat, of course." He then explained that not only did the "Human Squid" live in the makeshift village, but he also shared a trailer with the "Human Blockhead."

Hearing Raeford talk of where people were staying in the park just made Brick's interest grow. To him, everything was surreal; he was becoming hooked on the carnival. Raeford explained the village of trailers served as home, at least until the next move. Brick then commented, "That has got to be interesting!"

Raeford just smiled and said, "Interesting is not the word I would choose, but for some I guess it is. It can also be a pain in the ass." They all laughed, and Brick and Ray were beginning to feel as if they belonged.

They had not reached the office when Brick noticed two young women walking their way. The women were both brunettes and looked to be in their early twenties-—one was a full-figured girl and the other was tall and slender. Both possessed a smile that could melt a block of ice that only added to their beauty. Brick hoped they were employees of Howard's Amusements. When the girls met up with Raeford, they asked about his new friends. With the flirtation, both Brick and Ray began to blush. Raeford told the girls, "These boys are thinking about working with us this week, so y'all need to be nice."

Brick was the first to say hello, and Ray smiled as he said, "Ladies." Brick wasn't sure his hello held up against Ray's greeting. When it came to girls, Brick was always a bit awkward.

One of the girls quickly smiled and said, "Good looking and polite—how nice."

Raeford joked with the girls, saying, "I'm hoping Brick and Ray here are going to be with us for a while." That sounded great to Brick.

The tall, slender one smiled and said, "We could use a few fresh faces around here."

The other one added, "Maybe they can work our tent."

Raeford chuckled, "Let's get them to agree to work, and then we'll see where they go."

The girls began to move away, but as they were leaving, they told the boys that hopefully they would see them around.

Once the young women were out of earshot, Raeford shared with Brick and Ray that if they had not figured it out, Misty and Sugar were two of the girls from the revue. Hearing these ladies worked the revue was exciting and made the possibility of working the fair even better. Brick thought how much better looking the ladies were than those who worked the revue last year. The boys were grinning when they told Raeford they would probably have to check out the show. Ray made the comment that it looked like this year's revue would be better than the one last year. Raeford then smiled and said, "That's the carnival business; things are always going to change. I will agree with you that this year's showgirls are an upgrade from the last couple of years, and I promise you, you won't be disappointed."

Raeford invited them into the office to get their pay. The office was a trailer in the middle of the residential area. Raeford pulled out a gray metal box and counted out twenty dollars for each of them. As he handed them the money, he said, "I think this is what we agreed on."

Brick was first to say, "Yes sir, but are we done for the day?"

Raeford replied, "Yeah, you can enjoy the rest of the evening. Not a bad payday, huh?" He then opened a cabinet door pulling out of a couple of badges for the employees of Howard's Amusements. He told the boys if they were going to continue working, they would need the badges. He then added, "Guys, it seems y'all have a good head on your shoulders, and from what I can tell, neither of you is afraid of work. So, if you are interested, I could use some help here in the office. If that sounds good, I will need you back here tomorrow morning. We've got plenty to do before opening the gates. The choice is yours, but I can guarantee you it will be an experience—something to tell the grandkids about one day."

Brick and Ray eagerly accepted the offer and told Raeford he could depend on them. They then asked where they should go the next morning.

Raeford said, "Just come to the office; I'll be here."

With that, Ray put the twenty in his pocket saying, "This job already pays better than any of our other summer jobs."

Raeford laughed and replied, "We try to take care of our employees. I guarantee you, if you are willing to do the work, you are going to be pleased with the pay." He then told them he should get their full names since they would be coming on board. He pulled out a yellow legal pad and said, "This is about as official as it gets around here."

He wrote down their names, Brick Kirby and Ray Hill, and told them he felt sure they would be happy with the decision to join the team at Howard's Amusements. He then added, "This week—the carnival, next week—college. Not many can say that."

Raeford then indicated he had some things that needed his attention. He shook their hands, and they all agreed they would see each other the next morning. Brick and Ray were so excited, and quickly told Raeford they were looking forward to the work.

As they left the office, Ray speculated, "Raeford must be management."

They decided to walk around the midway before heading out. Both were looking to get a feel for what to expect in the coming week. On the backside of the fairgrounds, they passed a food trailer. The lady working was pulling an electric cord, and they asked if she needed help. She was very appreciative and told them she needed to lay some plywood over the electrical cord once she hooked it up. Before moving the plywood, she began duct taping the wire down to a board underneath. Ray pulled the cord evenly over the board, and Brick helped tape it down. Once they finished taping down the wiring, they placed another piece of plywood to cover everything in order to prevent someone from tripping over the cable. With everything connected she threw the switch, and the trailer lit up like a Christmas tree. The neon sign read, Hot Dogs and other Delights. She thanked them for their help and offered to pay them for their trouble.

Ray said, "No trouble—no need to pay us."

She responded, "At least let me get you a soda." She was waiting on an ice delivery, so the Pepsi was lukewarm, but to them it was still wet and refreshing.

As they started to leave, the lady asked if they were looking for work. Ray told her about helping Raeford and that it looked like they would be working for him. Brick added, "Yeah, he told us to be here around seven o'clock in the morning, and he would have us doing something."

She responded, "Raeford is a good, honest man. I am sure he will have plenty for you to do, but if by chance it doesn't work out, come see me. And if you find yourself in need of a corn dog, just come on by. I'll take care of you at no charge." They thanked her, and she asked them to call her Glenda. She then asked for their names.

Glenda was an older lady, and judging from her weight, it was safe to say she enjoyed the food she sold. As they left the stand, Glenda shut off the power and pulled down the protective covers, explaining she had done enough for the day. Ray noticed Glenda walking toward the trailers and said, "I wonder how many people live in the trailer park." Neither of them had any idea, but from the looks of things, there were plenty staying on the grounds.

Neither boy was ready to leave and decided to make one more loop. Brick laughed and said, "Who knows? Maybe we will see "Tonya, the Gorilla Girl," and with some luck maybe we'll run into some of the ladies of the revue." They slowed their pace down as they approached the assembling of the "All-Girl Nude Revue." Fortune shone on them as they noticed Misty and Sugar talking with another group of girls near the site of the revue. They made a beeline toward the girls, hoping for a little interaction; however, they were awkwardly aware if there would be any conversation, it would need to be instigated by the girls. Both were a little starstruck and a bit intimidated by them.

Happily, Misty noticed them and spoke, "Well, look what the cat dragged in."

A nervous smile came to Brick's face and in a feeble attempt to be funny, he said, "Meow."

Other than the lame joke, Brick was stumped for words, but Ray, always cool under pressure, didn't miss a beat. He responded, "Evening ladies."

Misty turned her attention toward them, "Are you guys going to be working with Howard's for a while?"

Ray answered, "Yes, at least for a few days. Raeford feels he can find us some work."

The full-figured girl told them how good that sounded, and she then seductively smiled and introduced herself as Sugar. They both, of course, remembered the girls' names from the brief encounter earlier.

Brick and Ray gave them their names. They resisted using aliases, which would have been something they would do at the beach when meeting girls outside their comfort zone. Using fake names gave them a strange sense of confidence, especially when talking with the opposite sex. Tonight, they would stick to their real names. This was a smart thing to do as Raeford had already told them their names, and they hopefully would be working together. Misty gave them her name, but it was evident she felt the guys already knew hers. She was right; their brief exchange had made an impression on both. Brick felt the girls appeared to be just old enough to fulfill the older-woman fantasy shared by many teenage boys.

The other two girls soon joined the conversation with one asking Misty if she was going to introduce her new friends. Brick wasn't sure what to expect, but the interactions were innocent. The conversation was as wholesome as a Jimmy Stewart movie, and yet the boys were talking with strippers. The girl with light brown hair—thin and wearing short shorts and a T-shirt—introduced herself as Tammy. The other, a tall blond, was wearing shorts and a blouse that failed to conceal a rather lovely figure. She introduced herself as Mary Jane but said some call her MJ. Tammy and Mary Jane both appeared to be a little younger than Misty and Sugar.

Brick, trying to maintain his cool said, "Nice to meet you. Do y'all work with the fair?" He knew the answer, but he was looking for conversation—not facts.

Brick couldn't help being lured into Misty's seductive ways when she indicated they all worked for the Revue. She questioned if he and Ray had ever heard of it. Brick knew he was now blushing and could only assume Ray as well. But both took time to smile and indicate their knowledge of the Revue.

Brick heard Ray in his self-assured manner answered, "Matter of fact, we're both big fans of the show."

It was then Brick became even more entranced with Misty's responded, "Well, that's nice to hear." She was by far the most seductive and had no problems promoting the revue with her talk and actions, which only added to the boys' fantasies.

Brick joined the conversation saying, "We're looking forward to the work, and hopefully we will be able to take in all the attractions."

Brick was asked by Tammy if they were from Sanford?

It seemed a strange question to Brick, but it didn't take him long to figure out why she wanted to know. He replied, "Yeah, I hate to say it—Sanford born and bred." Tammy told them she was glad to hear that. It turns out she wanted Brick and Ray to promote the revue. She believed both would have friends who would enjoy the show, and word-of-mouth advertising would be good for business.

Returning to her seductive ways, Misty said, "If we do our jobs right, I'm sure your friends will want to come again and again. They will not be disappointed, and maybe we can even make it special for both of you."

"Damn!" was all Brick was thinking. What started out so innocently had taken an exciting turn. He was now feeling a little more daring and said, "With you ladies being part of the revue, I'm sure we can get our friends to come."

Tammy laughed, saying, "That's sweet. I hope you both plan on attending as well."

"Oh, we will be there," Ray replied.

Misty caressed Ray's face in her hands and said, "Maybe you would like a special show."

Brick was becoming jealous of the attention Ray was getting. Misty was a looker, and Ray was now the object of her affection. Her focus seemed to take Ray off his game as he was taken aback by her aggressive flirtatious style. He, however, quickly recovered with a smile, saying, "I would like that very much."

She then kissed his cheek and said, "So, it's a date. I'll be looking for you."

Brick thought, Damn you! He was now jealous indeed.

His feeling changed when Mary Jane said, "Now Misty, you know you cannot have them all to yourself." With that statement, they all laughed.

Mary Jane looked at Brick, possibly seeing his disappointment, and told him not to feel left out as she was sure Misty would get around to him. Misty then added, "MJ, you are going to give them the wrong impression."

Again, all were laughing.

Brick and Ray were becoming more comfortable with the talk and the ladies.

Mary Jane turned her full attention toward Brick and asked him once again to spread the word about the show, and she guaranteed him it would be worth it. Sugar and Tammy joined in, saying, "Best show on the midway."

Ray excitably replied, "it all sounds very inviting."

Once again, there was laughter.

The flirtation was back and forth, and Brick and Ray were enjoying every bit of it. The girls had a sales pitch that made them both anxious for show time.

Mary Jane then took Brick's hand and kindly said, "It's always nice meeting new people, but I will look forward to seeing you again. It should be a fun week." She then leaned over and kissed Brick on the cheek, adding, "I don't want you to feel left out."

When the interchange was over, all four girls said they hoped to see them later. It was a friendly exchange that could have taken place at any beach in the country where young people come together looking for a summer romance. The difference with this exchange was that it took place at the county fair, and it was with strippers. The boys felt the week was shaping up to be an exciting one.

In a short time, Brick and Ray were finished walking the midway. Most of the construction was complete; only a few games still needed to be assembled. The Batmobile had arrived, although it was covered. Brick told Ray he might have to see that one. Ray shook his head, saying, "You want to see the Batmobile?"

"Oh yeah, you know me. I'm a sucker for that kind of stuff," replied Brick.

Before they got into the car, they both looked back at the lights of the midway. They knew if all went as they hoped, it should be a hell of a week. Ray remarked, "It's going to be interesting, and if the ladies of the revue are part of our week, it could be great." Both were feeling hyped up with the excitement of the coming days.

On their way home, they decided to stop by Morton's, one of their favorite hangouts, in hopes of seeing some friends and sharing their story. Morton's was a small diner directly across from the city pool and tennis courts. It was in a prime location for all the teenagers in Sanford, and it stayed open late. To the students of Central High School, Morton's was a destination as much as a restaurant. With a small soda fountain and a few booths, Morton's served good, reasonably priced food. Dave, the owner, was a rather gruff individual who probably failed charm school, but he certainly knew how to cook. In Sanford, his cheeseburgers and fries were legendary. Marylyn, the waitress, was a staple at the restaurant and always seemed to be working. She was a pleasant lady who appeared to enjoy the loyal following of the students.

While Brick and Ray waited on their burgers, a couple of friends came in. It was not unusual to see someone you knew at Morton's, especially on a weekend night. Their two friends, Andy, and Donnie, sat down with them. Andy was the first to speak, asking the standard question, "What's up?" Brick seized the moment to tell them about going out to the fairgrounds and getting work.

Their friends laughed at them, saying, "No way." Brick and Ray quickly pulled out their employee badges, and their friends changed their tune.

Ray took the opportunity to tell them, "Not only are we working, but we've already met some of the ladies starring in this year's nude revue." Their friends were then immediately impressed.

Andy asked eagerly, "You met some of the dancers?"

Ray, smiling like the cat that ate the canary, answered, "Yes, we did! And I can promise you this, if they dance as good as they look, the show will be worth the money. The girls are not only good looking, but they also have great bodies." Now their friends were envious and began asking about going to the show.

Brick took the lead, telling them, "I think we should get a large group and go to the shows together. Trust me, we are going to want to go more than once for these girls."

Ray added, "Here's the deal. If you guys get to go and we are not with you, do me a favor. Tell them we sent you. It may help us out with the ladies if you know what I mean."

Brick knew they had made an impression on Donnie when Donnie declared both he and Ray were full of shit.

No one needed to be encouraged to go, but Brick and Ray were doing it anyway. They had learned from last year that there was a better chance of getting in if you were with a large group. Ray, feeling empowered, said, "Maybe we can introduce you to the girls if we all go together. Of course, that depends on whether you want to meet them or not." Ray was hoping that attending with a large group could give him some credit with Misty and the others. Neither Brick nor Ray lacked an active imagination, and when it came to these girls, it was on full speed. Their new aquaintances were now the center of their conversations and fantasies.

As the boys drove home, they discussed everything about the fair. Excited or not, they knew they may have a challenge in telling their parents about their new jobs. Brick felt his folks would be happy, knowing he was making money as opposed to spending it his last week at home. Ray was confident his would be okay with the idea, especially considering Russell would be at the fairgrounds often due to his role as an officer in the Lions Club. Both laughed, feeling everything should be okay. They just hoped their parents wouldn't find out about their new friends who were working the "All-Girl Nude Revue."

Brick's dad was still up when he got home. He knew Brick had been at the fair, and he wondered how the evening went. Brick gave him an abbreviated story about helping with the tents and games of chance, but he failed to disclose anything else. Brick told him it looked like he and Ray would be able to work the entire week.

"Today we hardly worked four hours and made twenty bucks; that's hard to beat," Brick shared happily. "The man who hired us was pleased with our work and feels they will have plenty for us to do." His dad was supportive of his working and even commented on the boys' initiative. He did question, though, what type of work they would be doing. Brick told him he wasn't quite sure, but he imagined they would be running games or cleaning something—whatever scrub work needed to be done.

Brick's dad liked the idea and saw no problems with the work. After all, when he was Brick's age, he was in the Army preparing to go to war. His only advice was not to let anyone take advantage of him. Being supportive, he said to Brick, "You should get good pay for good work." Brick assured him he would take his advice. His father then added, "You'll be starting college soon, so be careful—also have some fun."

Brick had feared all along that his mom might think he was getting into something he couldn't handle. His dad told him he would talk to Brick's mom about the job, but he was confident she would be okay with everything. He assured Brick, "As far as your mother is concerned, don't worry about her; she'll be fine. If she has any concerns, I'll remind her of how much she loves the fair." They both laughed. Brick thanked him and said he hoped to make some money and learn something about the life of a carnie.

Brick's mom had heard them talking, and she joined them in the living room. It was evident she was curious about their conversation. Brick began telling her about how he and Ray had gotten jobs at the fair, quickly adding they were hoping to work all week. Like most mothers would be, she wasn't thrilled with the idea. Brick's dad sensed how she was feeling and told her not to worry as Brick could take care of himself.

Brick said, "Mom, it's something I feel I will enjoy doing. I've always had a fascination for those who make the fair come to life. Maybe by working this week, I can learn about the fair from the inside out and satisfy my curiosity. I'm hoping to make a little extra money, and let's face it, it should be fun."

Brick's dad laughed and said, "Don't let her concern fool you. I'm sure as much as your mother loves the fair, she's a bit envious." She had a look of disagreement on her face, but she only asked that both boys be careful. Brick told her they would; all they planned to do was work hard and make some extra money, and he promised to keep his nose clean.

Brick knew keeping his nose clean would be a challenge, but he wasn't about to address this challenge with either of his parents. There was no need for them to know the whole story. He knew he should be respectful of his parents' wishes; after all, he was still living under their roof.

Brick told his folks he probably should get some rest as he was expecting a busy day come morning. Before he left them, he asked if someone would wake him the next morning, giving him plenty of time to get to work by seven o'clock.

In his room, Brick could hear his mom telling his father that she didn't think it was such a good idea. His dad quickly assured her that Brick was a grown boy and that it may do him some good. He reminded her that at Brick's age he was in a bomber over Europe, explaining further that the war was a bit more dangerous than running the Tilt-a-Whirl or selling cotton candy for a week. His dad once again told her not to worry as Brick would be off to college soon enough, and that would present a whole new set of worries.

⚜

Brick at Home

Although it was late, Brick decided to give Ray a call. He was wondering how Ray's parents took the news of the new jobs. Ray told him, "We're good to go. Mom wasn't crazy about the idea, but since dad will be there off and on during the week, she gave in." Both laughed, wondering if their mothers were worried about the fair or about their friends seeing their baby boys working at the carnival.

Brick said, "Speaking of work, I wonder what we will be doing?"

Ray laughed and said, "I sure know what I'd like to be doing."

With that, Brick replied, "Dream on big boy. Tell you what, I will come by around six thirty in the morning to pick you up."

After talking with Ray, Brick decided to give Emily (his on-again, off again girlfriend) a call as she was already off at college. The two had dated most of their senior year and throughout the summer. Brick felt Emily was different from his other high school romances; she was special. She had a spell on him, and unfortunately, he never really knew what to expect. Brick hoped tonight she might show some interest, or even some concern, after learning he would be working at the fair. It had been painfully obvious to Brick that his feelings for Emily were much stronger than hers for him. His common sense told him he should not feel this way.

Brick and Emily would be attending different colleges, and Brick knew that no matter how strong a connection may be, time and distance always creates hurdles for a successful relationship. Brick wasn't ready to throw in the towel though. When it came to his feelings for Emily, he had never felt such affection for someone.

Emily was already in her second week at Peace College in Raleigh. Freshman rules prevented her from going off campus for the first month, so it would be another two weeks before he would be able to see her. All their interaction was now dependent on the occasional letter or phone call. He made the call to Raleigh, hoping to catch her in the dorm.

Brick was lucky. The girl who answered the phone felt certain Emily was in her room, and she went to get her. Waiting for Emily to pick up the phone, Brick wondered how she would react to the news of him working at the fair. Even though Brick felt love for Emily, he was battling youthful hormones and quite aware of the excitement he felt about meeting the girls of the revue.

Brick was especially interested in the blond named Mary Jane as she had made quite an impression on him. Was it her flirtatious style or just the fact that she gave him some attention? He didn't know, but what he did know was it felt good. He also knew the feelings he had for Mary Jane were more lustful and had little to do with love.

When Emily picked up the phone and Brick heard her voice, his thoughts of the revue were quickly replaced by his love for Emily. He loved talking with her. She had the ability to make him smile and lift his spirits with a simple hello. To Brick, she had it all. She was smart, beautiful, outgoing, and very self-assured. The downside, however, was that everything he admired about her intimidated him. He often wondered if his feelings were the result of the two of them being from different areas of town. She was a downtown girl, and Brick was from the other side of the tracks—an area known as Jonesboro.

The two sides of town were only separated by a few miles; Jonesboro was considered the country and Sanford the city. Brick allowed this so-called social divide to bother him much more than it did Emily. He viewed her as someone who had it all together and was surely out of his league. It all added to unhealthy insecurities when it came to their relationship. She was not concerned with images; she had enough self-confidence to overcome any such hurdle. Brick struggled, thinking he was not quite good enough for Emily. She was smart and attractive with so much to offer, and he was a boy from Jonesboro with little direction. He feared one day she would come to her senses and see him for what he was (or what he thought he was) and move on to someone more in her class. But all the fears he had over the two not being compatible did not keep him from loving her.

Emily never gave Brick any reason for his paranoid feeling. Even though Brick knew his insecurities did not present a foundation for a healthy, lasting relationship, he continued to have them. Unfortunately, this seemed to be a constant battle raging in his mind. He knew he should look for ways to make the relationship stronger. Instead, he often allowed his fears to dictate his actions, creating more self-doubt and less confidence in their relationship. His biggest fear of Emily waking up and finding someone more self-assured and more her equal was always in the back of his mind. His negative thoughts prevented him from being genuine with her even when he knew it was unhealthy.

The silly thing was that Emily was first attracted to Brick by him just being himself and not pretending to be something he was not. He was a basket case when it came to her. He knew that at eighteen he was socially challenged and more than a little insecure when it came to girls. If there was a bright side, it was that Brick was aware of his shortcomings and was trying hard to change. He knew he needed to give himself some credit; after all, they had been dating for nearly a year.

Brick was pleasantly surprised by how happy Emily sounded when she heard his voice. She talked about her week and how it had been a long one, telling him her classes would finally be starting and things should get better. She then reminded Brick that his time was coming soon, and she was excited for him. He appreciated her thoughtfulness and told her he was anxious to get to Elon but not necessarily ready for the classes. He also shared that it was a bit slow around town, and he was missing her.

Emily said, "That's nice, but I know you are also missing some of the guys."

Emily asked Brick what he had been up to since he wasn't painting anymore. Brick laughingly told her that he and Ray had decided to run off and join the circus. Emily, not sure how to respond, questioned, "You're what?"

Brick then explained, "Well, maybe joining the circus is a stretch, but we are going to work this week at the Lee County fair."

Emily, somewhat puzzled, said, "You're joking, right? You and Ray will be working at the fair? It sounds to me the two of you have lost your minds. Do you have any idea what you will be doing?"

Brick answered, "I'm not exactly sure yet, but we did some work tonight helping to assemble some of the tents and rides. It was interesting and looks like it could be fun. We must have done something right; they asked us to come back tomorrow."

Emily seemed rather taken aback by the news. She questioned if he and Ray were sure they knew what they were doing. Brick responded, "Since things have been slow, and like you said, a lot of the guys have already gone off to school, Ray and I felt working the fair would be an interesting way to finish off our summer."

Emily replied, "It should be interesting all right; just be careful."

Brick, liking the fact that she was concerned, said, "Who knows? Maybe I'll run one of the games or be guessing someone's weight and finally see if those elusive teddy bears are ever won. I really don't have any idea what to expect. I guess we will find out tomorrow."

Brick changed the conversation, telling her he was looking forward to seeing her soon. She concurred but not as convincingly as he would have liked; that was his ugly insecurities rising once again.

Brick said, "I hope to have a story to tell you next time we see each other."

She then surprised him, telling him again to be careful. She thanked him for calling and added she was missing him. Just hearing her say those words almost made Brick's heart jump out of his body. Maybe his adventure had stirred something in Emily. It didn't matter though; her words of protection only made him care for her more.

Sleep would not come easy.

Brick was excited about working at the fair and what the coming week may hold. He wasn't sure if it was the excitement of working the fair or the thought of meeting a whole new group of people. All of it was thrilling to him.

He then began thinking of Mary Jane and hoped he would see her again—maybe even get to know her better. Brick thought, You just talked to Emily and you know how much she means to you, and now you are fantasizing about Mary Jane. Damn! He was one screwed up teenager

⚜

Odom's Sunday

The day had already been a long one for Odom. Most of his energy had been focused on the sermon and his passionate plea for the church to rise and take a stand. Although disappointed with the turnout, he felt good about his message. His sermon had unveiled a different man—a leader with responsibilities. He was preparing to take his place as the leader of a protest that would not only impact the church but the community as well.

After he finished eating his Sunday lunch, he and Beverly began discussing the protest and all he planned to do to ensure its success. Odom was so riled up about the protest coming up that he decided to drive out to the fairgrounds and get a better feel for how the attractions were being laid out. He was anxious and felt going to the fairgrounds would do him some good.

After the short drive, he arrived at the fairgrounds and began walking the midway to get the gist of how it was being transformed for the coming week. No one recognized him, and why would they? Few in town knew of him or his church but come Monday things would begin to change. People would start recognizing him, and it wouldn't be long before everyone would know his name.

Odom failed to see what he was looking for and returned to his car to wait. He watched various trucks arriving with the numerous attractions. After some time passed, he finally saw the one attraction he was hoping to see. The "All-Girl Nude Revue" was pulling onto the grounds. With the arrival of the revue, Odom knew there would be a need for the protest. If the revue was not included in this year's attractions, Odom's dream of relevance would have to be put on hold once again. But there it was—a lime green truck pulling a trailer advertising the erotic dancers. Odom thought the sign might as well read, Sin for Sale. He watched intently as the truck drove onto the grounds.

The workers quickly began unloading the tent and preparing the stage for the week's upcoming performances. Odom left his car to make one more walk around the midway, pausing for a short time at the revue. He took notice of the workers. He felt like a soldier readying for combat, putting his target in his crosshairs. His adrenaline began to rise, knowing the battle that was coming, and he was ready for victory.

It wasn't long before Odom returned home and reported to Beverly that the revue had arrived, and its home was being set up. She smiled, knowing this gave Odom a mission and a cause. They talked some more about the coming week, and he tried to hide his nervousness by taking a walk into Jonesboro just to pass the time.

When Odom returned from his walk, he felt he should get some rest; however, sleep would not come easy for him. No matter how hard he tried, his mind was full of anticipation for the coming week's protest. He was anxious—but confident—that the planned protest would mark a new direction for him and his church. The protest would be a unique experience for Odom, and he was optimistic about his ability to lead. His need for success had never been matched by his desire to work, but he was ready for the challenge that lay ahead of him. Although he had always wanted recognition and money to come his way, he had resisted working for it. It wasn't so much laziness as it was his lack of knowledge and direction. This time, he had a cause to pursue and a mission to support.

Before going to bed, Odom gave Hinson a call to check in and report on what he hoped Monday would bring. Hinson too was excited about the prospects and was supportive of Odom and his plans.

Still unable to sleep, Odom went to his office and once again began going over his plans for the week. In the dimly lit office, he stood and thought of chants and signs that could possibly help in gaining traction for the protest. It would be a busy week, but he was confident his efforts would be rewarded and well worth the work. It would not be long before the citizens of Sanford would welcome The Revival Revolutionary Church as a part of the community. The church would be recognized as a leader in the battle against sin and the evil being promoted by the revue. The roots of sin were long and robust, but he and the church were up to the challenge. Odom felt the time had come to hold Howard's Amusements accountable for their attractions. He looked over the homemade signs of protest and couldn't help but smile, feeling things were about to turn in his favor. His dream of wealth and influence would soon come true. He and his church would become well known in the city of Sanford.

He took a seat at an old wooden desk and began looking over a roster of church members. The names gave a clear indication of his struggling congregation, which was made up of a variety of transient citizens of various ages and backgrounds. Most of them had stumbled upon The Revival Revolutionary Church while looking for something possibly not found in a traditional church. Many had pledged their support for the protest, but he questioned how many would actually come to the fairgrounds. He remained optimistic as he had a feeling that participants in the protest would grow with each day. He feared some members had signed up only out of loyalty to him and not out of a commitment to the cause, but Odom didn't really care what motivated them. He just hoped they would follow through with their promise.

The Revival Revolutionary Church represented a place for nontraditional churchgoers to assemble and seek God's guidance. Odom was confident the names before him would only be a small sampling of the numbers the protest would draw. He believed that when word began to spread and people learned of the movement, it would grow. Odom envisioned the citizens of Sanford gravitating to the campaign once they grasped the importance of such a movement. He started making a mental checklist of all the news outlets contacted—radio, television. and newspapers—leaving no stone unturned. Although a little nervous, his confidence remained. Before long, he would be recognized as a community leader. He was going to lead a movement that would transform the Lee County fair for years to come.

Odom had never been so optimistic. Before now, his life had been a series of failures and missteps; he now felt his half-empty glass was overflowing with goodness. He believed success was near, and his future was bright.

Beverly entered the room, telling him he needed to come to bed. She reminded him of the big day. Odom was pleased with the attention he was getting from Beverly, and he was certain his life was beginning to fall into place. He had a loving wife and now had direction. It may have been the first time in his life he felt so confident about his future.

❧

Monday Morning

Ray was waiting in his driveway when Brick arrived. He was as anxious as Brick for the day to begin. Both wore jeans and a knit shirt—neither certain what to wear. The weather for the day was predicted to be overcast with a chance of rain and a high temperature in the eighties. Brick's parents were early risers, usually up around five o'clock in the morning, and his mother had told him what to expect weatherwise. Brick felt she was hoping he would change his mind once he heard it could rain. It was clear his mom had her concerns and was a bit apprehensive about his new job.

As they drove to the fairgrounds, the boys talked about the upcoming day and wondered what it would be like. The talk was all about fun as they speculated on their new adventures.

Brick pulled into a lot near the fairgrounds that was designated for employees. Before he could say anything, an elderly man came to the car and asked, "You boys here to work?"

Brick showed the man the badge Raeford had given him the night before and simply replied, "Yes sir, we sure are." He motioned them to park behind an old blue pickup truck, and with that, their day was about to begin. They exited the car and headed to the office.

Although the opening ceremonies were still hours away, the grounds were full of activity. The boys' heads were full of questions about the workers and about their jobs. This was their opportunity to learn more about the people who brought the fair to life. Were they all looking for an adventure that came with a paycheck? Both boys felt the life of the carnie must be varied and exciting.

While walking to the office, Ray asked if Brick had talked to Emily about the jobs. Brick happily responded, "Yeah, I called her late last night, and surprisingly, she seemed glad to hear from me. Of course, she did question our senses for taking on our new jobs. She also said we needed to be careful and not get into any trouble. Did you talk to Donna?"

"Oh yeah," Ray replied, "And I think her words were something like 'you have no business working for a carnival'." I tried to tell her it wouldn't be any different than working for the schools, but she didn't see it that way. It's no big deal; she'll get over it."

No one paid them much attention as everyone was busy preparing for the opening. Both boys figured they looked legit as no one asked for any identification. Brick wondered if Ray's dad was going to be at the opening ceremonies.

Ray said, "Yeah, he told me he needed to be here about an hour before the gates opened. He was going to meet with the mayor and last year's beauty queen, Donna Thomas." Hearing Donna would be at the opening ceremonies piqued Brick's interest. Ray added, "I think Donna is going to Central Carolina and living at home." Both worked with Donna one summer at Southern Packaging, and there was no debate everyone agreed she deserved her title of Miss Lee County Fair. She was a dark-haired beauty from the country, and unfortunately, Donna had little interest in guys from town.

Brick said, "I wouldn't mind seeing Donna. Maybe I can get to the opening ceremonies as well. Who knows? She might be ready for a little city action."

Ray shook his head, saying, "Damn, you talked with Emily last night, and I'm sure you were thinking about the girls from the revue. Now you're talking foolishly about Donna."

Brick smiled and said, "Yeah, I know. I'm such a shit."

"Not only are you a shit, but you are also one hell of a dreamer," Ray laughingly remarked. "Yeah, you talk big, but if Emily said jump, you would say how high?"

Brick replied, "Sad, but true. As you know, there's a song—'Mixed up, Shook-up Girl'. Well, that applies to me as a guy."

Ray shook his head. "Let's find Raeford and get this day started."

As they passed the Ferris wheel, a large lady with red hair asked if they needed anything. They told her they didn't and showed their badges. Ray said to her, "We are on our way to the office to see Raeford. She smiled and welcomed them to Howard's Amusements.

At the office, they knocked on the door and heard Raeford yell, "It's open!" Raeford saw them standing in the doorway and said, "So, you boys decided to return to give it a shot." That was how Raeford welcomed them to a new day with Howard's Amusements. "You boys ready to work?"

Both quickly responded, "Yes sir."

Raeford wasn't worried about any paperwork or official application, telling them they could get it done later.

Their first assignment was at "The World Zoo." The attraction had arrived late due to engine trouble. He instructed the boys to go over to its location and help with the setup. The zoo was sort of a petting zoo where patrons could see the animals up close. Raeford told them to ask for Doyle and to tell him he sent them over to help. Before leaving, Raeford asked that they come back later for their next assignments. They thanked him and headed to the zoo.

They had no trouble finding the attraction. It was being laid out near the livestock barns, which is where they found Doyle and introduced themselves. Doyle said he hoped they didn't mind a little dirt. Both smiled and said, "Just tell us what you need."

Doyle pointed toward some fencing on a large flatbed truck that needed to be unloaded and constructed. They quickly became fully engaged in assorting the fencing and moving it into a tent that had already been assembled. The fencing would be used to designate a walking perimeter for those viewing the animals in cages. The whole process didn't take much over an hour.

Their next assignment was to help move the animals into their temporary home inside the tent. First, it was a llama to which Ray jokingly asked, "Is your mama a llama?"

Brick rolled his eyes and said, "Funny, let's keep moving."

They then placed a zebra in the viewing area, followed by some large and very heavy turtles. Then came a camel, a long-haired dog being passed off as a wolf, and a monkey cage with two rambunctious monkeys enjoying the move. Both Brick and Ray felt the most intriguing of the animals was a male lion with his mane brushed out to give it an even more fearful look. Although the lion remained in a cage, both boys were a little apprehensive when pushing the lion's cage to its designated spot. Of all the animals they moved, they were most concerned about the lion. Other than the monkeys, most of the animals appeared old and possibly drugged as they exhibited very little movement.

The tent itself gave the appearance of being a free attraction— appearance being the keyword. Once inside, donations were strongly encouraged. Apparently, it would take a cash offering to exit the tent. It was a real bait and switch operation; nothing is free at the fair.

It was getting close to the opening ceremonies when Raeford joined them at "The World Zoo." The attraction was the last to be assembled, and now the midway was ready for business. Raeford said he needed one of them to help distribute tickets and the other to help with the opening ceremonies. Since Ray's dad would be at the opening, he chose to go with Raeford to the front gate. Raeford liked the fact Ray's dad was a member of The Lions Club. He knew it never hurt to be in good with the host organization. Raeford then asked Brick to go back to the office and find a lady named Betty Anne. "Tell her you are there to help with the ticket distribution, and she will be able to tell you what needs to be done."

Brick found Betty Anne at the office, and she welcomed him to Howard's Amusements. She told him to let her know if he needed anything. Betty Anne reminded Brick of so many of his friends' mothers; she was polite and had that take care of others personality.

Betty Anne then asked Brick if he had filled out an application. He replied, "Raeford says we'll get to it, but so far, I haven't seen one."

Betty Anne smiled as she responded. "Typical Raeford! You leave it up to him, and you will go all week without one. Need it more for the payment process. No big deal unless you want to get paid."

She asked Brick if he knew of any others who were starting work and would need to fill out an application. He mentioned Ray, who was with Raeford preparing for the opening ceremonies. Betty Anne suggested she catch both of them at the same time. "When you get a chance to grab Ray, come back here and we will make everything official."

After that, Betty Anne began explaining the packets of tickets and how they would be distributed. Brick learned that each ticket window would get a pack of 3,000 tickets, and someone would need to sign for them. She said, "Just bring me the signed sheets when you come back so we can finish up the paperwork." For the start of the day, Brick had six packets of tickets to distribute with the understanding that if more were needed, an afternoon delivery would take place.

Brick learned the fair operated primarily on a voucher economy. All of the rides and most of the games did not accept cash, requiring the patrons to use tickets. One could purchase tickets at any of the six ticket booths, and the cost of the tickets was ten cents each or twelve for a dollar. The number of tickets required for each attraction was dependent on its appeal. The more expensive rides were the newer and bigger ones. The food vendors and most of the sideshows operated on a cash-only basis.

Brick's first delivery was to a grouchy old man at the kiddie rides. The man did not say much; he just took the tickets and signed off on them. Brick thought, Nice to meet you too. He could not figure out why this man of all people would be at the kiddie rides. He had no personality and appeared to be holding a grudge against everyone. This man surely wasn't a salesman and seemed a poor choice for the kiddie rides.

The next drop-off was to an older lady; of course, this was just an assumption on Brick's part. He felt most of the people working the fair looked older than their years— maybe a byproduct of the work. Not knowing many older people outside his family, Brick had little to compare with the workers when it came to aging.

When he reached the lady, she told him she had been looking for the tickets. She was talkative and said she hoped to need them all— and then some. Her booth was out from the children's' rides but still in front of the more tamed ones, such as the bumper cars, the giant slide, the haunted house, and the house of mirrors. The remainder of the booths were scattered out in a circular fashion, allowing anyone access to a ticket booth with limited walking. Once Brick finished delivering the tickets, he placed the signed sheets in his pocket and decided to go to the opening ceremonies.

His walk was rewarded when he spotted Mary Jane and Misty leaving one of the food trailers. Brick started walking toward them, hoping they would say something. His wish was granted when Mary Jane saw him and spoke, "Does this mean you are working?"

"Yes, Ray and I are now official employees of Howard's Amusements," Brick replied. He told her about delivering the tickets and that he wasn't sure what his next job would be, but he was ready.

Mary Jane said, "It's Brick, right?"

"Yeah, and you are Mary Jane?"

"That's right." She then asked where he was off too.

"I'm going to the opening ceremonies and catch up with Ray and Raeford to find out what I need to do next."

"Misty, maybe we should go with him, you know opening ceremonies can be interesting."

"You go ahead. I've got some things I need to take care of before we open," Misty replied.

Brick asked when the revue would be opening. Mary Jane said they would open their tent around four o'clock and would be there until no one is left to entertain. She then said, "Or, as Tammy likes to say, show our boobs to."

Brick, feeling flirtatious, laughed and told her, "That could be late into the night."

Misty told him he was sweet and that she hoped he was right. Before leaving, she told Brick to tell Ray hello, and she was sorry that she missed him. She then added, "Be sure to spread the word—best show in town." Mary Jane grabbed Brick's arm, telling him she did not want him to get fired before he even gets started.

Brick assured Misty he would spread the word and began following Mary Jane to the front gates. He then realized how tall she was, and although he had recognized her beauty before, her height now made her even more erotic. Brick's thoughts of Mary Jane were confirmed as she walked slightly ahead of him. She had quite a body! Brick enjoyed talking with her as they walked together. He viewed her as a mystery he hoped to solve.

Mary Jane wanted to know what folks in Sanford do for fun. Brick was beginning to feel more comfortable talking with her, and he said, "This week you're it, or at least it's the fair."

Mary Jane took hold of his arm and smiled as she said, "I liked it better when you said I was the excitement."

Brick assured her she was indeed the source of his enthusiasm. She leaned against his side and said, "Misty's right; you are sweet. But tell me, when the fair's not here, what do you do for fun?"

With little feeling, Brick replied, "I'm afraid Sanford is like most small towns in America; there is not much happening. We do a lot of riding around—cruising the block. There are a couple of movie theaters, and that's about it."

Mary Jane said, "Sounds a lot like my hometown."

Brick asked, "Where's home?"

"A place you've probably never heard of—Clover, South Carolina."

Brick responded, "You've got me there, but to be honest, if it's not on the way to Myrtle Beach, I more than likely wouldn't know. I don't know much about South Carolina. Do know about 'South of the Border' but little else."

Mary Jane sweetly said, "That's okay. I had never heard of Sanford until we pulled in yesterday. Sanford and Clover probably have a lot in common. Kids in Clover go to Charlotte and Rock Hill for excitement."

"Here, it's either Raleigh or Fayetteville," said Brick.

Both smiled at the common ground they shared.

Mary Jane then said, "Maybe you can introduce me to Sanford, and show me around a little bit." Brick liked the sound of that and assured her it would be his pleasure. She laughed flirtatiously and said she hoped so.

It was all new territory for Brick. Although Mary Jane could not have been much older than him, she was more experienced, and she was showing interest in him. He was excited by the flirtation and what it may mean. He tried his best to remain calm, hoping the talk would lead to more than just conversation. Maybe she was just a tease, but that didn't bother him. At this point in Brick's life, a little teasing wouldn't be all bad. They continued to walk toward the front gate when Mary Jane asked if he would be coming to the show later.

With a hint of excitement, Brick replied, "I sure hope so; I've been thinking about it since we met."

She smiled, saying, "I'm glad; I'm looking forward to seeing you there."

At the entrance, Brick spotted Ray standing with his dad. He and Mary Jane had arrived in time for the ribbon cutting. There was little going on (more standing around than ceremony), and from the looks of things, it appeared the opening was on hold. Brick found out from a member of the Lions Club that they were waiting on the mayor and a reporter from The Sanford Herald.

When Ray saw Brick with Mary Jane, he had to smile. He told his dad he needed to talk to them for a moment. Russell, Ray's father, looked over at Brick with Mary Jane at his side and waved. Mary Jane looked as innocent as any student from Sanford Central High. Brick was confident Russell had no idea what her current occupation was. One thing Brick was sure of was that Mary Jane's stunning, good looks and her innocent mannerism would bring a smile to anyone's face. Brick returned the wave without saying anything. Mary Jane followed Brick's lead and waved. Russell was probably trying to figure out who she was, assuming she was one of the boys' classmates. Mary Jane looked at Brick, saying he seemed sweet and maybe he would come to the show. Hearing this, Ray told her he didn't think his dad would be making an appearance.

Mary Jane smiled and said, "You never know." She then told Ray that Misty had been looking for him.

Ray looked at Brick, telling him, "I hope you told her we would be working all week."

"Oh, she knows," said Brick.

Then Mary Jane reminded Ray that Misty wanted him to spread the word about the show being the best on the midway. With a chuckle, Ray responded, "Don't you worry; I'm telling everyone."

It wasn't long before the mayor, Rick Blue, arrived and began shaking hands and apologizing for running late. Then the reporter from the Herald arrived with a photographer. Raeford pulled out a ribbon that looked as if it had been used numerous times before. There was evidence the fabric had been taped back together more than once. Raeford, Mr. Hill, Mayor Blue, and Donna Thomas-Miss Lee County

Fair posed for several pictures as they cut the ribbon. The 1969 edition of the Lee County Fair was now officially open.

Brick did take the opportunity to speak to Donna, who was dressed in a white shortcut dress that made her look stunning with her dark hair and complexion. They exchanged pleasantries, and Brick shared the news that he and Ray would be working the fair all week. It was painfully obvious that Donna had no interest in his work (or him, for that matter).

After the ribbon cutting was complete, Raeford asked the boys to go down to the office where they could complete the paperwork with Betty Anne. He then told both, "When you are done with Betty Anne, go down to the livestock yard and ask for Mr. Alexander. He's a local Lions Club member. He's overseeing the livestock display and might need some help." Ray asked if he was talking about Charles Alexander.

Raeford acknowledged, "Yeah, I think that's his name. Do you know him?" Ray told him that Mr. Alexander had been one of their teachers at their high school.

Raeford grinned and said, "Well, not today. He's working in cow shit, and he may need some help. Tell him you are working for us and are there to assist."

On the way to the office, Mary Jane walked slightly in front of Brick and Ray. Dressed in tight shorts and a cotton blouse tied at her waist, Mary Jane revealed enough curves to create fantasies for both. She carried herself with such grace and beauty, and Brick couldn't figure her out. Why would a woman with so much to offer strip for a living? In his mind, Mary Jane seemed to have the world by a string and could do anything she put her mind to. Brick knew he was being judgmental, and that wasn't fair to her or anyone. It was her life, and if she wanted to do it, then more power to her.

Mary Jane told them she would see them later and started walking toward some trailers. Brick took the opportunity to ask if that was where she was staying. Without hesitation she replied, "Misty and I share a trailer beside the barracks—the closer to the showers the better. It's our home for the week."

In the office, Betty Anne offered them a seat and handed both an official employment application. The form was little more than an information sheet asking for name, address, Social Security number, and a contact number. She made it a point to tell them they would be paid in cash unless they decided to come on full-time. She then gave each of them food vouchers that would get them fifty percent off at specially marked vendors. She suggested they come by the office every morning—unless Raeford said differently—to get their daily assignments. She repeated what Raeford told them: "The job determines the pay." She went on to say, "Your badges will allow you to ride the rides for free when you're not working, and the food vouchers will help keep your expenses down. If you wish to attend any of the sideshows, it is totally up to the operator whether you pay or not. The sideshows only accept cash—no tickets. Do you have any questions?"

Brick and Ray were both curious about how long the workday would be. She shrugged her shoulders and said, "That's a good question, but unfortunately, there is no way to determine the hours. You can rest assured it will not be your standard nine-to-five job. You can work as long as there is a need, and you can count on there being a need. Raeford will let you know for sure."

To the surprise of both boys, she then asked if she could give them some motherly advice. They, of course, were fine with it, so she said, "Listen, I want you to know that we have some good people working here and a few jack asses; you'll be able to tell the difference. No matter, you can learn a lot from most of the good folks, but you will probably see some things you will want to avoid. I know since both of you are young and adventurous, you will be interested in the girls working at the revue. Let me tell you, those girls are sweet, and they work hard. Do not assume they are anything but cute girls, even if they do work the revue. These girls are people too and should be respected just as everyone else here should be. If you show respect, you will receive it back. It is as simple as that. I like to think of Howard's Amusements as one large family, and we want to keep it that way. If I were you, I would stay away from the drinkers and the gamblers. No good will come from hanging out with them. Also, if you see something that bothers you, let me know, or tell Raeford. We both want your experience to be positive, and we want your moms and dads to be proud you chose to work with us."

At the few other jobs Brick had worked, no one had ever taken the time to share anything about the people he would be working with. It was very clear Betty Anne was a nice person, and she was proud of Howard's Amusements.

They thanked Betty Anne. She then told them they could usually find her in the office if they needed anything and not to hesitate to come see her if they had any questions. Before leaving, Ray did ask about any rules regarding the residents' trailer park they should know. She smiled and said, "We have a simple request that there be no loud music after midnight. It's home for many and needs to be treated as such. We do have security twenty-four seven. Be courteous and get to know the people. You should have plenty of work to do, but if you are shy, you could go hungry. Good luck fellows, and again, welcome to Howard's Amusements."

They thanked her again and exited the trailer. Ray suggested they drop by to see Misty and Mary Jane. He felt they should invite the girls to join them for lunch. The idea appealed to Brick, but neither knew which trailer was home for the girls. Brick got up his nerve and decided to knock on the one closest to the barracks, and luckily, he was right. Mary Jane opened the door slightly. With the door ajar, she asked if they were now official.

"That we are," said Brick. We are planning on getting something to eat and wanted to know if y'all would like to join us."

Mary Jane smiled and politely said, "No thanks. We are eating in and need to get ready for work. Maybe you can give us a rain check for another time." Brick was pleased when she mentioned the rain check and didn't hesitate to tell her she was on.

It was difficult for Brick to remain cool as there was so much about her he wanted to learn. She was not only sexy as hell, but she was friendly and reassuring. Brick knew he was beginning to like her as a person—not just as an entertainer.

Misty popped her head in the door and asked if they would mind doing them a favor, and of course, there were no objections. She asked if they would carry some items to the revue's tent. Brick and Ray were anxious to oblige. The girls invited them in while they gathered some things to send over.

In the small trailer, Brick took quick stock of the area. It was little more than three separate rooms. There was a bedroom at each end with no doors, just curtains separating the areas from the center space. In the middle of the trailer was a tiny kitchen with not much more than a hot plate and a small refrigerator. What looked like a closet stuck out from the side, and Brick assumed it was a bathroom. Misty and Mary Jane went back to their bedrooms, and Brick could see them laying out some clothes on the bed. They then placed other pieces of clothing in separate bags. Misty told Ray each of them had a bin at the tent, and she asked that they put the bags in the ones with their names on them. Misty very seductively said to Ray, "I hope you like my choices."

Ray only said, "I'm sure I will."

Mary Jane handed Brick her bag, and both girls stated they expected to see them at the show later. Ray—ever so cocky—replied, "I will be there with a smile on my face."

As they walked away, Ray told Brick that he thought Mary Jane might be a little sweet on him. Brick didn't want to give in to his hopes, but he certainly wouldn't mind if Ray was right. Brick found Mary Jane to be so inviting, and there was no denying he was becoming fond of her. Brick knew it wasn't just hormones, though, that played a significant role in his desire.

Out front of the revue stood a lady neither had met. Brick told her they had been asked to drop some things off for Mary Jane and Misty. The woman was older but very friendly. She quickly said they must be the new guys the girls had been talking about. Hearing that the girls had talked about them only added to the boys' already inflated egos. Brick as polite as ever said, "Yes mam, we started last night—hope to be working all week."

She introduced herself as Lucy and assured them there was always a need for good help. Brick and Ray gave their names, telling her they were looking forward to the work. Lucy smiled and told them it was always good to see a fresh face, and she hoped to see them again.

Lucy looked to be in her early forties. Judging from her appearance, Brick felt she must have had years of experience with the fair. Dressed in jeans and a red blouse, Brick was uncertain if she was a dancer or not. She didn't look the part, but that didn't mean much.

Lucy told them to follow her. They entered the tent where they saw the platform that would serve as the stage. The plywood platform couldn't have been over ten feet long and maybe five feet deep. Lucy led them to the far side of the stage and up some steps. There they saw a curtain that served as a border to the makeshift dressing room. On the side wall were six bins, all with names on them; some had two names, but Misty and Mary Jane had individual ones. The boys placed the items into the bins and thanked Lucy. Lucy then asked them how well they knew MJ and Misty. Brick told her, "We just met last night. We stopped by to see them, and they asked us to bring this stuff up."

Lucy said, "MJ and Misty are special girls—beautiful and talented. I guess you could say I'm like the house mother to the girls, and of course, I think they are all special. I have seen my share of girls come and go, and believe me, MJ and Misty are good girls. Of course, this year I feel that way about all of the girls." Ray told her they had also met Tammy and Sugar.

Lucy then said, "This week, you will meet a lot of folks—some good and some bad. Be respectful to the good ones and stay away from the asses, and you will enjoy your week." Lucy sounded a lot like Betty Anne, and Brick knew being respectful was good advice for anyone at any time. As they began to leave, Lucy said she hoped to see them later on. Both told her to count on it. She smiled, saying, "Great."

As the boys walked away from the revue, Ray said, "You know, I think I'm going to enjoy this week. So far, everyone has been good to us, and the work hasn't been that hard. And getting to know some of the entertainers; well, that's a bonus."

Brick asked Ray if he thought Lucy, was a stripper. "Who knows? I'll bet if she's not, she was at one time," answered Ray.

Brick said in response, "True. I wouldn't mind seeing her dance."

Ray shook his head and told Brick that he was so horny he wouldn't mind seeing "Tonya, the Gorilla Girl" strip. Brick was laughing and told him he might have a point. He then said, "I hope Emily doesn't find out about all our new friends. I have enough issues with her without her knowing I'm trying to pick up a stripper."

Ray told him, "No worries here—I won't say a word. No need for Donna to learn about our new friends either. I'm only hoping we have something that requires us to be quiet." Both were laughing as they walked toward the corndog trailer.

The boys used their discount to buy corndogs, fries, and a Coke. The food vendor knew they were new and asked when they started working. Ray answered, "We started last night and hope to work most of the week." The vendor told them to be careful as he started three years ago, looking to do one week, and has been working with Howard's ever since.

Brick said, "Sounds like you enjoy it."

"Enjoy it may be a stretch, but the money is good, and you see a lot of sights. So, I guess it's not all bad." He then turned his attention to a new customer. Ray and Brick found a place to sit down and eat. They ate quickly, knowing the crowds were beginning to arrive, and they needed to get moving.

Once they finished eating, they went straight to the livestock display. It looked like most of the animals had already arrived. They had no problem finding Mr. Alexander, and he was surprised to see them. Ray said, "You just can't get rid of us." They all laughed, and Ray explained how they had a week before college and decided to try working at the fair, adding how they both thought the experience would be good for them and how happy they were to be making some extra money.

Mr. Alexander smiled, saying, "I envy you boys. Your whole life is in front of you, and you decide to begin the journey here at the Lee County fair. Well, come on. You can help me with this display."

The display consisted of a small tent that gave visitors information on the scheduled judging of the animals. As they were asked to do, they spread out a few free coupons on a table for some of the attractions. It was a way to stir up traffic to the livestock section of the midway. The fair represented a total marketing effort—one item selling another. Although the works of the fair appeared rather simple in truth, it was a well-organized machine. Each attraction contributed to the overall success. When they finished, Mr. Alexander wished them luck and said he hoped to see them again.

Charles Alexander was a respected teacher. Brick hoped that when he told Emily about working with Mr. Alexander that she would see the job as being legit and a worthwhile adventure.

As the boys prepared to leave the area, a lady came up to them, asking if they were Brick and Ray. She told them Raeford had sent her over to tell them they were needed at the "Water Shoot" and the "Duck Pond" to relieve some of the workers. Ray asked, "Where do we go?" She told them they could find the games over near the "House of Mirrors," adjacent to the kiddie rides. The boys thanked her and once again said bye to Mr. Alexander. He told them to have a great week and to come back to see him sometime at the school.

Morning for Odom

Before leaving home, Odom again called the local paper and the radio stations. He felt confident this would be the day that would mark the beginning of his quest for publicity. He was sure the news outlets would soon be the ones contacting him after they learned of the movement and its importance. Odom believed things would begin snowballing as the community began to grasp the mission, the call for the protest, and his church.

Odom met a small group from his congregation outside the main gate at the fairgrounds. When everyone had gathered, he asked the group to bow their heads and join him in prayer. Odom wanted God to lead the group, helping them take a stand against the sinful activity found on the midway. He prayed, asking God for His guidance and strength for his group to defeat Satan today, tomorrow, and the remainder of the week.

After the short public prayer, Odom and his group made their mission clear by holding up the signs of protest. They were without a doubt striving to shut down the girly shows. Those taking part in the protest claimed the shows were immoral and sinful, and any decent God-fearing man would never attend such an attraction. For Odom, the early movement of the protest now gave him confidence his life was about to change.

Painfully, the truth was that Odom's efforts thus far had only attracted a handful of parishioners. He had been hoping for a bigger turnout, but he resisted being dissuaded by the small showing. Odom asked the assembled group to remain focused and show determination, and he called for them to be loyal to the church and the mission. He reminded the group that the Lord was on their side and that soon the movement would attract others. His belief had always been that once the word began to spread, others would join the fight, and the numbers would grow. Victory was just around the corner! Odom proclaimed, "We may be slight in numbers, but God's word will guide us to victory in the battle with Satan." Odom sounded more like a coach than a preacher, but he was putting his heart into the cause.

He had given protest signs to all of his followers, which were to not only share the message but to hopefully draw attention to the church's grassroots effort to shut down the girly shows. The signs read, Sin Must Stop/The Revue is Sin/Turn Away from Sin and Believe in the Lord. They were hand painted by Odom and Beverly, and of course, each sign identified the church. Soon, everyone would learn of The Revival Revolutionary Church. Odom was pleased that all the protesters had brought their Bibles; he felt holding a Bible in one hand and a sign in the other would help illustrate the strength of the message.

It would still be several hours before the revue would open, but Odom was hoping to get a few steps ahead by starting the protest early. He was looking to gain the attention of those early attendees. He envisioned the protest as a means to dissuade potential customers from the revue, making them think twice before paying for admission.

While Odom was waiting to move the protest to the fairgrounds, he noticed a reporter from The Sanford Herald who was there to cover the opening ceremonies. Odom was able to catch up with the reporter, Jarred Turner. He told Turner he would like to speak with him about their protest and what they hoped to accomplish. Odom was pleased when Turner showed some interest in the rally and asked him several questions, even taking a few notes. Their interchange made him happy, and Odom felt confident something would be in the next day's paper.

After a few hours of protesting at the entrance, Odom led his small group onto the grounds. They settled on a site adjacent to the revue, but they were blocking a food vendor; therefore, security asked them to move. They found a small vacant spot, and with the modest number of people in the group, there was plenty of room for everyone.

When the protest was in full swing, Odom noticed Jimmy Moore, the photographer from the Herald. Moore took a few photos of Odom and his followers holding their home-made signs while spouting the evil of the shows. Moore's attention to the group thrilled Odom. He was now more confident than ever that the paper would be featuring an article on the protest. The newspaper coverage would help grow the momentum of the protest, and Odom was on a personal high. He could now visualize the respect and acceptance he would gain from the religious community he so desperately desired.

Odom's Backstory

Before accepting the call to the ministry, Odom had lived a rather colorful past. He had always struggled with his career and identity. For the most part, no matter what direction his life took, he found it difficult to fit in. Even in the Army, Odom failed to adjust. After having been charged with insubordination, which landed him in the brig, he received a general discharge from service.

Once out of the military, he began a series of temporary and unsatisfying jobs. He had tried his hand at being a plumber's helper and did landscaping work (a skill learned while serving time in a Virginia prison for writing bad checks). Pastor Odom had many occupations but never a successful career.

Misguided reasoning could have been Odom's life story. It was while driving a cab in South Boston, Virginia, that he decided to try his hand at the ministry. It was his first attempt, and establishing a church was a dream of his; however, after struggling for a while, he was unable to find a foothold for his church.

Sadly, Odom's draw to the ministry was not out of a calling from the Lord but out of personal interest. Odom saw the church merely as a means to individual accomplishments. The church could be his vehicle to accomplishing what he wanted most—respect, recognition, and personal wealth. Odom had always been envious of people with wealth and notoriety, and from some illogical reasoning, he felt the church could propel him to the Promised Land.

Odom's infatuation with the church and its potential for him came full circle when he came upon a roadside revival in his native state of Virginia. He was driving a taxi for Red Horse Cabs in Norfolk when he picked up a passenger who would have a major impact on his life. The passenger turned out to be a minister, Alton Brown. He was immaculately dressed and oozed trustworthiness and self-confidence. They talked during the ride, and he invited Odom to attend the tent revival he was leading on the outskirts of town.

Odom was impressed with the man dressed in a gray silk suit, a white shirt with gold cufflinks, and a large gold cross hanging on a chain around his neck. He was mesmerized by the minister's positive self-image and charismatic personality. Brown had all the qualities that led Odom to make the decision to attend the tent service that night.

At the revival, Odom not only was able to witness the power of the church but also the power of the spoken word. He had limited experience with the church; he had always felt uncomfortable in a religious setting. It was that night at the revival that Alton Brown began changing Odom's perceptions and beliefs in the church.

During the sermon, Odom again was moved with Brown's mannerisms—and his message. He was especially awestruck by the attention others were giving Brown. It became clear to Odom that through the influence of the church, he could begin gaining respect and power by becoming a minister. The preacher was impressive, and Odom developed a desire to learn more about the man and his ministry.

Odom discovered Brown was a traveling evangelist from Memphis, Tennessee, and he was currently conducting tent revivals throughout the southeast. Even though Brown didn't have the notoriety of a Billy Graham, Oral Roberts, or even Jimmy Swaggert, he did have a strong following. It was clear they had helped support his lifestyle rather well.

Odom was so impressed with Brown that first night that he answered the call to give his life to Christ. When it came time for the invitational hymn, Brown called on the attendees to come forward and accept Jesus Christ as their Lord and Savior. As people began to move toward the front, Odom joined them; he took his place among many. He and the others were giving their souls to the Lord.

After the service, Odom waited around in hopes of meeting with Brown. He was successful, and the two of them began discussing the ministry as well as the biblical teachings. Odom was as much enthralled in the man as he was his message. The flashy veteran preacher, who

Odom so admired, told him he loved talking with others about the wonders of the Lord. Odom seemed to be looking for direction, and Brown promised one could always find guidance in the word of God. At that time, however, Odom wasn't looking as much for direction as he was a break.

Odom had been down on his luck for what felt like forever, but Brown's message gave him hope, and he returned the next night with his wife Beverly. That evening, they witnessed the wonders and the power of religion—blended with showmanship. More than the miracles of the church, Odom observed people giving money and shouting praise for the Lord—and also for Brown. He became intoxicated with the attention and money Brown was receiving, and he desired everything that Brown was getting—money, respect, and admiration. It was then that Odom started to believe the ministry may be the answer to his dreams, and it could help write his ticket to a better life.

Odom was hooked and returned nearly every night of the three-week revival. He wanted to know more about Brown and his ministry. He shared with Beverly his desire for what Brown had amassed, and she was seduced by Brown's power as well. Both began to believe the church held the answer to so many of their prayers. During those nights, Odom befriended Brown, and with Brown's encouragement and help, Odom formulated his plans for a new life.

Although Odom had never felt comfortable in church, often feeling out of place, his feelings for the church began to change while attending the revival. It was there that Odom discovered Alton Brown and the power of the gospel. He began seeing the church differently. It now felt the church could offer him a pathway to personal success, however, one could easily question his qualifications or sincerity of being called to the ministry. Odom at age forty-two was feeling the need for a change. He saw the church as a beacon of hope, holding the answers for success while providing a pathway to transformation. With the minister's help, Odom decided to embark on a new mission in life.

Brown suggested several avenues that would help Odom pursue a career in the ministry. Odom, never one with patience, felt Brown's suggestions would require more time and money than he possessed. The religious schools around Richmond would take years to complete.

Odom began looking for alternative ways to join the clergy. Good fortune came his way when he ran across an advertisement in Grit Newspaper. The ad offered religious training and official recognition through correspondence courses. The training was offered by The Revival Revolutionary Church and Bible College in Greenwood, Mississippi.

The credentials provided by the college were little more than a piece of paper designed to create tax breaks for its ministers and make money for the home organization. This arrangement suited Odom just fine. He was never one to be bogged down with details, and the school offered a quick solution to his needs. Odom sent away for the courses, most of which dealt with the religious doctrine of The Revival Revolutionary Church. The course work was limited, but he completed it and spent several hundred dollars for the certification. In a matter of months, Odom had become an ordained minister.

Once ordained, he quickly created a small storefront church, and he opened his church in a rundown strip mall in the suburbs of Norfolk. For Odom, however, reality was a cruel teacher. He promptly discovered there's more to running a church than just declaring yourself a minister and putting up a sign. Fortunately, he never stopped driving a cab.

He became frustrated by the lack of success, and he and Beverly decided they may need a fresh start. It was then that they decided to relocate the church and his ministry to Sanford. When they arrived, Odom announced he had come to Sanford, at the request of the governing board of The Revival Revolutionary Church, to create a branch of the church for the people of Sanford. This was, of course, a fabrication of Odom's.

✣

Beverly's Past

Odom had personal knowledge of the girly shows and how they operated. Beverly, his wife of twelve years, had various jobs while working one season for Arrington's Attractions. She managed rides, ran games of chance, and at one time even danced for the erotic shows. At that time, Beverly was on the run from an abusive husband and was vulnerable to such a lifestyle.

When Beverly met Patrick Odom, she was attempting to put her past behind her. She was waitressing at a café in Norfolk, and Odom was a regular customer. It wasn't long before they developed a relationship that grew out of need and want. She and Odom were able to look beyond their colorful backgrounds. Beverly saw Odom as a handsome and friendly man, and he saw her as a country beauty. They were two lost souls finding reassurance in one another. The partnership they formed through marriage may have been the most success either had ever experienced. Beverly seldom spoke of her past, wanting to leave it behind. She discussed working for Arrington's once, telling Odom she never wanted to talk about it again. She was now a different person, and the shame she felt was history.

When the call came from Hinson, Odom knew he would need to discuss it with Beverly. He hoped she would support the protest even if it meant revisiting tragic moments from her past. He told Beverly about the call from Hinson and what he wanted. As he talked with her about the protest, she began to cry. Beverly still had built up anger and feelings of shame from the year she had spent working on the carnival circuit.

Through her tears, Beverly expressed her support for the protest. She had never stopped worrying about the girls who worked the shows, always questioning their treatment. Beverly feared the women dancers were being taken advantage of and may even be subject to abuse. She didn't want anyone else to suffer the horror she had. Beverly's views of the shows were tainted by her experiences, and she now felt lucky she had escaped the business. Beverly wanted Odom to take on the mission and closed down the shows. She was there to support him. She shared Hinson's beliefs that the industry was evil and promoted sin.

Beverly had resisted speaking of her abusive past for many years, but with Hinson's call, the hate and pain she had endured all came back. Beverly's pain became a motivational factor in her desire to help Odom lead a successful protest. She believed if Odom could raise social awareness of the shows, more people would see the negatives of such entertainment venues. Beverly wanted the demonstration to be an educational outlet about the abusive lifestyle many of the dancers had to endure. Odom was thrilled with her encouragement.

Beverly also felt such an undertaking would be a noble cause for the church. She, like Hinson, saw the protest as a stand against evil. For Odom, however, it had nothing to do with social change and everything to do with raising him from a storefront minister to a respected member of the religious community.

At The Fair

B rick was surprised by the sight of the protest. He wasn't sure what or
why they were protesting. It wasn't until he began to read the signs
and listen to their chants, Stop the Temptation of Sin/End the Shows/
God over Lust, that he knew what the group was protesting. It was the
revue, and Brick questioned why. He began to study the protesters and
was thankful he didn't recognize anybody.

He had heard in the past that some disgruntled people in town
complained about the possibility that the games of chance were rigged,
but since he had been attending the fair, he had never seen anyone take
to the streets to protest any of the shows. His last year at Central he did
have a teacher complain about the girly shows. She warned the boys to
stay away from such shows, feeling they were exploiting women and
degrading society; however, few gave much thought to her concerns
or declaration.

Brick couldn't help but feel it was odd that the group was protesting
an entertainment venue that no one had to attend. He saw the war in
Vietnam and the civil rights movement being more likely targets than
the girly shows of a county fair. Brick believed the group's energy
could be better spent with other more pressing issues affecting society.
He reasoned the shows would only be in town for a short while, and
there wouldn't be enough time to create much trouble. He felt the
protesters were missing the mark when it came to challenging morality;
if anything was immoral, it was the war. Too many young people
were being sent to a land far away without knowing why or what they
hoped to accomplish. Many of those young people were returning to
towns across America in a pine box. This was immoral—not a group
of dancing girls.

Brick, like so many others, had registered for the draft at age eighteen, and the thought of going off to war scared him. His dad went to war at his age, and since his brother had finished college and no longer had a deferment, he was now considering joining the Army to satisfy his obligation to serve our country. Even with strong military ties, no one in his family felt positive about the war or its cause. It was a known fact that most of those attending the girly shows would be young men of draft age or currently in the service. Fort Bragg was only thirty miles away, and the revue would offer an escape from the threat of war and the Army.

The war in Vietnam was not the only root of social protests. Racial tension was ever growing, and integration remained a hot topic. Many changes were taking place. The fall of 1969 would be the first year Brick's high school would be fully integrated. Brick believed protesting the war and the civil rights movement were helping change society for the better, but opposing a girly show seemed misdirected and unnecessary. Brick was aware his views were a little biased, especially since he had met some of the dancers. But he still could not rationalize the need for demonstrations against the shows.

Brick hoped the group would quickly become bored and leave. He was looking forward to an exciting and enjoyable week and was not interested in distractions. His gut, however, told him this group might be in it for the long haul. His feelings were supported by the actions of the overweight and balding man he believed to be the leader. The man leading the protest seemed entrenched with his beliefs, and he seemed intent on having his message heard. At this time, Brick felt little empathy for the man or the protest.

Brick had no trouble finding the "Duck Pond" where he met Arty Crain, who appeared to be in the throes of battling a hangover and welcomed the relief. When Crain thanked Brick for coming in, it was evident he was ready for a break. Brick attempted to ask him a few questions about the operation of the game but with little success. Brick wanted to know if Crain had been busy, and Crain tried to be humorous when he said, "It's been slow, but hopefully things will pick up." With that, Crain picked up a duck from the flowing water and began to laugh.

The booth had a container of water that circulated the tub, aided by a large fan strategically located so that the air from the fan moved the ducks continuously around the tub. Hundreds of plastic ducks floated around with numbers painted on their bottoms. Customers would give two tickets and pull a duck, and everyone would be a winner. The size and value of the winning prize would be in direct relationship to the number selected. Awards ranged from pencils to oversized stuffed bears. If someone happened to pick a winning duck for one of the larger prizes, the duck was removed and replaced by one of the many replacement ducks under the counter that had numbers coinciding with the lesser prizes. Crain referred to these as the slum prizes (carnival lingo for junk). No one wanted to give too much away.

Although everyone was guaranteed to be a winner, it seemed as if ninety-nine percent of the ducks had numbers that produced a slum prize. The ducks were painted identically, and it would have been nearly impossible to use the process of elimination to win one of the larger prizes. Nothing prevented the customers from trying to outsmart the game, but it wasn't going to happen. These efforts only brought more money into the game. If someone claimed a big win, it was blind luck. Of course, there were times the attendant would steer the player to a winning duck, hoping to increase business. Such action was frowned upon, but it did happen. Each big prize had a tag declaring where it was won to create more traffic to the booth. Everything had a gimmick.

Brick knew he was getting an education on carnival life with each new assignment. When Crain did leave, he told Brick he wouldn't be gone long.

Brick had been running the booth for nearly an hour, and the biggest thing he had given away was a rubber snake, which did excite the young winner. He told Brick he could use it later to scare his little sister.

Crain reeked of alcohol when he returned and showed little interest in how busy the booth had been. He merely took his spot at the booth and thanked Brick again for taking over while he was on break.

Raeford had asked Brick and Ray to come to the office after the relief work. As Brick started walking that way, he was thinking how well organized the Howard's Amusements' operation was; everyone depended on each other for its success. In his mind, though, he did question Crain's value considering his alcohol use. Teamwork and responsibility were critical ingredients for success, but that goes with any organization—not just the carnival.

Ray was on his way to the office when he spotted Brick. He had been working the "Water Shoot" game where players shot a steam of water into a tube, causing a ping pong ball to rise to the top. The first ball to the top was the winner, and they could continue playing as long as they wanted to get a bigger prize.

The two began walking together, and their path took them by the "All-Girl Nude Revue." As they passed the revue, Ray made a remark that he hoped they could catch a show later.

Just outside the revue, the protesters were now in full force. Brick asked Ray if his dad had said anything about the protesters to which Ray replied, "No, but I haven't seen Dad since the opening ceremonies. I did, however, have someone stop by my booth asking about them. He must have thought that I knew something, but he knew more than I did. He told me he heard the group was from a church in Jonesboro." Brick wondered where in Jonesboro, but Ray didn't have any idea.

Brick, with a little bit of worry in his voice, told Ray, "I sure hope they don't gain much traction and spoil our week with the ladies."

Ray smiled, saying, "Damn protesters! This year of all years! Maybe they'll get tired and go home. Hopefully, they will see that no one wants them here. After all, the women in the shows are much more attractive than the protesters."

When they arrived at the office, Raeford was sitting at his desk and appeared to be doing paperwork. He took the time to stop and ask, "How's your first day going?" The boys told him things were good and how much they were enjoying the work.

Brick added, "This is quite an operation."

Ray followed, "I'm not sure I would want to make a living out of it, but for now it's fun."

Raeford laughed again and said, "I have told you this before. Be careful as that's what I said years ago down in Florida."

Brick responded, "So, you've been at this for a while?"

"Yeah, I made it to twenty years last month. Not sure I could do anything different now." He then told them he hadn't been with Howard's the whole time. In his early years, he had worked for a variety of shows, but for the last twelve, he had been with Howard's. He continued, "Howard's is in my blood. The wife's not crazy about it, but she enjoys the money."

Ray asked if Raeford's wife was with the carnival. Raeford looked off as if he was thinking about his answer when he said, "She was, but once the kids started growing up, we both agreed it was best for them to stay put. There have been times when we have all toured together, but that's become more infrequent because of their ages." Ray then asked about his children. "I've got two beautiful girls—not much younger than you two. I'm sure the day will come when they'll want to join the business, and I guess I'll have to put them to work," Raeford replied.

Brick asked, "Where's home?"

"I'm from the low country of South Carolina—down around Beaufort. Raeford answered. "I got out of the Marines and decided to stay, but work was tough to find. I heard of an opportunity with a traveling show in Pensacola, Florida, and decided to check it out. Now, after twenty plus years, I'm still working. I even met my wife with the Hudson Carnival out of Brunswick, Georgia."

Ray asked, "Where were you in the war?"

Raeford replied, "Well, I saw a little action in the Pacific, but it was toward the end. By the time I got there, most of the real fighting had stopped. Got out in '48 and wasn't called back during Korea."

The boys enjoyed talking with Raeford. He had a relaxed style and an honest approach to things, making both feel comfortable.

Raeford said, "Both of you boys seem to have a good head on your shoulders. I may need some brain power in the morning. I'd like for you to help with our daily audit. It's something we try to get done each morning."

They learned the audit consisted of reviewing the reported ticket sales. The system gives management a quick guesstimate of how the week is going. Raeford explained it was rather mundane, but it sure beat the "Duck Pond" and the "Water Shoot." They laughed and told Raeford it sounded good to them.

One day of working at the carnival, and they were already moving into management. Raeford asked them to come in at seven o'clock the next morning, and he would supply breakfast. Of course, the early start wasn't very appealing.

As they were talking, Raeford asked if they had noticed the protesters. Both said they had, but neither knew what to make of them. Raeford said, "Hopefully, they won't be a problem. I've had to deal with a few groups this summer, and they are usually more of a nuisance than anything else. Generally, they take a stand and remain relatively quiet while handing out flyers and trying to shame the patrons from attending the revue."

Brick told him he thought they were a bunch of nuts. Raeford replied, "I wish it were that simple; unfortunately, this type of thing is happening more and more. There seems to be a movement afoot. I believe a church is organizing them from down east. They are showing up way too much for me. Do either of you know if this group is even from Sanford?"

Ray answered, "I have heard they are from a church in an area known as Jonesboro. I just wish they would get frustrated and go home."

"That would be nice," Raeford replied, "but unfortunately, I don't see that happening. I hope they stay in their place and don't try to make any trouble. There have been a few times I've considered shutting the shows down—more as a precaution than anything else. Luckily, it hasn't come to that yet. No one other than those protesting seems to want the shows stopped, but I'm concerned with any group protesting. In other counties, the protesters have always stayed on the outside of the grounds. I have noticed this group is trying to get as close as possible to the show, and they seem to be rather loud. I'm worried they'll make everyone uncomfortable. I may try to get them to move, and hopefully, they will go quietly. I'm not sure what I can do, but I'm going to try to be proactive in dealing with them."

Ray said, "If you would like, I'll talk to my dad about it."

Raeford smiled and said, "Thanks, but that's not necessary. It's just part of the job. I know it's just a matter of time before the sideshows become extinct. Attendance is down, and this protesting is not helping. Just keep me posted if you happen to hear anything. Right now, I think most of the patrons see it just as an annoyance. It could get worse, though, and I don't need that headache."

The conversation quickly changed when Raeford said, "Let's get your pay." They went over the day's activities, and Raeford told the boys they were getting the real Howard's experience. They both just grinned. Raeford then counted out thirty-two dollars for each. They signed off on the money, and both were now done for the day. As they stepped out of the office, they thanked Raeford and told him they would see him the next morning.

Outside the office, Ray said, "Thirty-two bucks—not bad, not bad at all—and it sounds like tomorrow may even be better."

Brick commented that the work hadn't been hard, and the time went by quickly. He added, "I think I'm going to enjoy the work, especially the money. They stopped at a food stand to get a Coke and some fries. When they had finished with their food, they decided it was time to see the revue. "Tonya, the Gorilla Girl" would have to wait. Tonight, the boys had a date with the ladies of the revue.

✣

Not as Planned

Although Monday had started with such promise, Odom's optimism had turned sour. The lack of interest being shown for the protest was frustrating him. Few had paid them any attention; it was as if they were invisible. Those that did acknowledge their presence seemed to look at Odom and the others as if they were as much a sideshow as the revue. Odom's lack of patience was beginning to show. His group had dwindled down from the morning. Beverly was very tired, and even she left for home. She knew a long week lay ahead, and if she was going to help, she needed to get some rest.

Odom's confidant and friend, Jimmy Key, had come to the protest after getting off work. Key had worked a full day in the warehouse of Roberts Company but was still willing to help Odom. He was disappointed, however, upon learning that Beverly and her sister Gail left earlier. The only people remaining were Odom and Rooster Craig. Rooster was probably the strangest of all the members of the church. Neither Odom nor Key had any idea how he made ends meet. He was known to hang around the merchants in Jonesboro asking for work, from unloading trucks to washing windows. Rooster had found The Revival Revolutionary Church to his liking, especially when Beverly prepared meals for church meetings.

Key spoke to both, asking how it was going. Odom responded, "It's slow. I'm beginning to think no one even cares about the sin and evil these shows are promoting."

Odom tried to show his disdain for the shows, but it was the lack of attention the protest had garnered that bothered him more. Key asked if there had been any others at the protest, so Odom went over who had been there. He then added, "We've got to get more people involved. No one is going to pay attention to a small group yelling and waving signs."

Key said, "I'll be able to help out later in the week. I'm switching over to the late shift." He then asked if Gail would be coming back. Odom knew Key was sweet on Gail and may have been motivated by her presence more than the mission of the protest, but he didn't care where Key found the motivation. He just wanted him there. Higher numbers would bring more attention to the protest and the church.

Odom, Key, and Rooster remained on the grounds for a while longer before deciding to stop for the day. Odom knew he needed to reach out to some of his members and didn't want it to be too late. He told Key he would make some calls when he got home and suggested Key do the same. There was no need to ask Rooster to call anyone. Odom wasn't even sure Rooster had a home—much less a phone.

When Odom returned home, he could tell Beverly was anxious. Odom tried to conceal his disappointment as Beverly told him how proud she was of the work he was doing. He told her he had hoped for a better day, but he recognized it was still early. Although he knew it could take some time to grow the protests, he just wasn't happy with the day's results. His disappointment began to show as he explained how little had happened after she left—just a lot of standing around, waving signs, and chanting. He added, "If tomorrow is as slow as today was, we are going to be way behind schedule. Things need to change the fair is only here for a few days."

Odom's sour mood was evident, and he knew Beverly was trying to ease his pain when she sweetly said, "Patrick, it's just the first day. Things will get better." But Odom didn't need pity; he needed action. He rose from his chair and told her he was going to make some calls.

His first call was to Hinson, hoping for a little support or at least some recommendations on how to improve the participation in the upcoming protests. Odom suggested Hinson bring some of his followers to Lee County to strengthen the numbers, but Hinson balked at coming to Sanford— at least for now. Hinson was repeating what Odom had already heard way too many times—it's early and things take time. Hinson shared with Odom that he had contacted many of the media outlets and shared the story of the protest, and he was confident some publicity would be coming. Talking with Hinson helped ease Odom's mind, especially after he learned of Hinson's calls. Odom believed Hinson had more pull with the news outlets than he did and welcomed his help.

Hinson did quiz Odom about the day, and Odom shared that for the most part no one paid them much attention. Odom became agitated when Hinson asked if he had used any signs. Making every attempt to hide his frustration, Odom assured Hinson he had done everything he thought possible. He made it clear to Hinson that what he needed was for more people to become involved. Hinson may have been trying to appease Odom as he told him that he would see about getting a busload of protesters to come to Sanford, but it would have to be later in the week. Odom hoped it would be sooner than later.

Odom did tell Hinson about being interviewed by The Sanford Herald and was confident it would be in the next day's paper. Hinson asked if they had taken any pictures, and Odom assured him once again that they had. Although Odom was feeling a little better about things, he was getting frustrated with Hinson and his questions. Did Hinson think he was an idiot?

After he finished his conversation with Hinson, Odom pulled out his roster and began calling some of the members of his church. He phoned members who he knew didn't work outside the home as he needed everyone possible for the protest. Unfortunately, because church membership was small, Odom had limited options. A few said they would try to join him the next day. Odom told those he spoke with he would pay their admission into the fair, hoping a little conning would help motivate them to come. They could protest a while before maybe spending some time in the exhibit hall and enjoying some of the other attractions.

Odom was encouraged after making his calls. He wasn't sure if they would help, but he was pleased that those he spoke with were happy to hear from him. Odom knew he should be satisfied with his efforts, but the need for more publicity was beginning to haunt him.

After a while, Beverly asked him to come to bed. She assured him the next day would be better, and Odom was too tired to argue. It had been a long day, and his disappointment only added to his fatigue. He crawled into bed and thanked her. Beverly smiled and told him, "You don't need to thank me. I am so proud of you Patrick. No matter what the results are, I know you are doing the right thing."

Odom lovingly replied, "Your support means so much to me, and I am lucky you are in my life."

Beverly gave him a kiss, told him she loved him, and then encouraged him to get some sleep.

⚜

The Revue

B rick and Ray were happy to see that the protesters were no longer outside the revue when they arrived. Their timing was perfect. The girls were just coming out front for their introductions, which were fun and humorous. Mary Jane was introduced as Jana the Swedish Princess; Sugar as the sweet girl from the exotic Far East; Misty as the big-hearted girl from Texas, where she learned to tease and please; and Tammy was billed as the girl next door, who everyone wanted as their neighbor. As soon as the barker had finished with the introductions, he told the girls to go on back and prepare for the show. He then turned his attention to the crowd and yelled through his microphone, "It's time to step up and come see the beauties of the midway! For only two dollars, you can see it all, and I mean SEE IT ALL! Two dollars for a show you will never forget!"

It wasn't long before a small crowd gathered around the man taking up money and began paying their way into the tent. Ray looked at Brick and said, "We may as well join the fun." At the same time, they were wondering if the man would recognize them as employees or friends of the girls, but it didn't seem to matter. He took their money and told them to enjoy the show.

The boys claimed a spot near the entrance side of the stage. Both were anxious for the show to begin. They could hear laughter coming from behind the curtains, and music was playing on a portable record player. The song playing was something by Booker T. & the M.G.'s (at least that was Brick's guess).

Before long, the curtains were pulled back and out walked Sugar. Wearing an unbuttoned blouse tied at the bottom and with what appeared to be blue gym shorts, Sugar waved to the crowd and asked if everyone was ready to have some fun. The crowd broke into applause. Sugar gave the group a mocked disappointing look and said they would need to do better than that. She then added, "The louder the applause, the better the show." The noise level quickly rose. For anyone standing outside the tent, they would have believed the crowd was much larger than it was. The men were looking for a good show and were loud and appreciative. Sugar was serving as the master of ceremonies for this show, and once the crowd noise died down, she got the group going again as she introduced Misty.

Misty came onto the stage waving her hands as the applause rose with each seductive move she made. Misty was dressed in a red cowgirl outfit accented by a white cowboy hat. It wasn't long before her top dropped, and she began playing peek-a-boo with her hat, revealing, and covering her breasts. She then stepped out of the outfit and made her way to the front of the stage with hat in hand and only wearing a small bikini bottom and a smile. Brick and Ray both blushed with excitement as they were mesmerized by her beauty and dance. Once she spotted Ray, she moved over to greet him and Brick. Misty leaned over and gave Ray a kiss, thanking him for being there. Her actions made the crowd scream for the same treatment. She smiled, wiggled her finger back and forth, and said, "Not tonight." As quick as her dance had started, it came to an end and the music stopped. Misty waved to the crowd and quickly exited the stage.

Next up was Jana, the Swedish Princess; the boys knew her as Mary Jane. Mary Jane's outfit was short white overalls. The overalls helped accent her breasts, complemented by her red pouty lips and blond hair. Mary Jane did have the look of a Swedish Princess. At first, she appeared disinterested—just going through the motions; however, once she spotted Brick and Ray, her energy seemed to pick up. Of course, this could have been Brick's wishful thinking, but she appeared to light up once she saw them. It wasn't long before she began dancing in front of both boys. Brick was shyly embarrassed, thinking she was the most exciting and beautiful woman he had ever known. What an odd feeling for Brick, taking into consideration she was the one taking off her clothes. The top then came down. She leaned over and whispered in Brick's ear, "You like?"

Brick could only muster the word—"Beautiful."

She then squeezed his hand and said, "Thank you."

When the music ended, she vanished behind the curtains, and it was time for Tammy. Tammy had chosen a short plaid skirt and a white blouse, accentuating her girl-next-door appeal. With dark-rimmed glasses, she looked as if she was preparing for school, but all that changed when she tossed the glasses and removed the top and skirt. She came to the boys smiling and seductively told them she hoped they were enjoying the show. Brick and Ray were feeling privileged with all the attention they were getting.

She now was off the stage, and it was time for Sugar. Still wearing the white blouse tied at her waist, Sugar returned to the stage and began her dance. She quickly pulled the top off and started making her way around the stage. She would stop for a moment to allow everyone to take in her beauty and large breasts. But like the others, once her music ended, she retreated behind the curtains. The lights came on as she was leaving the stage, and everyone began making their way to the exit. In less than fifteen minutes, the entire show was over—four dancers and four songs. A new crowd would appear in a matter of minutes, and the show would start all over.

The instrumental music began to blare once again. As Brick was leaving the tent, he could not help but laugh as none of the men who attended the show were making eye contact or talking—just exiting quickly to the midway. Brick and Ray moved slowly, hoping the girls would come out to see them. Their efforts failed; maybe the girls didn't realize they were hanging around. When the boys reached the outside of the tent, it was obvious to them that their night was coming to an end.

As they walked toward the car, the boys talked about the revue and their fantasies. They both wanted to get to know the ladies better, and hopefully, it would be soon. Brick, thinking of Mary Jane's introduction as the Swedish princess, said in a partially joking manner, "I have always wanted to go to Sweden, and now I know why."

Ray replied, "I hope to be roped by Misty the cowgirl if you know what I mean."

Both boys began to laugh. They knew they were big talkers, but they also knew it was fun to dream. They had their fantasies, but the only thing certain was that they would be working the fair the next day.

Brick dropped Ray off, telling him he would see him around six-thirty the next morning. Before turning in for the night, Brick wrote his parents a note asking them to please wake him up around five-thirty the next morning as he was sure they would be up by then. Once in bed, Brick could not stop thinking about the show—and Mary Jane.

⚜

Odom's Day Two

O dom was up early. He had trouble sleeping as his thoughts of the day's protest had kept him up most of the night. His desire for success had always clouded his thinking, but now it was worse than ever. He was extremely anxious for him and Beverly to get to the fairgrounds.

Before making his morning coffee, Odom walked into the large room that had been converted into a sanctuary. The room was once the waiting room for the dental office as well as the reception area for an accounting firm. When Odom moved into the house, he felt the room could be renovated to meet his needs. To make this happen, he had a wall taken out in order to give the room ample space for the church services. The makeshift sanctuary was far from impressive, but sadly, it was all Odom needed.

He acquired the pews from a salvage yard in Sanford. It was his understanding they had come out of the Jonesboro Baptist Church when they built a new sanctuary several years ag0. Odom was forced to modify the pews, sawing off sections to make them fit. The result was less than ideal, but it was all he had.

As he surveyed the room, reality began to seep in, forcing him to realize his dream of success wasn't any closer than it was two years ago. It was no wonder few came to the church as everything gave the appearance it belonged in a third world country—not Sanford, North Carolina. He and Beverly had tried to grow the church, but with limited money and less talent, it was evident that failure was once again at his doorstep.

Odom was now looking for the protest to be the spark that would reignite his dream. Although it had only been one day at the fair, he was left questioning his actions and his resolve. As he began to walk around the large room, there were reminders of Sunday's service on the pews. No one had been in the area since he made his passionate plea.

Odom took a seat on the front bench and gazed upon the homemade wooden cross. He reflected on his excitement the day he molded the cross. It was the same day he created a sign to hang out front declaring The Revival Revolutionary Church was open. He was now thinking of how naïve he must have been. Why would he even think a sign and a wooden cross would be the key to a thriving church? Was he so naïve again, being so excited about leading the protest?

Although Odom wasn't much on silent prayer, he fell to his knees from the pew, folded his hands together, and through the cross he looked to the heavens and asked God for help. He prayed that God would lead others to the movement, and with the spirit of the Lord, they could together put an end to the shows. If anyone had heard the prayer, they might have thought Odom was sincere, believing he was looking to make a difference.

That was the dichotomy of Patrick Odom; he was a complex man. Odom genuinely wanted to make a difference, but he also craved success and the finer things in life. Was he so different from other ministers? Did they not desire to grow their church? Didn't these ministers want to have a good life while honoring God? Although Odom was feeling pulled, he had to realize his prayer to shut the shows down was weak in comparison to his craving for respect and material items. As Odom remained on the floor, his prayer complete, he began to weep. His tears were brought on by his internal struggles with God and success.

Beverly entered the sanctuary after a short while and was surprised to see Odom sitting on the floor. She could tell he had been crying. She came to his side and in a calm, gentle voice asked, "What's wrong, Patrick?"

He just shook his head. Beverly didn't need words to recognize the protest was already taking a toll on Patrick. She worried if he was feeling this unstable now what he would be like when his mission was finally over, especially if it didn't turn out the way he visualized. Beverly was still in her nightgown and robe, and she sat on the floor beside him, placing her arms around him and asking him if he was okay.

His response was not short in coming. He stared into her eyes and finally managed to say, "I'm worried. I'm worried the protest is not going to work, and our efforts will be for nothing."

"That's nonsense, Patrick," she said. "People see the movement; they are talking about it. I assure you things will get better, and they will recognize you as a creator of change. You will be the one who helped bring an end to the sinful operation of such shows." That was Beverly. She was a source of constant support for Patrick. She only wished he could believe in himself as much as she did.

They rose from the floor, and Patrick once again looked around the sanctuary, but this time with Beverly by his side, he said, "You're right, we are making a difference. Our church may not be one of grandeur, but it does offer a religious home to many."

"Patrick, you have helped create a home church for individuals who may not have had one before," she replied.

Her words of encouragement helped bring Odom's confidence back. He once again felt empowered for the coming day. He thanked her for being with him and once again told her he loved her. Beverly smiled and said, "Things are going to be all right." She took him by the arm, saying she could use some coffee. The two then left the sanctuary and went into the kitchen.

When Odom and Beverly and her sister Gail arrived at the fairgrounds, he noticed two members of his church, Shelton and Joanie Clingstone, were there. Shelton was a part-time farmer and a full-time drunk. Joanie had dragged him to the church nearly ten months ago, hoping to change his ways. Odom had spoken to him about his drinking but was not qualified to offer any real help. He had suggested Shelton attend AA and even offered the use of the church for a meeting place. Thus far, there had been no takers for meetings. Odom wasn't sure Shelton had made any progress in his battle with the booze. Hopefully, he had at least slowed down on his drinking. Odom thanked them for coming.

He then noticed that Rooster Craig was back and was standing away from everyone. Odom called him over and asked him to help hand out the protest signs. Odom then led the six who were there in a prayer, asking God for His guidance and success for the day. After the prayer, the group walked to the area adjacent to the revue for the day's protest.

It would be hours before the revue would open. The morning crowds were sparse, with few attendees making their way to the area. This only added to Odom's frustration as they stood around with little to do. Beverly sensed Odom's nervousness, and she came to his side, telling him again that everything was okay and not to worry. She once again assured him the protest was worth it, and he was making a difference.

Odom wished he could see things the way Beverly did. She was the rational one who always saw the glass half full. Odom not only saw the glass half empty, but he felt it might even have a hole in it. It was tough for Odom to recognize good things as he had struggled most of his life seeing failure far more often than victory.

The protest had dragged on for a few hours when the revue finally did open. It was then that Odom and his group became more energized. They now had a target for their protest—not just an empty tent. Unfortunately, the Clingstones needed to leave. Not only were they tired as they had given the rally four solid hours, but they also had other things to do.

Jimmy Key arrived after he finished work and was pleased to see that Gail was still there. Key and Gail spent more time talking than protesting. Odom and Rooster did the most chanting, and Beverly walked around with her sign, Stop the Offering of Sin. The S's and O were enlarged and at first glance looked like an SOS sign. Even for Odom, the sign was rather amusing. Still, very few people paid them much attention. Some stopped and stared while others appeared to be laughing at them. A few did wish them well but weren't willing to commit themselves to the cause.

As the afternoon began to turn into night, two more couples came to protest. Odom now had the most participants yet, and it was still under ten people. He knew he should be pleased but pleasing oneself was always tricky. This was especially true for Odom.

Beverly could see Odom's uneasiness, so she asked him to take a break, telling him she wanted to walk around the midway for a while as she thought the time away from the protest would do him good. Odom agreed, and the two told the others they would be back shortly. They soon were walking the aisles of the exhibit hall.

As the two began walking the midway Beverly reiterated how well she felt things were going. Patrick knew he took things too personal, and she was trying her best to be positive. Maybe she was fearing what he would do if he failed to be successful. Odom stopped the walk and said, "I know I should be proud of what we're doing, but I want it to be more. I want people to take notice, and I want the protest to make a difference." Beverly reminded him everything worth doing is worth waiting for, and he was putting down the first installment toward a change. She pointed out again that change would come, and he needed to believe in himself; he was making an impact on the community. Odom anxiously responded, "That's just it; we don't have that much time. Something needs to happen, and it needs to happen soon."

❧

Brick and Ray's Day 2

The next morning, Brick's dad wanted to know how his first day went. Brick couldn't help but smile when he answered, "It was good. The work was different, but the people we met and worked with were friendly, and I'm making good money. Not sure what I was expecting, but so far, so good."

When Brick saw his mom, she too wanted to know how his day had been. She asked if there were any other friends working with him and Ray. There was an obvious difference in how each approached the issue. His mom seemed worried and his dad curious.

Brick told her, "No, it's just me and Ray. But thankfully, for most of the day, we worked together. Not sure that will be the case here on out, but I hope so." He grabbed a piece of toast and a couple of strips of bacon and headed out. As he was leaving, he said, "I'm not sure when I'll be home, but you know where I am."

His mom smiled and said, "Yes, that's what concerns me."

Brick turned back to her and once again tried to put her mind at ease by saying, "Mom, everything is fine, and it gives me something to do before I leave for Elon. Don't worry, it's all good."

Ray was out front when Brick arrived to pick him up, and Ray's first question was, "So, did you dream about the lovely ladies of the revue?"

Brick answered, "No, but not because I didn't want to." Ray echoed his sentiment, and Brick continued, "Well, it's a new day, and with a new day comes more opportunities to see the ladies."

Ray just grinned and said, "Oh yeah."

Brick had been thinking about the protesters and asked Ray if he had said anything to his dad about them. Ray replied, "Nope, didn't even think about it, and dad didn't mention it. Must not be a big deal."

Brick told Ray he hoped he was right and that maybe they would just go away. Ray responded, "Yeah, it's a damn shame! The one time we have the opportunity to get to know the ladies, we have to deal with protesters. The protests are a pisser for sure." They both laughed, neither thinking of anything other than what they hoped to experience in the coming days, and that included the ladies of the revue.

They were at the office right at seven o'clock. Raeford was fixing himself a cup of coffee and told them he liked their punctuality. He then added, "Unfortunately, punctuality is not a well-known trait in the carnie business." He was glad to see they were anxious to start work, so he began sharing with them what to expect.

Brick noticed several cloth sacks sitting on a folding card table. The bags were marked for each of the ticket windows he had delivered to the day before. The boys learned the sacks contained the unused tickets from the previous day's operation and a receipt of how many tickets were received and sold. The money collected had already been placed in the office safe. The tickets and receipts would give Raeford a good indication of how much business they had done the day before. Brick and Ray's job would be to count the tickets and subtract the number from those that were given to start the day. He would then calculate how much money was made and compare it to the money that was turned in.

Raeford said, "It's a primitive system, but it works well enough and is somewhat accurate. I need you to do two counts, making sure we don't have any discrepancies. Each ticket is worth ten cents, so you can get an idea of how much money each booth should have turned in. There should also be a numeral count of the number of twelve ticket sheets they sold. I will match it all up and see if we have any problems, but it usually works out."

Raeford then pulled out several sheets of legal paper, and his instructions continued, "At this point it gets a little iffy. The number of patrons is supposed to match up with the money collected. On these sheets, the numbers will reflect the traffic the sideshow had, and there should be times listed when the show operated. Each show is expected to operate three times an hour from the time they open until closing. I need you to give me the total number of shows and the number of patrons, and that will give us an estimate of how well each show did. I can then check it against the money that was turned in. If any of the operators of the shows wanted to cheat the house, they could alter the count to go along with the money. I just have to trust they are not skimming off the top too much. And let me remind you to check your math twice." Brick thought this was a strange check and balance system, but it evidently served its purpose. It all sounded so simple and shouldn't take long.

Raeford pointed out another batch of cloth bags, saying, "...and now for the real fun!" Each bag had the name of the attraction on it from the "Balloon Pop" to the "Ring Toss." The bags contained the tickets each game took in for the day. Raeford explained, "I need you to count the tickets and multiply by ten with each ticket representing a dime. This should give us the amount of money each of the games brought in. We know there will be some discrepancies since we sometimes do the twelve tickets for a dollar, but it will be a good indicator of how each game did." Brick felt the system was a bit convoluted but knew it would give them a better idea of which games and attractions were popular and how successful the day had been.

Raeford added, "While you're figuring out how much business the games did, I'll be working on the count for the rides. Look at it this way; we have several money streams, and getting adequate numbers is important. Hopefully, when we have finished with all the calculations, we will have a close estimation of how we did yesterday—which shows were popular, which games were played, and which rides were ridden. It is not all that difficult; it's just time-consuming. Once we have the audit done for yesterday, we can begin distribution of today's tickets, and the fun will start all over."

Brick said, "So, you do this every day?"

Raeford smiled and said, "Let's put it this way; we attempt to. There are days it doesn't get done, and when that happens it gets carried over to the next day. It then can be a real pain in the ass."

Ray, still interested in learning more, said, "It seems to be a hell of an operation, but what about the food vendors?"

"That's a bit simpler," Raeford answered. "They pay us a flat rate each day; it makes it a hell of a lot easier. The booths we operate keep a running tab of what they make and how much they sell, and they can skim some off the top. We order the supplies for our vendors, and we keep a close look at the inventory. These things work together to give us a good indication if they are attempting to cheat the house. Keep in mind, we do not look kindly at being cheated. The workers are paid handsomely for their talents and time. Like I said yesterday, a lot of what we do is dependent on the honor system, and we try to make it easy to be honorable." Raeford then handed each of them a pencil and paper and told them if they needed anything or had any questions, he would be in the next room.

Brick and Ray were somewhat surprised to finish up the numbers so quickly. Once they gave the results to Raeford, he began calculating the day's earnings. The way Raeford used the adding machine made him look like he should be working in Vegas—or at least a bank.

Once Raeford finished up, he said, "I'm sure there are better ways to determine our success, but so far, so good."

Ray questioned how opening day was.

Raeford looked over everything and said, "It wasn't a bad day. According to ticket sales, we had 1,207 adults and 396 children in paid admissions. Of course, there is no charge for kids under six, so we don't have their numbers. We collected close to $2,900 from the sideshows with 'Tonya' being the biggest money maker."

Brick was surprised that the revue didn't bring in the most money. He asked Raeford if he felt their numbers were affected by the protesters. Raeford reminded him and Ray, "The other sideshows, such as 'Tonya,' do not have an age requirement, so parents can take the kids in if they want to. The revue is for eighteen and older and generally does most of its business in the evenings—and just for men. Hopefully, the protesters didn't have much of an effect on attendance."

According to Raeford, it was a good start, but he had hopes attendance would pick up, expecting bigger crowds and more money on Friday and Saturday. The boys learned from Raeford that Wednesday was the least profitable day as that was Senior Citizens' Day, and there was no charge for senior admission. He then pointed out that seniors do not have much interest in the rides or the sideshows, which doesn't generate a lot of profit; they generally come for the food and the exhibits.

Brick and Ray were starting their second full day as fair employees and had already learned a lot about the business. Both boys felt their experience was not only educational, but it was also fun.

Next up was ticket distribution. The tickets for that day had changed colors, but they learned that tickets from the previous day would still be honored. It was another means to track attendance and success. Raeford wanted the tickets to be distributed before the gates opened at ten o'clock.

Once the tickets had been delivered, the boys reported back to Raeford. He suggested they get something to eat, maybe at The Biscuit Barn, as this seemed to be a favorite for employees and should be open. He said to the boys, "I spoke with Wayne at The Biscuit Barn last night, and he is expecting you this morning. He has agreed to feed you at no cost." The Biscuit Barn catered to the employees' appetites before most of the other food vendors started serving.

As Raeford had said, it was one of only a few food vendors operating at that time of the morning. The others were preparing for the day but would not start serving until the gates officially opened. There was a decent number of employees at The Biscuit Barn, and they were quite busy. The country ham biscuits were as good as advertised—very salty, supporting the need for a Coke.

Although the boys had been on the lookout for the girls of the revue, they had not seen anybody they had met. While they were eating, they did see Lucy (the self-proclaimed house mother of the revue), and she looked to be a little out of sorts. She spoke to the boys and went straight for coffee, getting nothing to eat. She came back to where Brick and Ray were sitting, asking if they made it to the show the previous night. Brick quickly answered, "Yes ma'am." Lucy smiled and told them she was not old enough to be called ma'am. She then asked how they liked the show.

Ray was the first to answer, rhetorically asking, "What's not to like?"

Brick followed Ray's comment, saying, "Yeah, fifteen minutes of fun and excitement." Brick felt it odd that they were talking about a nudie show like it was a baseball game, and they were speaking to a woman as well. Brick could not help but think how different life is at the fair, especially compared to his high school days.

Lucy was pleased that the boys enjoyed the show. She then asked if they had seen any of the protesters, to which Brick replied, "They had already gone by the time we got there, but I did see them earlier." She wanted to know what the boys thought about them, and Brick, as he had before, replied, "I feel it's a few people with too much time on their hands."

Lucy said, "I hope you are right." She then echoed Raeford's statement, saying they were seeing more and more of them lately. She told them she had heard of a group protesting Sattler Amusements out of Camden, South Carolina, which resulted in the shows having to be shut down for a few weeks while they were in Georgia. Brick asked if she knew what had happened. Lucy shrugged her shoulders and said, "I'm thinking the protests got larger and more vocal to the point that the company couldn't deal with the negative publicity and decided to shut it down. I'm sure they were also worried about the safety of the girls. You can bet they lost money those weeks. Fortunately for us, at this point the protesters have been less threatening. We haven't had to shut anything down. I hope it doesn't come to that this week."

With a smile on his face, Brick said, "Yeah, I'm just beginning to enjoy the shows."

Lucy laughed and said, "I bet you are." She then told them she had to get moving and hoped to see them later.

After Lucy left, Ray asked Brick, "What do you think she was up to last night?"

Grinning, Ray responded, "I'm not sure, but whatever it was, I'll bet there was some alcohol involved."

Brick leaned back, crossed his arms, and then said, "What a life!"

Raeford told the boys before they left for breakfast to come back to the office after they had finished eating, and he would have their next assignments. On their way back, the boys began talking more about the protesters. Ray tried to rationalize the protest and said, "You know, we studied civil disruption in civics class. Maybe this is just an attempt to create awareness while hoping to promote change."

Brick responded, "But the protests we studied and the ones we see on television are about the war and civil rights. They're not about a bunch of women showing their tits."

Ray replied, "I know, but who's to say these protesters don't feel their cause is just as important. Maybe to them the girly shows are their anti-war movement. It's possible it is something they honestly believe in."

"I don't think you can compare the two, Brick said. "One deals with human tragedy and death and the other a little entertainment for a bunch of horny guys."

Ray told him, "I know that's how we see it, but maybe the preacher sees it differently. He may see it as the downfall of morality and the rise of the devil."

Brick shook his head, saying, "Please don't tell me you agree with them."

"No, hell no! I'm just trying to see it from their point of view," replied Ray. "I heard dad tell mom he felt they should have lobbied to stop the shows before they were contracted to be in Sanford."

Brick thought for a minute and responded, "You know, your dad's right. Everyone knew the shows would be coming with the fair. They have for years. So, if the protest was more than a publicity stunt, they should have started earlier. I hate to think they are just a bunch of opportunists trying to get some publicity for their church." Both boys were giving the protesters a lot of thought and agreed that they and the preacher seemed hell-bent on spoiling their fantasies.

Ray laughed and said, "That preacher probably got shot down by a stripper last year, and now he's trying to get back at them."

Brick agreed, "Yeah, it would be funny to learn that the root of the protest was planted due to rejection. Maybe we should spread that rumor."

They both enjoyed an awkward laugh, and Ray said, "No matter what, I don't plan on talking to my dad about the protest. I sure don't want him to know I have a personal interest in the shows—if you know what I mean."

Brick replied, "I'm with you on that one. There is no need to let the folks know about our new friendships."

Being a little curious, Ray said, "Speaking of our new friends, do you think we should drop by and give them a surprise visit? I don't think Raeford is going to miss us for a few minutes." Brick thought it was tempting but feared they may still be in bed, to which Ray replied, "Even better."

Brick smiled and said, "We don't want to appear desperate."

Ray began laughing and said, "But we are desperate, and I certainly wouldn't mind seeing what they sleep in."

Brick just shook his head, saying, "Damn, Ray! Let's try to be cool. With any luck, we'll find out before the end of the week." Ray hoped he was right and agreed they should probably get to the office and pick up their next assignment.

Brick felt Ray was one of the most easy-going friends he had. He didn't let much get to him. It would not have been a bit surprising to Brick if Ray had gone to the trailer and talked himself inside. That was Ray. He was not at all worried about expectations; he created his own. Brick envied Ray's self-confidence and nerve, but what Brick liked best about Ray was his relaxed view on life.

Although the boys didn't stop by to see the girls, they did walk by their place somewhat deliberately, hoping maybe the ladies would be out and about. But the walk was for naught; there was no activity. When they reached the office, Raeford appeared to still be going over some of the figures from the previous day. Apparently, there was a ton of paperwork when it came to operating the fair.

Raeford noticed them and said, "Guys, it seems you are going to get the entire Howard's experience. I am going to need you both to run some of the games today. You seem to be learning the business from all angles." Both had enjoyed the short time working the games, and they were ready to try it again. Raeford instructed them to go to the row of games across from the petting zoo and the exotic reptile's display.

He told them, "I'll need one of you to operate the Dart Throw (or Balloon Bust) and the other the Softball Throw. I'm assuming you each know how these games work; if not, someone will help you learn. The games are near the Water Gun Game you worked yesterday, Ray.

Once you get there, you will find both booths covered with a tarp. You only need to flip the tarp back, and you should be good to go. Under the tarp, you will see a metal box with what looks like a coin slot; it's for collecting the tickets. But I guess since both of you used the boxes yesterday, you are aware of its purpose. Under the counter, you will find other supplies if you need them. Prizes are on the shelves with explanations as to how to win and how players can trade up by continuing to play. Do me a favor and make sure the boxes are empty. We try to secure a clean count for each day. You will be working beside each other, giving you a chance to switch off and take a break when needed. Unfortunately, I haven't heard from the fellows who were supposed to be running the games today." He shook his head and said, "If I had to bet, they are probably laid up drunk somewhere and are trying to sleep it off. I wish this was unusual, but it's not." Ray and Brick felt this was an issue Raeford probably had to deal with on a regular basis.

Raeford's instructions continued, "Let me share a few trade secrets. First off, there should be some balloons already in place, but if you must replace any, try not to over-inflate. As I would think you already know, the tighter the balloon, the more likely it will burst. At the Softball Throw, try to position the heavier bottles on the bottom and put them toward the back of the platform. You'll be able to tell the heavier bottles. All this makes the games a bit more challenging." He also asked them to talk up the games, "Don't hesitate to invite players over. Try to entice the public to come to the booth to show them just how easy it is to win. You'll have time to craft your skills at the booths and have some fun. Let people know how much fun it is to play."

He emphasized they should show the folks plenty of energy, and went on to say, "If you haven't had a winner for a while, change things up to try to get one, especially if there is decent traffic in front of your booth—heavier bottles on top and tighter-closed balloons. Remember, at this point you are looking for a winner. And a winner gets everyone excited."

The boys also learned that the softballs were heavier than normal, and the darts were a little off-center, making the games even more difficult. He emphasized these are games of chance, but the house wanted the odds tilted in their favor—always wanting to make more money than it gives out.

Ray asked, "Is all this legal?"

Raeford shrugged his shoulders and said, "Probably not. But hey, no one has to play the games, and the same rules apply to all. Just remember to talk it up and have fun. Each game takes three tickets or four tries for ten. You may be there for a while, so don't hesitate to give each other a break."

Outside the office, Ray commented, "So, that's how the games work."

Brick said, "I always knew they were rigged but just didn't know how they pulled it off."

Ray then added, "All I know is I never won a prize at any of those booths. But it appears we are now going to get plenty of practice. Who knows? Maybe while waiting on players, we can learn the tricks and become experts for the next fair we attend."

Brick laughed as he said, "Now that's something to be proud of— becoming a professional dart/balloon buster or softball thrower and being paid in stuffed animals."

Trying to be serious, Ray replied, "Don't knock it. You never know when that skill might come in handy. We are always trying to impress the ladies and what better way than with an overstuffed teddy bear."

They had no trouble finding the booths, and once they flipped back the tarps, they discovered everything was in place just like Raeford said. They were ready to open.

Each booth was about the size of an oversized walk-in closet. The balloons were placed on a large sheet of plywood. The softballs were thrown on two different lanes, meaning two people could play at the same time, and the bottles were placed about eight feet back from the counter.

Brick was taking charge of the Balloon Bust game. Under the counter was a box full of more balloons, some already inflated and the air seeping out. This, Raeford had told them, made it difficult to bust with the off-centered darts. Ray would run the Softball Throw (or the Milk Bottle Game as some preferred to call it). The boys were now ready for the fun to begin. Ray tried his hand at throwing the softballs and missed every time. Brick then tried the darts, and he too failed miserably. They were laughing at their lack of skills but felt by the end of a long day running the booths that with practice their skills would surely improve.

Ray saw Jill Lewis. He met her the day before while he was working at one of the booths, and he took a liking to her. Not only was she young and attractive, but he also just enjoyed talking with her. Today, she would be running a different Water Gun game than the one Ray had relieved her from the day before. Jill asked about working together, maybe helping each other with breaks. She explained to them that they usually try to cover for one another so that everyone can have some time away from the games. Both boys said that sounded good and that Raeford had made the same suggestion for the two of them. Everyone was going to need a break at some point.

Once the gates opened, the crowds began to trickle in. Brick and Ray tried to drum up players for the games. They saw it as a competition to see who could attract the most players, and they found that the early crowd seemed more interested in looking than playing. Brick gave it his all, calling out to all those passing by, inviting them to step up and win a prize. For most of the morning, business was slow with only a few folks stopping to play. It appeared that Ray had less activity than Brick, but each of them had ample opportunity to enjoy practicing and playing the games.

They had been staffing the booths for a little over an hour when Jill asked Ray if she could take a break. They were glad to do so and arranged themselves in such a way to offer full coverage with no problems.

During the short time Ray had worked with Jill, he learned a few things about her. He shared with Brick that Jill was new to Howard's and was learning her way around the business. She had been hired on with the team a couple of weeks ago when they were in Monroe, North Carolina. Brick's first question to Ray was, "Did she say where she was staying?"

Ray answered, "I think the barracks for the time being. She said something about the living conditions not being great, but at least for now she had a place to sleep and shower." Brick was curious about the barracks and wondered if she said how many people were staying in them.

Ray replied, "We didn't discuss that."

When Jill returned, business was still slow, allowing the three of them plenty of time to talk. Brick asked Jill about home, and she told them she was from Union, South Carolina. Neither of the boys had ever heard of the town, but then again that was not unusual. She laughed and said, "Don't worry. I can assure you, more than a few folks in South Carolina don't know about it either. Do y'all know anything about a town named Tarboro? I think that's where we go next."

Brick said, "I just know it's near Rocky Mount, and I only know that because I have an aunt who lives there. It's in the eastern part of the state. I would imagine it to be about a two-hour drive from here."

Brick asked if she enjoyed the work and the travel, and Jill replied, "Well, I've only been doing it for three weeks—so far, so good. I needed the work, and the money's not bad. So, here I am. Thus far, I have only met a few people and no young guys. Are y'all going to keep working?"

Ray answered, "No, we are just here for the Sanford run. We're both off to school next week."

She was impressed to learn they were going off to college. The news seemed to surprise her. She then added, "I know I'm new to the business, but I have to tell you, I don't think many college guys choose this type of work. You're the first I've met."

Brick laughed and said, "Well, we're not college guys yet, but hopefully, we will be soon."

Jill asked if they thought they would enjoy college. Ray replied, "Sure hope we do. If it keeps me out of the Army for a while, then I will be a college man. They won't draft you if you're in school."

Jill then told him she knew plenty about the draft as her ex-boyfriend back in Union County was facing the draft last year when he decided to join the Army. She hadn't seen him since. Brick told her he was sorry to hear that and then asked if he was in Nam. "Not that I'm aware of," she said. "Like I told you, I haven't seen him for a while. We fought about his joining. I couldn't handle how eager he was to enlist. Maybe I was selfish, but I didn't want him to go; I sure wanted him to stay home. But he was all for the idea of going to war. That crazy bastard wanted to go to Vietnam and fight."

Brick, with a look of wonder, said, "Sorry, but I've got to tell you something. That is one fight I'm not interested in being a part of, but his desire seems admirable."

Jill then said, "I know. I should have been proud of him, but he could have cared about my feelings. He didn't, and now I miss him and feel so alone. It didn't have to be this way."

Ray echoed Brick's statement, "I'm with Brick. Joining the Army is not something I want to do. I hope to put it off as long as possible."

Jill, with tears in her eyes, said, "I wish he would have felt that way, but I guess I loved him more than he loved me. That's one reason I joined the fair circuit. I'm trying to find a new direction that doesn't include an old boyfriend."

Their conversation was interrupted when a young couple came up, hoping to play darts. They were close to Brick's age, but he didn't recognize either of them. Brick welcomed them to the booth and held out the darts as he was not sure who would be throwing. The girl took the darts and told her date she would show him how to do it. She smiled at Brick and asked if he had given her the sharp darts. Brick jokingly informed her they were all sharp. Of course, his flirtatious smile may have indicated otherwise.

Telling her date to step back, the girl aimed and let the dart fly, missing everything. Laughter broke out all around. Brick smiled, telling her she still had two more tries. The second dart landed a little to the right of the target, prompting her boyfriend to say, "Let me throw that last one."

His throw was a little better; his dart at least struck the plywood backboard. They both laughed, and she said, "Let's do it again." This time, Brick was handed enough tickets for both to play, and he gave each of them three darts. The boyfriend missed the balloons with his first effort and quickly began complaining about the quality of the darts, but his complaints were then muted when his date popped one of the balloons.

Brick smiled again and said, "One more for a win." She failed on the next try, but her boyfriend popped one. Now, both needed only to pop one balloon to win a prize. The boyfriend's throw was on target, but he threw it so softly that the dart bounced off one of the balloons, only adding to his frustration. The girl sailed her dart into the board, and a balloon popped. It made Brick happy that he was able to offer her a prize. She selected a small stuffed dog and laughingly pulled her boyfriend away, saying she would give him another chance later, but for now she wanted to ride the Ferris wheel.

A few more people tried their luck, and business was picking up for everyone. There was no time for conversation, which disappointed Brick. In an effort to find out more about Mary Jane and Misty, he was hoping he could get some information about them from Jill. It was probably for the best, though, as he wasn't sure she would have appreciated his questions about other girls. She appeared to be a loner, and Brick didn't want to impose on her friendship.

After a few hours of work, Brick and Ray were both hungry. The crowds had grown, but action at the games remained hit or miss, so Ray offered to go pick up some food for them if Brick would watch over his booth. They would be able to eat while working. Ray asked Jill if he could get her anything. She thanked him but told him no as she had fixed herself a sandwich to eat a little later.

Before leaving, Ray told Brick he would try to check on the girls—to see if they were out and about. Brick laughed at him, saying, "I had no doubts where you would be going. So, how do you propose to see the ladies?"

Ray said, "I'll walk by the tent and see if they are open. If they are, maybe I'll take in an afternoon show."

"Ah, you are such a good friend, Brick said. "You're always willing to step up just to see if the ladies are doing okay."

Ray responded, "That's me! Always looking out for my fellow man."

Brick asked Ray to bring him the famed sausage dog all the way with fries and a Coke. Ray told him he would be back shortly; of course, that was dependent on what may be happening at the revue. Brick reminded Ray he would be working two booths while he was away and besides, he was hungry.

While Brick was working both booths, a friend of his from high school came by. It was Mike Harrington, Brick's tennis partner from last year. Mike was a year younger and was starting his senior year at Central. When Mike spotted Brick working, he immediately began to laugh, saying, "Is this what I have to look forward to after graduation—a career in the Softball Throw?" Brick told him not to knock it until he tried it.

Harrington said, "I heard you and Ray were working here, but I wasn't sure it was true."

Brick shook Mike's hand, saying, "Oh, it's true. We have joined the carnival, and so far, it's been a blast. Who told you about us working?"

Harrington laughed, "Hell, I don't remember. Everyone is talking about it. You guys are legendary. It's true; Toby Tyler did run off to join the circus."

Brick smiled and said, "It's not the circus, but its damn close. It's only for the week, then we are both off to college. But I've got to tell you this; thus far, it's setting up to be a hell of a send-off."

Harrington wondered if Brick would be working the games all week, and Brick told him, "I certainly hope not. So far, we have done a few different things. It is kind of go where you are needed, and today we are needed at the booths. Ray just left to get us something to eat, but he should be back in a few minutes."

Harrington sheepishly asked if he and Ray had met any of the traveling professionals. Brick knew immediately what Harrington was referring to and took great pleasure in answering, "Not only have we met the ladies, but I would also like to think we've become friends."

Harrington responded, "Damn man, tell me more."

"Let's just say we have gotten to know them," Brick continued, "and I suggest you take in a show. And if you do, drop our names. I'm sure you will be pleased."

Harrington just laughed and said, "I believe I'm going to have to call bullshit on my friend for that."

Brick shrugged his shoulders and replied, "Suit yourself man, but I am telling you, it will be worth it."

Harrington replied, "I just hope I can get into the show."

Brick assuredly said, "I'm pretty sure you can get in. I think the only ID you need is a couple of Washingtons."

"Well, if that's the case, Harrington said, "I'm in. Maybe I will get some of the guys to come with me." Brick thought that was a great idea and reminded him to drop his name— and Ray's.

Harrington, wanting to know more, asked Brick, "What about the girls?"

Without hesitation, Brick responded, "They're not only good looking, but they have bodies to die for. I can promise you that. Ray and I are hoping to get to know all the ladies a little better, especially after what we saw last night."

Harrington laughed and said, "A couple of days at the fair makes you delusional, huh?"

"It may only be a dream, but I can't think of a better way to finish up the summer," Brick replied with a look of satisfaction on his face.

Harrington agreed and then asked what Emily thought of Brick's new job. Brick replied, "She is okay with it, but let's keep the talk about the ladies with the boys—the less she knows, the better."

Harrington smiled and said, "No problem. When do you head out to school?"

Brick replied, "I'm hoping to go up this coming Monday. Registration and orientation begin next Tuesday, and classes start the following Monday. We should finish working here on Saturday."

Harrington told Brick that he was considering Elon for college and maybe he could come up and visit him to check it out. Brick said, "Sounds good to me. Just let me know."

When Ray returned with the food, Harrington was still talking with Brick. After saying hello, Ray immediately told Harrington he needed to get up with some of the guys and go to the revue and to be sure to let the ladies know he and Brick sent them. Harrington began laughing as he said, "So I understand. Brick just told me the same thing."

With a grin on his face, Ray said, "Well, let me assure you it will be well worth your time, and you will want to go more than once." As Ray was giving Brick his food, Harrington asked how many times they had been.

Brick excitedly replied, "Not nearly enough." Harrington grinned and said he needed to run as he was helping his girlfriend, Jo Ann, prepare for the beauty pageant.

As he was leaving, both boys called out to him, "Don't forget what we said. And be sure to tell Jo Ann good luck."

Harrington looked back and waved, telling them, "Will do."

Between the ever-growing number of customers, the boys were able to enjoy their food. Although they had been working close to four hours, Brick had less than ten winners and Ray even fewer. Ray shared with Brick that the revue wasn't open when he wandered by, and he didn't see anyone.

Sounding a little disappointed, Brick said, "I hate to say it, but it looks like we may be here for a while. I haven't seen Raeford since this morning."

Ray replied, "You take the next break, and bring me back another Coke when you do."

They relieved Jill again, and with the increased business, the time passed quickly.

It was almost five o'clock when Brick decided to take a break. He told Ray that he would pick them up some drinks and check on the revue. He went straight to the revue and was happy to see they were in full operation. Unfortunately, the protesters had returned and were much louder than the day before. The size of the crowd had even increased, and the protests were becoming less calm and more obnoxious.

Brick saw Lucy out front, and he asked her how things were going. She replied, "Things could be better. Those damn protesters are not helping at all. I wish they would just go and find something else to do."

Brick told her he had seen some friends and encouraged them to come to the show, and he added that he was hoping the night would be better. Lucy thanked him for spreading the word but then said with a little fear in her voice, "I just hope we are still operating then."

She then asked where they were working. Brick told her they were running the games, and she smiled, saying, "Not the best assignment, that's for sure, but you do see most everyone who comes to the fair." She then asked if they had met the new girl, Jill, who was running one of the games. Brick told her Jill was working a booth beside them, and they had talked some—nothing more.

Lucy said, "She seems to be a sweet girl. She is a little shy and appears to be a loner, but it's tough getting used to this business. I have asked her about joining the revue. We are always looking for girls, but she seems a bit nervous and apprehensive." Lucy suggested to Brick, "Maybe you can talk to her, and tell her she has the looks and body to become part of the show. The way girls come and go, you can never have too many. Also, you might want to tell her the money is a lot more than what she's currently making."

Brick was beginning to feel like he belonged with Howard's, telling Lucy he would try to talk with Jill. He then added that he believed Jill was angry over an old boyfriend and was running from his memory. Lucy smiled and said, "Honey, they are always running from something— boyfriends, parents, or the law. No one just joins the fair circuit; you do not need a degree in psychology to figure that out. I do believe, though, joining the revue could be a good fit for Jill. We can give her a sense of family here; we all care for one another. That, and it's not all bad to have men wanting you, especially when you have been wronged or you're running from someone or something." Brick thought to himself how strange that sounded, but he was way too young to know what she may have meant.

Brick asked if Mary Jane was working. Lucy told him she was and if he would wait a minute, she would get her for him. Brick thanked her, but quickly said, "I need to get back to the games. Just tell her I said hi, and I will see her later."

"Suit yourself, but she should be out for the preview shortly," Lucy responded.

Hearing she would soon be out, Brick decided he had time to wait and at least take in the preview and catch today's sales pitch.

It wasn't long before all the girls were introduced, and there was Mary Jane as Janna, the Swedish princess. Mary Jane noticed Brick right away. She waved and mouthed the words, "You coming to the show?" Brick indicated he needed to get back to work and silently said he was sorry. He was surprised when she threw him a kiss and mouthed the words, "See you soon."

Before leaving, Misty and Tammy both waved, and once again Brick felt he was part of the team. Some of the men standing around noticed the attention he was getting, and Brick could not help but smile. The silent exchange was fun, and Brick hoped it might be an indicator of what the night may hold. Brick hoped the protesters had not noticed the interactions between him and the girls. After all, the last thing he wanted was a confrontation with the group.

Before leaving, Brick counted the protesters. Eight people were carrying signs and demanding the show be shut down. Once again, Brick saw the overweight man and was now convinced he was the leader of the protests. He was holding a sign in one hand and his Bible in the other, moving about the empty lot as if he was preaching and the Bible was his shield. He was challenging the crowd to avoid the temptation of the evil and sinful activities found behind the curtains. Brick could not see that the protests were having any effect at all; he saw it more annoying than anything else. There were plenty of good ole boys who wanted to see some naked women.

Brick picked up a couple of sodas and made his way back to the games. Ray was moving quickly from one booth to the next with organizational skills that would make anyone proud. It wasn't long, and Brick was back in the flow. Once the initial surge of business had slowed down, he told Ray the revue was open for business and that he saw the girls. Ray gave him a thumbs-up and indicated he would need a break soon. Before he could get away, Jill asked them once again to cover for her for a short spell.

Ray said, "Sure, we've got it covered. Take your time." She thanked him again for being so sweet.

As Jill walked away, Brick told Ray what Lucy had said about trying to talk Jill into joining the revue. Brick said, "Thus far, she has resisted the temptation, but Lucy feels she has got what it takes and hopes she will consider joining the others. Lucy feels all she needs is a little persuasion."

Ray replied, "I've gotten to know her better. Maybe I'll ask her about it to see how she feels."

Brick shook his head, saying, "And I'm certain you would only be doing it for the good of the show—no ulterior motives, right?"

Ray laughed, "None whatsoever. You know me better than that. I'm only looking out for the lady's best interest. That, and the fact I wouldn't mind seeing her naked either." Brick smiled, knowing Ray was full of himself. But that was Ray.

Jill was gone longer than expected but was apologetic when she returned. Ray told her no worries; they had everything covered. She explained how she had gone to the barracks to check on her belongings. It wasn't that Jill did not trust people. She knew they had security, but she preferred to check on things just the same. She thanked Ray again for being so nice, telling him it had been a while since she had been as comfortable with someone as she was with him. Ray was flattered and again said, "No problem."

Jill then asked Ray if he had a car, to which Ray replied, "Not today, but I do have one. Is there something you need?"

Jill said, "I was going to ask if you could take me to a store. I need a few items, and I don't even know where to look." Ray told her he would be happy to take her wherever she needed to go. He told her he would drive in the next day, or he could borrow Brick's car after they got off, and he would be happy to take her into town. He added Sanford had a couple of stores close by, and it would be no problem. Jill was pleased with Ray's willingness to help her, and she seemed a little surprised by his kindness. She even asked, "You'll do that for me?"

Ray smiled and said, "Of course." She thanked him, and he told her they could figure it all out later.

Ray told Brick they could bring his car the next day as Jill needed some supplies, and he had offered to take her to the store. Brick sarcastically said, "You're a good man, Ray Hill—no matter what others say."

"Yeah, and I figure maybe I can get the scoop on whether or not she would consider working the revue," replied Ray. "Like I said, sure wouldn't mind seeing those tits."

Brick, trying to be funny and disgusted at the same time said, "Just when I think you are a good humanitarian, you bring up her tits. Damn, is that all you think about?"

Ray said, "As if you don't. It's not all I think about, but they do demand some attention."

Brick gave a sly grin and said, "Yeah, what can I say? I wouldn't mind seeing them either. I just hope Emily and Donna don't figure out what we are up to."

When Raeford finally did stop by, both boys were tiring of the games. Brick wanted to say there is just so much fun one can have with darts and milk jugs, but he resisted. He was happy, though, to hear Raeford say how much he appreciated their dedication. He was even happier when Raeford promised he would try to find them a different experience the following day.

Raeford gave them instructions on shutting down the booths and told them they should be able to close everything down after ten o'clock. He did ask that they restock the balloons and make sure everything was good for Wednesday before they closed out.

Raeford stopped by Jill's booth and checked in with her. Running one of the booths was her regular gig for the week. The idea of running a booth for twelve hours a day for six days was less than appealing to Ray, making him wonder how she could do it.

Both boys were tired when it was time to close for the evening, having spent close to twelve hours at the games. But for them, their workday started three hours earlier at seven o'clock in the morning. They were learning the carnie life was not always as they had thought. Once the booths were secure, they still needed to take the tickets to the office. Jill walked with them, and once they dropped the tickets off, Raeford told them not to worry about the count as he could tell they were tired.

Jill headed back to the village, and the boys walked outside the tent. Even though they were tired, they decided they weren't quite ready to head home. Brick suggested they stick around the village for a while, hoping to see Mary Jane. Ray was cool with that and asked Brick if he could borrow his car to take Jill into town while he visited with Mary Jane. Brick, with his usual grin, said, "That's my man Ray—stepping up to help others. I'm certain you don't have any ulterior motives."

Both were laughing when Ray said, "Just give me the keys."

Brick handed Ray the car keys and jokingly said to him, "Now don't be late."

Ray said, "It shouldn't take long. I'll probably just go to Wicker's Grocery; they should have all she needs."

Ray called out to Jill, and she came back to see what he wanted. He told her he could take her to the store if she would like. He explained

Brick was hoping to stay in the village a little while longer. Although Jill was tired, she was thrilled with the offer. She asked Ray if he could give her a few minutes, and she would be ready.

Jill stepped inside the tent to let Raeford know Ray had offered to take her to a nearby store to pick up a few things, and they would be back before midnight. Raeford was okay with that.

Ray asked Raeford before they left what time he and Brick needed to come in the next day. Raeford responded, "How about seven o'clock again? I know you both have had a long day, but I promise I won't work you quite as hard tomorrow."

As Ray and Jill were leaving, Raeford told Brick, "I appreciate Ray taking an interest in Jill. She has had a tough time adjusting to our lifestyle. Maybe some time away will do her some good."

Brick was impressed that Raeford took so much interest in the employees. Not only did he care about how the fair operated, but he also had concern for the people. Brick knew Raeford was a good man.

After Ray and Jill had gone, Raeford invited Brick into his office. He asked if he had time to talk. Brick had been hoping to catch up with Mary Jane, but an invite from the big boss was a plus. He followed Raeford into the office, and Brick was surprised when Raeford offered him a beer. Brick thanked him and sat down to talk. Raeford wanted to know what he thought about work so far. Brick said, "I've got to tell you, I have enjoyed it. Everyone's been so nice—almost like a family—where people look out for one another."

Raeford smiled and said, "That's great to hear. I was hoping you would see it that way. Sometimes, the carnie life gets a bad reputation. I guess it's our nomadic lifestyle that folks don't understand. We are still people." He then asked Brick if he had made it to the revue yet.

With a smile as big as a Cheshire cat, Brick said, "Yes sir, we went last night." After a short pause, he continued, "And I've got to say, it was quite enjoyable."

Raeford laughed and said, "I'mmm sure it was. Were you able to meet Lucy?"

"Yes sir, I've talked with her a couple of times. She seems pleasant," Brick responded.

In his usual kind-hearted manner, Raeford said, "She's a good person. She may drink a little too much, but she's a sweetie. We couldn't do without her."

While they were talking, other vendors began dropping off their tickets, and a few of the sideshows checked in as well. Brick wondered how long the drop off lasted, and Raeford told him he would be there at least until midnight. Hearing that, Brick asked if he ever slept. "Sleep, what's that? Seriously, it's the nature of the business. You learn to adjust," said Raeford.

He told Brick he would have some help soon as the advance team would be returning from Tarboro, and things should slow down for him. When they return, he could spread around some of his responsibilities. Raeford then pulled out a strongbox and began counting out the boys' pay for the day. Raeford told him he figured they had worked the entire day and asked how sixty dollars sounded. Brick did not hesitate to say it sounded great, and he knew Ray would be happy with it as well.

As Raeford finished up his beer, he told Brick how much he appreciated the work he and Ray were doing. He went on to say, "A lot of people want to work the fair and then when they get here, it's not as exciting as they had hoped and quit as quick as they started. So, if you guys hang in there, I am sure the money will continue to be good. I don't want either of you to forget how much fun a fair can be. We will figure out when you guys can have some time off to give you an opportunity to enjoy the fair as well as work it. Maybe you could take one of the girls out. We try to give everyone some time off; it helps keep the energy up." The idea certainly appealed to Brick, and he had no doubt Ray would agree.

A few minutes went by, and Raeford pulled another beer from the fridge and asked Brick if he needed another. Brick answered, "No sir, I'm still working on this one." The two continued to talk, and Raeford shared some war stories about the work. After a few minutes, Brick asked Raeford how he felt about the protesters and if he was concerned.

With a little sadness in his voice, Raeford said, "We see it more and more, and yeah, I'm always concerned when someone wants to challenge how we do business. I've come close to closing down the shows, but hopefully it won't come to that. I'm going to try to meet with the pastor and give him a chance to voice his complaints. I would like to see if there is anything we can do to appease him, but short of shutting down the shows, I'm not sure we can do that. Unfortunately, his kind always wants to legislate morality, and we both know that is an impossible task. That never keeps people from trying though. It's just a show. We're not promoting prostitution or other illegal activities. But that does not always satisfy the morals police. You have met some of the girls; they like to flirt and have fun. If anything, they are running a more legitimate business than the games you were operating today."

Brick knew he was right. The games were tilted to favor the house, but with the shows, you get what you go for.

Raeford continued, "Who knows what's motivating him. Maybe he had a parishioner run off and join the shows, or maybe he's just a stick in the mud. No telling, but it does concern me. I'm afraid that the girly shows will soon be a part of carnival lure. Clubs are popping up in the larger cities, and it will not be long before they make their way to the smaller towns. With the clubs opening, the novelty of the girly shows will wear off. As more outlets for adult entertainment open up, it's only natural there will be less interest in such shows."

Brick then said he had heard some refer to the protesters as opportunists, hoping to get their name in the paper and maybe stir up some controversy. Raeford agreed with Brick, telling him that may be part of it, but no matter what the motivation may be, the results are never good.

After a few minutes, their conversation was broken up by some commotion outside. Raeford went to the door where he saw Lucy and a few of the girls talking. When Lucy spotted Raeford, she said, "You may need to speak to those protesters sooner than you think. Tonight, the fat one was yelling at the girls, and I don't like it."

Brick noticed Mary Jane in the group and wanted to talk to her, so he told Raeford he would see him in the morning. He thanked him for the beer as he left the office. Brick went over to where Mary Jane was standing and asked if she would like some company. She told Brick that would be nice and then needled him about not making it to the show earlier. Brick explained, "I'm sorry we didn't get over, but we had to work the entire night. We haven't been off long."

Mary Jane smiled and said, "I'm just kidding. It's been a long day for everyone. So, where is your friend?" Brick told her Ray had taken Jill into town. Mary Jane confirmed, "You met Jill?"

Brick responded, "Yeah, she was working the booth next to Ray."

Mary Jane continued, "What did you think of her?"

"To tell you the truth, she seemed sad and alone," Brick replied.

Mary Jane said, "I know the feeling. I was the same way when I started. It is not that easy to make friends, especially for a girl. It takes some time to get used to everything. You don't know who to trust, and you don't know what to expect. I have tried to reach out to her, but like I said, it takes time. Maybe Ray can bring her out of her shell. I know Lucy would like for her to join the revue as there is always room for new girls."

Mary Jane spoke of the show as if it were the same as working at the Winn Dixie. She didn't seem to mind peoples' perceptions at all. She was fine with her current job. Brick was impressed with her self-confidence and wondered if she had always been this self-assured. He wondered if she had joined the fair with such confidence, or did it grow out of her ability to dance and show her body to an adoring unknown public? She then asked what time Ray was supposed to get back.

Brick said, "They should be back before midnight. That's about all I know." Mary Jane then surprised Brick by inviting him into her trailer to wait for Ray. Of course, Brick was thrilled with the invitation.

As they approached the trailer, Misty was coming out. She told Mary Jane she was on her way to take a shower as she needed to cleanse herself; one could only take so much drooling. Mary Jane laughed without responding. Brick, realizing he would be alone with Mary Jane, couldn't help but feel excited by the prospect. Mary Jane was wearing shorts and a loose top with only a few buttons fastened, allowing her beautiful breasts to be somewhat exposed. Brick could not tell if she was wearing a bra and then thought, Well, when you show your tits for a living, a bra would always be optional.

When they were inside, Mary Jane pulled out a couple of beers from the fridge and handed one to Brick. He had never been much of a drinker, but tonight was a different story. He did fear, though, how the beer might make him act, but he was not about to pass up Mary Jane's offer. He thanked her and took a small sip. The middle of the trailer had limited room, so Mary Jane suggested they go into her room. Brick's heart began to race. Was she just being nice or was she coming on to him? The room was small and filled primarily with her unmade bed.

Looking around, Mary Jane said to Brick, "Now don't be judging me on my housekeeping skills. I just haven't gotten around to cleaning yet."

Brick nervously said, "Hey, it looks great to me."

She smiled and took his hand, and they sat at the end of the bed. She looked at Brick and said, "I hope this is okay. We don't have any comfortable chairs." Brick just grinned and told her not to worry about him.

He hoisted his beer, saying, "Here's to uncomfortable chairs."

Mary Jane laughed and told him, "You're funny, and I like that. In this business, you don't meet many people who take the time to be nice. We go into towns and do our shows, and it is as if we are zoo animals. No one wants to get too close. They just want to stare. But you and Ray seem different—reminds me of the boys I used to know back home."

Brick tried to remain cool and said, "You're telling me that you knew some boring boys back home."

She laughed as she hit him on his arm and said, "That's not what I said."

He then told her, "I'm enjoying getting to know everyone, and spending time with you is a bonus. I have always enjoyed the fair, and you and the others have just added to that enjoyment. And today, working the games, well, that was sweet! I've always been somewhat of a ham, so that job was right up my alley."

She laughed again, telling him, "I love your perspective. You don't seem to be very judgmental. I guess you noticed that we don't have many young men working, and those that are can be complete jackasses."

Brick said, "Well, that is their loss," and besides, he enjoyed the attention. He asked her how long she had been with the show.

"It's hard to believe, she replied, but I'm closing in on a year. It does get lonely. That's why it's nice to meet someone like you."

Brick's heart began to race—enough talk! He wanted to kiss her. But he resisted and said, "I wouldn't think someone as nice as you would ever be lonely."

Mary Jane looked into his eyes and said, "That's sweet, but many things can contribute to loneliness, and there are times it's hard to avoid." She then said, "Enough about me. Tell me more about you."

Almost apologetically, Brick said, "I'm afraid you would find my life rather dull. But I can promise you, this week it has been getting better." Mary Jane smiled and once again spoke of how nice Brick was. As she was smiling, Brick found the courage to lean over and kiss her. He surprised himself as he had never been much on first moves, but things were different with her. He was pleased that Mary Jane offered no resistance. She even seemed to welcome his advances. The kiss turned into kissing, and it intensified as they placed their drinks down. Brick found it magical as he held her in his arms and kissed her sweet lips. He was about to burst. Could his fantasy be coming to life? They had been kissing for a few minutes when Mary Jane suddenly broke his embrace. Brick, now stunned with her actions, asked if everything was okay. Mary Jane told him, "I'm fine, I just wanted to look at you. It's been a long time since I have enjoyed being with someone and being with you feels special. Thank you."

Brick smiled and held her hand, saying, "You don't need to thank me. I can't believe someone as special as you could ever be lonely. Someone like you should have plenty of friends and lots of company. You are such a beautiful, intriguing lady." She seemed to blush as Brick shared his feelings, telling him she could not remember the last time someone called her a lady.

She then picked up her beer, took a sip, and said, "Maybe we can spend some time together away from the fair. I usually get one night a week off. If you could get the same night off, we could go on that date we talked about."

Brick was taken aback by the proposal and all he could say was, "It would be my pleasure to show you the sights of Sanford."

Mary Jane told him, "It's been a long time since I've been on a date. It would be fun."

Brick told her she might find Sanford lacking excitement, but he would try to entertain her. Mary Jane smiled and told him she could not wait. She then leaned back with one arm on the bed, and Brick followed her lead, leaning back as well. They soon began kissing again.

Brick wondered if she was teasing, but even if she was, he didn't care. He was enjoying it way too much to worry.

Brick allowed his instincts to take over as he began to explore her body. Through the cotton blouse, Brick could feel the firmness of her breasts. Mary Jane then moved in a way that gave him greater access to her body. Things were moving so fast that he was having a difficult time remaining composed. Brick found her unbelievable as he pulled open her blouse, exposing her breasts. She smiled and directed his head down to her hardening nipples. Brick's tongue began exploring her exposed flesh. He could not imagine anyone being sexier or more beautiful at that time. He was surprised—and thrilled—to soon feel her hand exploring his arousal. She began to stroke him lightly through his jeans, only adding to Brick's euphoria. As Brick continued exploring her body, their love session was abruptly interrupted by the opening of the trailer door.

Mary Jane backed away from the embrace and said, "That must be Misty. Maybe we should stop." Brick was somewhat relieved. Lacking any real sexual experience, he was scared he may ruin their moment together. She told him she hoped they would be able to go on that date. Brick kissed her once again, telling her that sounded like a plan.

Mary Jane sat up and said, "Misty, is that you?" Misty answered, and before Mary Jane could tell her they were in the bedroom, she pulled back the curtain door. Once Misty saw Brick, she told them she was sorry to disturb them.

Mary Jane told her, "No problem. We were just talking."

Brick thought, well, if this was talking, then I can hardly wait until we start fooling around.

Misty said, "Brick, I think Ray's looking for you. He was outside the office."

Brick questioned, "Oh, he's back?"

"Yeah, he was with Jill when I saw him," said Misty.

Misty excused herself as quickly as she came in. As she went to her room in the front of the trailer, Mary Jane told Brick he probably should go. Brick felt as if he was unconscious to his desires; he didn't know what to do. She reached over and took his hand, "Maybe we can talk some more tomorrow," and with that she kissed him again.

Brick squeezed her hand in response. He wanted to thank her for the evening but feared that would be inappropriate. He decided to thank her for the beer instead and told her that he looked forward to seeing her the next day.

Brick was then surprised when she said, "Brick, you are so sweet. Please don't think I do this at every stop. It's been such a long time since I've been with anyone."

Brick kissed her gently and told her he was happy she decided to be with him. She then jumped up and said, "Go find Ray, and I will see you tomorrow." Before exiting the room, Brick smiled and told her to sleep well.

Outside Mary Jane's trailer, Brick spotted Ray and Jill embracing. When Jill noticed Brick, she broke from the embrace and immediately thanked him for letting Ray use his car. Brick told her, "Not a problem. I hope you were able to get the things you needed."

"I was. Thanks again," she responded.

Brick said it was his pleasure. Little did she know how much of a pleasure. Ray told Brick to give him a minute, and he would be right back. He wanted to walk Jill back to the barracks. Brick just said, "I'll be right here."

Brick could tell there was something going on between the two of them. Ray was being very attentive to Jill. Brick had to smile, knowing both were now experiencing something far different than anything they had enjoyed before.

While waiting for Ray, Brick took a seat on the office steps and could only think about how great the week had been so far. Ray wasn't gone long, and after a very brief exchange of words, they both agreed they needed to get home as it had been a long but eventful day.

Brick said, "seven o'clock in the morning is going to come mighty early."

Ray shook his head, saying, "One thing's for sure, this is not your average summer."

Brick then reminded Ray, "They did warn us that it wouldn't be a nine-to-five gig. It might not be nine to five, but it's damn good pay. He then handed Ray his share of the money that Raeford had given him. Both felt it was funny that they were having such a good time that neither had given the pay much thought.

As they were walking toward the car, Ray asked if he had missed anything when he was away. Brick was now so full of himself and anxious to tell Ray what he had been up to, especially about his time with Mary Jane. Without missing a beat, he quickly replied, "Oh, not much, unless you consider making out with Mary Jane something."

Ray slapped a high five and said, "All right!"

Although Brick was excited about the short time he spent with Mary Jane, he wanted Ray to know there was more to her than her looks and her body. Strangely enough, Brick wanted to talk about Mary Jane's wholesome side as much as he did her sexual side. He told Ray how much he enjoyed Mary Jane's company, and added he was having a hard time believing she was a stripper.

Ray grinned and said, "Do we need to go back to the revue to remind you?"

"No, we don't," Brick replied. "I know that's her job, but I'm telling you, there is more to her than the obvious. She has a wonderful personality and seems genuinely honest. I guess I am saying there is so much more to her than either of us realize. She is as much a lady as any of the girls in our class at school."

Ray laughed and said, "A strange lady you just happen to be getting it on with." Brick returned the laugh, and Ray responded, "My man" and gave him another high five.

Brick continued, "I'm telling you; she is something else. If things keep moving in the direction we're headed, this could be one of the best weeks of my life."

Ray said, "Damn." There was nothing else to say.

Brick decided to change the subject and began telling Ray about his short visit with Raeford and how impressed he was with their work. "Raeford really likes our willingness to do what's needed. Oh, he also said he appreciated your spending some time with Jill. He feels she could use a friend."

Ray agreed, "Yeah, I think he's right. She seems to be going through some stuff right now. I'm not sure what, but I'm enjoying getting to know her."

Brick then told him how Raeford had given him a beer while they talked. Hearing this made Ray grin as he said, "You were drinking with Raeford? Damn, man! That would never happen with Milton at the school."

"That's for sure," said Brick as he laughed. "It's so crazy that we are making damn good money and drinking a few beers with the boss. What a week!" Brick added he and Raeford did not talk long before he saw Mary Jane and walked her back to her trailer.

Ray, with a little sarcasm in his voice, responded, "That's my friend—always a gentleman. I'm sure you had nothing on your mind besides making sure she got home safely." They both laughed, and Ray wanted to know more. "So, tell me what happened with you and Mary Jane."

Brick replied, "Let me put it this way, we had some fun. Or at least I did." Ray asked for details, and Brick was happy to oblige, "For the most part, we just talked. We did go to her room, though, and some real magic took place." He had a grin on his face that said it all. Brick saw no need to go into detail, leaving it up to Ray and his imagination.

Ray smiled and said, "All right, my bud was getting lucky."

As if he was still trying to convince Ray (and maybe himself) of Mary Jane's wholesomeness, Brick replied, "I know it sounds that way, but I also enjoyed being with her. Like I said, she is not much different from the girls in our class. I am telling you, she could fit in with no trouble at all. She seems to be very much like a normal girl."

Acting rather cool, Ray reverently said, "Again, like I said, a normal girl who happens to strip for a living."

Brick was tiring of Ray's talk. He did not need to bring up the stripping constantly. Brick was aware of her job, but he was also able to recognize her other qualities. He then said to Ray, "That may be true, but it doesn't define her—at least in my eyes. Maybe I'm just foolish, but I feel there is a lot more to her than meets the eye."

Ray's mind was still in the gutter, but he smiled and said, "Yeah, but you have to admit, what meets the eye is quite nice."

Brick, still being defensive, told Ray, "That may be true, but I'm telling you again that there is more to her than her incredibly sexy appearance."

Ray began to wonder if Brick might be falling for Mary Jane. It sure sounded like he was. Brick told him, "No, I don't think that's it. Hell, maybe I am, but I have got to tell you that there is something about her other than the obvious. Maybe it is my insecurities with Emily that make it difficult to believe someone like Mary Jane could be interested in me. Mary Jane wants me to take her on a date. She wants to see the sights of Sanford."

Ray laughed and said, "Well, that won't take long."

"Funny! I guess the old saying, 'You can't judge a book by its cover' applies to her," said Brick in a caring way. "When we met on Sunday, all I could think about was the possibility of getting her into bed, and now I want to know her for who she is and not for what she does."

Ray replied, "You are what some would call a hopeless romantic, and like I said before, it appears you may be falling for her." Brick assured him that even though he was interested in Mary Jane, Emily still had his heart. But he also recognized that Mary Jane was teaching him that first impressions are not always correct. He continued talking with Ray about how much he was enjoying getting to know her.

Ray agreed with him, even commenting that it seemed most everyone they had met while working at the fair did not fit their expectations of carnie folks. Ray added, "I'm not totally sure what I was expecting, but it wasn't this." Both boys were pleasantly surprised with the people who brought the fair to life for them.

Before they drove off, Ray asked Brick if he was okay to drive. After all, between the beer and Mary Jane, he had had quite a night. Ray told him he did not want Brick's logical approach to life to affect his ability behind the wheel. Brick assured him he would have no problem driving as he had hardly touched the beer Mary Jane had given him. Besides that, he had other things on his mind. He then laughed as he said, "My philosophical approach could be a result of guilt," but he certainly was not going there.

Brick felt they had talked enough about his evening with Mary Jane, and he wanted to know about Ray's time with Jill. Ray told him, "There's not a lot to share. I took her to Wicker's Grocery since it is open late. We walked around the store for a while, and she bought a few items. She is interesting for sure, still learning about working the fair and questioning if this kind of life is good for her. I feel she is avoiding something from her past. Who knows? Maybe it's the boyfriend she talked about."

Brick asked Ray if he had seen anyone he knew while they were out. Ray replied, "Thankfully, the store was empty, and Wicker wasn't around at such a late hour. It may have been difficult to explain why I was out grocery shopping with a stranger. I certainly don't want Donna to find out about all of our adventures this week. Jill shopped for some personal items, telling me it's hard keeping things for a long time since she did not live in one of the trailers. She picked up some snacks and some fruit. Funny, but she says what she misses the most is not having fruit available. I have not thought about that, but she did tell me other than candy apples, there is little, if any, fruit to be found on the midway."

Brick, trying to move the conversation along, said, "Blah blah blah, that's all well and good, and you are certainly a good man, but I want to know what happened between you two. I don't believe her improved mood is entirely the result of some fresh fruit."

Ray, with a look of contentment, said, "Well, you may be right, but the fresh fruit did help. I'm happy to report that you weren't the only one having a little fun tonight." Brick already knew something was up by the way Jill said goodnight to Ray, and he was anxious to know what happened. Ray began to tell him that when they got back from the store, they stayed in the car for a while, and it was a good way to end the evening. Apparently, Jill was happy having someone show her some attention.

Brick then had to have his say by adding, "And, of course, you were more than willing."

"Hey, I'm just a nice guy. What can I say?" responded Ray proudly.

Brick asked Ray if he talked with Jill about working the revue. Ray told him he did and felt it is just a matter of time before she would seriously consider it. He felt the only thing holding her back was her lack of self-confidence. Ray added, "She told me the only man ever to see her naked was her former boyfriend."

Brick, somewhat surprised, said, "She told you that? what did you say?"

Ray responded, "I assured her she had the looks and the body for it, and I knew plenty of people who would love to see her dance. Of course, when I told her that, she said I was just being nice."

Brick was giving Ray a hard time and said, "Yeah, that's Ray, Mr. Nice Guy—always looking out for the ladies. You, of course, have no desire to see her dance."

Ray shrugged his shoulders, "I can't help how Jill heard my words." He then acknowledged he would love to see her naked, maybe even without her dancing. Brick simply smiled. The boys were having an adventure of a lifetime.

Both boys were all smiles as they drove out of the parking lot. There would be no stopping anywhere tonight. They headed straight home, knowing the next day promised to be just as eventful. Brick dropped Ray off at his house and told him he would see him the next morning around six-thirty for another day of fun and adventure. Both agreed if the next few days were anything like what they had already experienced, it could only get better.

Odom Returns Home

B efore returning home, Odom made a stop at the convenience store. He picked up a copy of The Sanford Herald, anticipating seeing an article and maybe some photos of the protest. As soon as he got inside the house, he quickly began to flip through the newspaper. It didn't take him long to discover the newspaper had failed to cover the protest, and there was no mention of it in any of the articles concerning the fair. Odom became enraged with anger and threw the newspaper across the room screaming, "What does it take; just what does it take?"

Odom's breathing became shallow as disappointment overtook him. His anger began to grow as did his frustration. He now believed the fair must be paying off the newspaper. What other reason could there be for not covering the protest? If the paper would do its job, people would learn of the movement as well as the evil infiltrating Sanford. He needed the citizens of Sanford to join him and his movement to stamp out the revue. Odom knew it would take publicity; after all, it was a key to driving a successful protest.

With no coverage of the protest, Odom began to think irrationally. His anger was evident as he sat down and screamed, "Why?" He was infuriated, and his anger only added to his determination to fight harder. He refused to allow the lack of coverage to discourage him. The movement would live on and succeed. Unfortunately, his desire for publicity was beginning to fuel his antagonistic thoughts. He was going to get noticed, even if it meant changing tactics, as desperate times call for desperate measures.

Beverly heard Odom screaming and went into the room, hoping to calm him down. She said, "Patrick, you need to give this some more time. It's still early in the game, and we have just started. It's not worth making yourself crazy."

Odom in a harsh tone said to her, "Crazy? Is that what you think I am? I'll tell you what's crazy; it's this town. The people of Sanford need to wake up and see the evil of those shows. They need to know The Revival Revolutionary Church will no longer merely exist. I'm tired of taking a back seat to the other churches. We have something to offer, and it's time our voices are heard. Tomorrow will be a new day, and we are going to be louder and stronger. By God, I promise you, people are going to take notice!"

Odom's words were scaring Beverly as she feared what may become of his talk. His declarations were making her uneasy, and she didn't know what to think. She reminded Odom she was on his side, and there was no need to attack her.

Odom realized he was wrong in taking out his frustrations on Beverly, but he had a need to vent. He apologized for his outburst and told her he would give Reverend Hinson a call as he could possibly offer some support. Beverly hoped the call would do some good; maybe Hinson could calm him down. She knew for sure that Odom needed some reassurance and positive reinforcement, and she felt a talk with Hinson could do just that.

Unfortunately, Odom had long passed being calm when Hinson answered the phone. He was still angry and never gave the preacher a chance to speak before he went into a rant about the fair and the lack of newspaper coverage. Beverly heard Odom tell Hinson, "No one is paying us any attention. It has been two days, and this town cares more about the shows than the sin." He continued complaining, telling Hinson that people were looking at them like they were a group of crazy hillbillies who didn't need to be taken seriously.

Hinson allowed Odom to sound off, knowing it was probably best to just let him get it out of his system. Odom's talk, though, was becoming a little unnerving, and Hinson now feared what Odom might do.

Hinson finally was able to get a word in and calmly said, "Patrick, you know God's work takes time and patience, but in the end we shall win the battle." Such talk was of little comfort to Odom, and Hinson had failed to soothe any nerves; if anything, it just added to his anger. What Hinson didn't know when he reached out to Odom was just how fragile Odom was. He also failed to understand Odom was looking to do much more than teach God's word. Odom was looking to grow his church. He believed the protest was the vehicle for growth, and the lack of success was now wearing him down.

Odom continued, telling Hinson, "Everyone acts as if we don't exist; no one is paying us any mind. I'm telling you; things have got to change." Wanting to let Odom know he felt his pain, Hinson tried to ask about the protests, asking where they were setting up and the time of day they were protesting. There was little Hinson could do to avert Odom's anger; if anything, the questions Hinson asked only added to Odom's frustrations.

Odom was not letting up, and he continued, "Look Hinson, we're not stupid! We've been at the front gate and moved onto the fairgrounds, setting up just outside the venue, and the only thing I have to show for it is the money we've spent."

Hinson feared Odom's outrage and now had to question his decision to reach out to Odom in the first place. He wondered if he had picked the right man to lead the protest. Hinson asked Odom to listen and told him that hopefully they could come up with some new ideas that would help get the protests noticed and the show closed.

Odom lowered his voice and even acknowledged his irrational behavior. He apologized for his tone and told Hinson it had just been a disappointing day; he only wanted someone to take him and the protests seriously. Odom said, "I fear time is running out. People walk by and look at us as if we are part of the show. Some even act as if we are the ones in the wrong, while those women continue to parade around half naked."

Odom wanted Hinson to hear him out, so he kept on talking. Odom continued his rant about how the newspaper had not covered the protests and how the local radio stations had not even contacted him much less the ones in Raleigh. Odom showed his exhaustion when he told Hinson, "I fear we are not doing any good. I'm just so frustrated with such little success."

Hinson reassured Odom that he was doing the right thing and pleaded with him to remain patient, adding that Rome wasn't built in a day. Hinson also stressed that when they've had some success with the protests in the past, it usually wasn't felt until the latter part of the week. The show they shut down in Eden closed for the weekend. He again emphasized that it takes time.

Hinson started building Odom up; he was now playing the role of a coach. He told Odom he would soon begin seeing progress, and he was sure the movement would gain momentum. He assured Odom that in the end the protesters would win out and that he would be rewarded for his efforts. Odom once again said, "It just seems like no one cares."

It was then that Hinson said, "You care, Patrick, and that's the most important thing. You are laying the foundation for success. It will not be long before the citizens of Sanford will recognize you and your mission. Please be patient and know that God is on your side." Hinson assured Odom he would continue to try and get the movement some publicity, and he then added, "It is a process; keep the faith."

Odom had finally calmed down, and he thanked Hinson for listening. He also reminded Hinson that if they didn't get some coverage soon, nothing would happen as the fair was only in town for a few days.

Hinson then said, "No, Patrick, it will happen. You just need to believe. It will happen; I promise."

Odom was disappointed with the conversation he had with Hinson. He wasn't sure what he was hoping for, but at least he had calmed down. Although Odom felt Hinson offered little reassurance, he understood he needed Hinson and his support. If things changed and the protest became a movement, both men needed each other.

Before Odom told Beverly about his call to Hinson, he again apologized to her for his outburst. This wasn't unusual as his outbursts were often followed with an apology. Odom was a conflicted man, and he struggled with his emotions. He knew he could be guilty of letting his anger get the best of him, but he wanted success so much that he was losing sight of the real goal. He then began telling Beverly about his conversation with Hinson and how he hoped Hinson would again make some calls to the media to help stir up some much-needed publicity.

Beverly said, "Patrick, I know how frustrated you must be, but don't allow the protest to change who you are. Nothing is worth the pain you are feeling. You ARE making a difference. You need to remember there are those of us who believe in you. I know we can make it, but it will take time and faith in each other."

Odom thanked her, gave her a peck on the cheek, and said he just wished Hinson shared his anger. As if he was trying to convince himself, he said, "Maybe I should take more action. If you want to create change, sometimes it takes more than words; it takes action." Odom felt Hinson was too passive, and he told Beverly, "I think I may need to take a bigger role in the movement. I don't think I can rely on Hinson to step it up."

Hinson had proven to be of little help by just telling him to be patient and give it time. Although Hinson said he would bring some protesters to Sanford, he had done nothing thus far; all he had gotten from Hinson were signs and words. Odom no longer had the patience nor the time to sit back and wait; he needed to act. If Hinson couldn't get any publicity, Odom was going to have to do something different.

Beverly didn't care for Patrick's defiance and told him, "Patrick, you know I believe in you, but the way you are talking is beginning to frighten me."

Odom shook his head and said, "Listen Beverly, I can't, and I won't, just wait to see what happens. This protesting is for both of us. You know how things need to change, and we both share the dream of building our church."

Odom was to wound up to rest and started thinking about his next move. He needed to make things happen, so he decided to call Jimmy Key. He knew Key would listen, and he also knew Key felt obligated to him and the church. Several months ago, Key had lived with the Odom's while he was going through a nasty divorce.

Key had a somewhat interesting past, including a few run-ins with the law. Odom didn't know much about Key's criminal history, and he didn't care. Odom was looking for someone who was willing to push the envelope a little more when it came to the protest. With Key adjusting his work schedule to give the protest more time and support, he may have some fresh ideas for making it stronger. Odom called Key and asked if he would meet him the next morning at Kelly's Truck Stop for breakfast. He ended the conversation, saying, "Let's just you and I meet—no one else. We need to discuss where we go from here. I'm tired of just holding signs and chanting slogans. I'm ready to step it up, and I need you to help me."

Brick Returns Home

When Brick got home, he was still keyed up. His thoughts were on Mary Jane and the short time they had spent together. He was feeling more a part of Howard's Amusements each day, and Mary Jane was only adding to that feeling.

No one was awake at his house, so Brick went straight to his room. Unfortunately, he was brought back to reality when he discovered a note his mother left for him. The note read, "Emily called." That was all it said. There were no details—just the message that she had called. Brick immediately began thinking about Emily, and his thoughts of her were now making him feel guilty; he had been in the arms of another.

The lack of details in her message only increased his anxiety. It was not like her to call, and he hoped nothing was wrong. He knew Emily would only call if it was important, and although he knew it was impossible, it didn't keep him from wondering if somehow Emily had found out about Mary Jane. At this point, he wasn't thinking straight. There was no way she could have known about Mary Jane, but Brick couldn't help but feel uneasy.

It was too late to call her back, so he would have to wait until morning and try to catch her even though the note said nothing about calling her back. Unfortunately, it also meant Brick would worry about Emily—all the while thinking about Mary Jane. In a strange way, he was happy she had called. Was it possible she was feeling a little homesick and was missing him and just needed to talk?

It didn't take long before Brick's self-doubt began creeping in, and he started envisioning the call being a bad sign. He was so insecure when it came to girls, especially those he had feelings for. Brick had had other girlfriends in the past, but he never truly felt completely comfortable with them either. His feelings for Emily were stronger than any he had felt for the others, but these feelings only increased his uncertainty. His stupid self-doubt and insecurities made it difficult for him to enjoy any relationships. Brick was smart enough to know he was screwing things up, but that failed to keep him from being a victim of his thoughts. Regrettably, he felt Emily looked at their relationship as a strong friendship—not a romantic connection. This, however, didn't prevent him from wanting more.

Brick also knew his self-description of being an emotional mess would be an understatement. After spending what one could only describe as a wonderful time with Mary Jane, Brick comes home and begins to worry about a phone call. He had no right to be worried. He was the one doing wrong and not acting like someone in a committed relationship. He had no right to even be concerned about what she may need or want. Brick knew the guilt he was feeling was a direct result of his actions with Mary Jane and his feelings for Emily. He also felt that at eighteen he shouldn't be so damn fragile. And if he cared for Emily so much, why didn't he act like it?

Brick laid in bed and thought of both girls. It occurred to him that maybe Emily represented that forbidden fruit. He had always placed her on a pedestal, viewing her love as something that was always just out of reach. Brick felt this way although Emily had never given any indication that she was different from any of the other girls he had dated. He suffered from self-inflicted turmoil.

Ray and other friends had grown tired of Brick and his woe is me attitude when it came to Emily. They had told him repeatedly that if Emily was the one, he needed to stop whining and start acting like it. Ray more than anyone felt Brick spent too much time looking for reasons for the relationship to fail and never considered why it should work. Brick knew Ray was right and thought maybe Ray should be the one studying psychology.

⚜

Wednesday Morning

When Key arrived at the truck stop, Odom was working on his second cup of coffee. The coffee only added to his jitteriness and his anxious feelings about that day's protest. Over breakfast, the two talked of ways to jump start the protest and how they could get more recognition from the media and the public. Key could tell Odom was now desperate for public awareness.

Key was an original member of The Revival Revolutionary Church. Odom's uncle had known Key and suggested to him that he help Odom get started with the church. It turned out to be a good partnership as Key learned to appreciate Odom and his church. If the membership was made up of lost souls, Key certainly fit the description. His life had been full of trouble and miss-steps, and he found a friend in Odom.

Key was in full support of the protest, seeing it as an opportunity to raise his presence and statue in the church while also helping Odom with his mission. Although Key was anxious to help, he too had his own motives. Key hoped his involvement with Odom and the church would gain him some recognition with Beverly's sister, Gail. At breakfast, Key was by far the more upbeat of the two, telling Odom he was there to help and wanted to know what he needed him to do.

Odom was becoming a broken record, talking about his frustration with how slow things were progressing. Once again, he shared how tired he was that no one seemed to be taking them seriously. He hoped Key might have some ideas to drive the protest. Odom gave Key a rundown about his call to Hinson and how it only irritated him more.

All that Key knew of Hinson was what Odom had shared with him previously. It was apparent to him that Hinson was cautious; he did not want to be destructive, but yet he wanted to be visible.

Odom continued to talk of Hinson, saying, "Hinson wasn't much help. He just kept telling me to be patient and to be positive. He kept reminding me that I was doing God's work, and we shouldn't push it. But I'm tired of being patient. Something needs to happen, and it needs to be quick!"

Key gave it some thought and suggested to Odom, "Maybe we've been going about it all wrong. Think about this; all we've done so far is make a few signs and stake out some ground to demonstrate. Don't get me wrong as those things are important, but maybe it's time to take a different approach. How about this? What if we blocked the entrance to the show? You know how those nuts in California chain themselves to trees, trying to prevent them from being cut down. Well, maybe we can do something like that. We join in a human chain and prevent others from attending the show. They would probably have us taken off to jail, but we would get some attention."

Odom, still pessimistic, asked, "How do you think we can block the entrance when we hardly have enough people to hold signs?"

Key acknowledged Odom's doubt and said, "Granted, it may be a challenge, but if we made a human chain standing arm-in-arm, we could block the entrance. I can assure you it will get us noticed. We could wait till early evening when more people are at the fair and wanting to attend the revue, and then move arm-in-arm to the entrance. I'm telling you—that would work!"

As Odom contemplated the human chain, Key offered another suggestion. He reminded Odom that Wednesday was Senior Citizens' Day, and they could move the protest to the exhibit hall where those attending the luncheon could see them. Key said, "You know how old folks like to talk. Well, once they notice that we are protesting the revue, the talk will grow, and it will help our movement. Seniors from all over the county will be coming in later today. Although they won't be attending the show, they can have a voice in bringing an end to the sin."

After he gave Odom a chance to consider moving the protest, he reminded him that the press would be covering the luncheon, and it would give them another chance to get some press coverage.

Odom liked Key's ideas. He was especially impressed with moving the protest to the exhibit hall for the senior luncheon. Key had made his point and it was good one. If they protested there, all those attending the luncheon would certainly see them. Once the protesters were in place, those attending would have to walk right past them. The seniors would not only learn of the protest, but they would also have a chance to see The Revival Revolutionary Church in action. In addition, the rally could possibly influence a few to visit. This could be a win/win situation for Odom and his church.

They now had a plan. Key told Odom to call the others and let everyone know they would be meeting at the Fulton Exhibit Hall. He also suggested to Odom that he tell the church members to be ready to step up the involvement as it was time to make some noise.

Once they had discussed the protest, Key revealed his real interest by asking if Gail would be at the protest. He was delighted when Odom assured him that she would be there. Key continued, "You know, Patrick, I think Gail is a fine lady, and I've been thinking about asking her out—maybe for dinner or a movie. Do you think she would be up for something like that?"

Odom responded, "I don't know why not. Beverly tells me she hasn't been out in a while. It may do you both some good."

Odom supported the idea for various reasons. The main reason, of course, would be to his advantage. If Key and Gail became a couple, it would ensure that Key would remain active in his church, and he needed someone with Key's energy. Odom picked up the bill and told Key he would see him around eleven o'clock outside the exhibit hall.

As Key was leaving, he said to Odom, "I still think you should give the human chain some thought; it just might work." Odom did like the idea, but he also was aware it would take more people than what had shown up so far to make it happen.

Odom returned home and once again began working hard on the phone, calling nearly everyone he knew. He told them they would be moving the protest to the exhibit hall in order to get more attention. He was much more relaxed after meeting with Key, and he saw the senior luncheon as an ideal setup for their protest. He was hoping to make it a banner day. Unfortunately, he was not having much luck with the members of his congregation, as he continued to run into excuses (from work to family obligations). Although not happy with the responses, Odom remained energized. He finally got commitments from eight parishioners, and he asked them to try and find someone to bring with them. This gathering needed to be the biggest yet.

Odom knew for him to be successful it would be dependent on the support and knowledge of the community. He remained puzzled by the lack of attention they had received thus far. Why didn't others view the evil of the shows as he did and understand why they must be stopped? His real disappointment was in the religious community and their response to such a need. The other churches seemed more complacent and showed little interest in helping to get rid of the shows. Other ministers so far had only given lip service to the movement, expressing the thought that the shows offered little harm. Some told Odom the shows had been a staple of the fair for years and would only be in town for a few days. Such logic frustrated Odom, and he tried to tell them that much harm can be done in a week; after all, God created the earth in seven days. Odom realized he had a challenge and was fighting an uphill battle, but he was resolved in his belief that things would change.

Wednesday for The Boys

E ven with morning coming early for Brick, he was still unable to catch his mom before he left for work. He had hoped to talk with her about Emily's phone call. With nothing to go on, he decided he would try to reach her later in the day.

When Brick saw Ray, he couldn't help but notice Ray was dressed a little nicer than usual. Brick brought this observation to Ray's attention, wondering if Jill had anything to do with the new look. Knowing what Brick was getting at, Ray smiled and said to him, "No, just felt it would be a good day to change the look—maybe step up my game."

Brick laughed and replied, "Yeah, of course, that's all it is."

Ray pretended to be shocked that Brick was questioning his sincerity. Brick continued needling him, saying he was just pointing out his observation. Both laughed and started for the fairgrounds.

Ray, eager to get on with the day, said, "I feel today is going to be a good one and not just for the senior citizens.

Brick responded, "I hope you are right."

As they were driving in, Brick told Ray that his mom left a note for him that Emily had called, and he was not sure why or what she may have wanted. Ray suggested he try to call her during the day as he knew Brick would not be happy until he talked with Emily. He also knew that, for whatever reason, Brick would make more out of it than he should. Ray was aware of how screwed up his best friend was when it came to girls.

They got to the office right at seven o'clock. Raeford was working on the previous day's count. He offered them a cup of coffee, and they both declined. Raeford told them they needed to learn to drink coffee as, from what he had heard, they would be needing it when they got to college—especially after a few of those long nights partying or possibly studying. They all smiled.

Raeford turned his attention to Ray and said, "Brick feels things are going well—how about you?" Ray told him he was enjoying it all. Raeford continued, "Yeah, it's not all bad, and if you stayed longer than a week, you would learn that it's not all good either." Brick joined the conversation and commented that few things were. Raeford, pointing his finger at Brick, said, "Good point."

Raeford continued with instructions for the day, "After you have finished up in the office and the ticket distribution, I will need your help at the senior luncheon. Senior day is usually a slow day on the midway, and unfortunately, the forecast for the day is heavy rain. I am just hoping the entire day is not a washout. If it does rain like they are predicting, you both may be able to take the rest of the day off after the luncheon is over. The guys that normally work the booths y'all did yesterday are back and asking for another chance. I know they will probably be good until the next time they have some extra money. That's the nature of our business. It would give you an opportunity to enjoy the fair without worrying about work." This made Brick happy as it opened the door for him and Mary Jane to go on that date they had talked about.

The ticket count was becoming routine; they completed the job a little before nine. Like most things—the more you do it, the easier it becomes. While working on the count, the rain arrived in full force and picked up its intensity. Raeford cussed the storm and said, "It doesn't look promising; some are saying it will be raining all day. I hope they're wrong, but I am afraid we are in for a slow day." After finishing up the count, Raeford told them to go to the Fulton Exhibit Hall and help with the setup, and he would join them later.

For many years, one of the staples of Senior Citizens' Day was the recognition of the Grandparent of the Year. The luncheon was a Lions Club sponsored event, and the club would start taking nominations for the honor about a month in advance. The submissions consisted of a short composition written by a grandchild, giving reasons why their grandparent should receive the award. The winner would be voted on by a committee of volunteers who would review each nomination, and they would announce the winner at the senior luncheon. The prize for the winner was a small silver tray engraved with the winner's name and date of the award. It was a nice touch and made the luncheon a popular venue for the seniors in Lee County. It had been a banner year for nominations with over one hundred received. With so many submissions, it was hoped there would be a lot of people attending the luncheon.

Brick knew of a pay phone just outside the barracks, and he decided to try and catch Emily. Luckily, she was still in her dorm. When she picked up the phone, Brick tried his best to remain cool as he said, "Hey, Mom said you called last night. What's up?"

Brick was glad to hear her voice and was relieved when she said, "Oh, thanks for calling. You didn't have to, but I'm glad you did. I was wondering if you could do me a favor."

Brick was once again on his roller coaster of emotions; he felt both disappointment and relief at the same time. He was disappointed that the only reason she had called was for a favor but very relieved it was not anything negative. It was nice knowing she needed something, and he was the one she called. It turned out Emily was looking for a copy of the book, The Electric Kool-Aid Acid Test, by Tom Wolfe. They had studied the book in their senior English Literature class, and she wanted to know if Brick still his copy had as she could not find hers.

Brick was certain he knew where his was and wondered why she needed it. Emily said, "I don't know what happened to mine, but it's on my required reading list for my English III class. I was hoping to review it."

Brick laughed as he asked her to confirm, "It's on your required reading list?"

Emily replied, "Yeah, I know it sounds strange, but it's actually in a section on Pop Culture. Maybe Mrs. Vail had more going for her than we realized."

Brick responded, "Now that's a scary thought."

Emily simply replied, "Be nice. She was a good teacher, and you know it."

Brick was loving the banter and told her, "Yeah, but remember, she liked you."

Emily laughed and said, "And well, she should have."

Emily then started talking about the book, telling Brick she had talked with her mom, and she could not find it either, and she didn't know where else to look.

Brick said, "Don't worry. I'm sure I can find mine, and if not, I'll ask Ray if he has his copy."

Emily went on to say, "That would be great. My parents are driving up for Parents' Orientation on Saturday. If you could get it to them before then, they could bring it to me."

Brick assured her, "That won't be a problem. I will get a copy to them by tomorrow. I promise."

Emily thanked him and said, "You can take it by Dr. James's office. Mom's working all week."

Brick jokingly responded, "And not see your dad? I'm just kidding. I'll drop a copy off at your mom's work; it'll be nice to see her."

The conversation then turned to how things were going at the fair. Brick shared with her how much he was enjoying the work and how he was meeting some interesting people. Emily commented, "Well, that's what you were hoping to do, right?"

Brick then said, "Yeah, that—and meet 'Tonya, the Gorilla Girl.' So far, though, that hasn't happened, but the week is still young."

Emily questioned Brick, "Don't tell me Tonya is back for another year?"

"Oh yeah," said Brick. "She's here, and so is your all-time favorite, "Human Blockhead."

Emily laughed and said, "Oh no, I believe those were your favorites."

Brick said, "Guilty, but I've got to tell you this. It has been fun—not at all what I was expecting. Most of the people we have met have been friendly, and the whole operation resembles one large family. I'll have lots to tell you; that's for sure."

Emily told him she could not wait and then asked about Ray and if he was enjoying himself. Brick knew if she could see his grinning face, it would say oh yeah. He said, "Yeah, we're both having a lot of fun. But I will have to admit, I think I've found a cure for the Toby Tyler syndrome. I don't think there is any danger of either of us running off to join the circus anytime in the near future."

Emily said, "Well, that's good to hear. I talked with Joan last night, and she asked about you. I told her how you and Ray had joined the fair, and she thought it was hysterical."

Brick said, "I hope you set her straight that it's our last adventure before the cruel world of college comes crashing down on us." They both laughed.

Brick was enjoying talking and laughing with Emily; she always made him feel good. Sensing the time, he told her he knew she needed to get to class, and he had to get back to work. He then told her she might need to let her mom know that he would be coming by with the book. Emily said, "I know Mom will be happy to see you."

Brick then got serious and told her how much he enjoyed talking with her, saying he wished they could do it more often. Emily, in her sweet voice, responded, "I enjoy hearing about your adventures. Take care. I'll let mom know to look for you, and thanks again."

Once again, Brick was left wondering what her feelings were for him. Maybe it was just karma, considering his thoughts about Mary Jane, and he was getting what he deserved.

While Brick was on the phone, Ray went to the games thinking he may catch Jill before she got too busy. Since Raeford told them earlier that they had some time before they needed to be at the exhibit hall, Brick decided to see if Mary Jane was up. When he arrived at her trailer, he feared he might wake her but decided to knock anyway. He was pleasantly surprised when the door swung open, and there stood Mary Jane, wearing shorts and a flannel shirt. Brick once again was drawn to her poise and beauty. The silence broke when she smiled and said, "Hey, you're up early. You already working?" Brick told her he had been there since seven o'clock. She smiled and asked if he wanted to come in.

They stayed in the living area, and she offered Brick a Coke. He thanked her and said, "It looks like the rain will keep us from being too busy today, and Raeford said Ray and I would probably have the night off. I thought maybe, if you could get the evening off, we could enjoy that date we talked about."

Smiling, Mary Jane told him that sounded great, adding she would see if she could get the night off too. She then said, "If the rain continues, I don't see any problem. And then, you can show me how exciting Sanford is."

Just the possibility thrilled Brick. She wondered if he was already off or still had some work to do. Brick told her he and Ray were on their way to help at the exhibit hall for the senior luncheon, but he wanted to try and catch up with her first. She said, "Well, I'm glad you did. Where's Ray?"

"He went by to see Jill," answered Brick.

Mary Jane asked if Ray had a good time last night with Jill. With a smile, he replied, "I'm sure he did."

Mary Jane commented, "You guys are having quite a week with your county fair romances."

Brick was not sure how to take her remark, so he just said, "Oh, so it's a fair romance, huh?" She gave a flirtatious smile and asked what he would call it. Brick tried to be noncommittal with his response by saying, "Okay, I'll go with a fair romance."

Mary Jane smiled and again told him he was sweet. Brick found her willingness to joke and to own up to her feelings were just more of her characteristics he was attracted to. He could not help but think maybe there was something to this romance; after all, it take two to tango. Grinning, he hoped that their brief romantic encounter the night before might have been their first dance.

Brick heard Ray outside talking with Lucy, so he said to Mary Jane, "I should be going. Hopefully, I will see you later." Mary Jane reminded him she would see about getting some time off and reaffirmed her desire to enjoy some Sanford hospitality. Mary Jane then hugged him and the two kissed. Brick felt she was such a temptress, and he was being pulled into her world and enjoying every minute.

When Brick came out of the trailer, Ray noticed him right away, and they both shared a grin. They were all having their own special moments at the Lee County Fair.

Walking to the exhibit hall, Ray asked Brick if he had talked with Emily. Brick responded, "Yeah, I was able to catch her before she went to class."

"And?" Ray was looking for some details of why she had called.

Brick told him, "It's all good. She wanted to know if I could find my copy of The Electric Kool-Aid Acid Test. She hasn't been able to find hers and wanted to borrow mine if I still had it. It is on her English required reading list this semester."

Ray, a little surprised, laughed and said, "It's on her required reading list? I sure hope it will be on ours. That is one I did read."

Brick, also laughing, said, "Well, we were supposed to have read it. Anyway, Emily wants me to drop my copy off at her mom's work so she and Mr. Dixon can take it up to her this weekend." Ray told Brick if he couldn't find his, he was sure he still had his copy.

Brick then told Ray that Emily asked about him and wanted to know how he was enjoying the fair. I told her we were both enjoying it and had met a lot of interesting people. Ray, pleased with Brick's clever response, laughed and said, "A nice evasive answer—not telling her too much, yet not lying either. You, my friend, are a smart man."

While they were talking, the rain began to fall harder by the minute. The heavy rain made the boys start running to the exhibit hall, but Brick continued talking about Emily. He said, "I wonder if she did know about Mary Jane, would it even bother her?"

Ray replied, "Damn Brick, you are pitiful when it comes to her. Do you think she would have dated you this long if she did not have some feelings for you? After all, she is an attractive, smart, and fun girl. And you, well, you are just you." Brick knew Ray was right, and he also knew how foolish he was being. Sadly, though, that is just the way his mind worked.

Ray told him he would be fine once he got to Elon and met a whole new set of friends, including the new girls, and Brick hoped Ray was right. Ray suggested for now he should enjoy the company of Mary Jane; after all, she seemed to have more than a passing interest in him.

Brick knew that Ray, as usual, made a good point; if things continued with Mary Jane as he hoped, he should be in for a memorable time. But even the excitement he felt for Mary Jane did not prevent him from worrying about a high school relationship—a relationship that he feared was never going to be what he wanted it to be.

As they arrived at the exhibit hall, Ray firmly said, "Brick, it seems rather simple to me. You want your cake and eat it too, and that is not going to happen. What you need to do is make a commitment, get on with it, and stop being so fickle." Brick thought that maybe Ray was on to something knowing the time, he was spending with Mary Jane could be the start of a new chapter in his life—one he should begin living as soon as possible.

There wasn't much going on inside the exhibit hall, so they tried to find someone to get some instructions. Ray spotted Betty Anne (from the office) and asked if she knew who they needed to speak to about helping with the setup. Betty Anne, friendly as usual, said, "I'm glad to see you both. Just wait here, and I'll try to find someone in charge."

Both boys were surprised when Peter Campbell appeared. Campbell was a member of the Lions Club but also ran a record shop on Horner Boulevard in Sanford. Brick and Ray had shopped there many times. He was surprised to see them also, and once again they were questioned about their work at the fair. They told him they were enjoying it and the reasons why they decided to go on this adventure. Campbell simply said, "Good for you." They then noticed others they knew from the Lions Club.

The exhibit hall had a banquet room at the front of the building, and it was there they began putting out tables and chairs. Each table was then covered with a tablecloth and decorated with fresh flowers, and there was plenty of help from members of the Lions Club and their wives. The boys knew many of those helping with the setup, and all were surprised to see Brick and Ray working. Both, now tired of telling their story, had to politely explain how they were waiting to go off to school and trying to pick up some spending money at the same time.

After finishing the setup, Campbell began talking about the luncheon and some of the changes the club had made for this year's event. A decision was made by the Lions Club to use a few of the food vendors to cater the luncheon. This would be a first as in the past the luncheon was catered by a local restaurant. The club members believed it would be a special treat for many of the seniors, giving them an opportunity to enjoy authentic fair food. It would also demonstrate support for the vendors and allow them to serve up their specialties. Of course, there were those who felt the effort may backfire as there was a chance some may get sick from the corn dogs, hot dogs, French fries, and other fair delights. In the end, the fair food won out.

Raeford came by just as they were finishing with the setup. He asked Campbell if everything was going okay and then said something about Brick and Ray. Raeford was pleased that the Lions Club had decided to use the food vendors for the luncheon. He felt it helped cement a positive relationship between the Lions Club and Howard's Amusements. It was a nice touch.

While they were setting up for the luncheon, Brick could hear the hard, steady rain and knew most likely it would keep the day's attendance down. Raeford, on the other hand, was optimistic that the senior luncheon would at least bring a few people to the fair.

The Lions Club realized the wet grounds could be a concern for many, so they decided to use golf carts to aid anyone arriving for the luncheon. The club could pick up as many of the seniors as possible at the main gate and transport them to the exhibit hall. It was a nice effort to help keep as many of those attending out of the rain as much as possible.

Raeford gave Ray a list of vendors who would be preparing food and asked if he would alert them when it was time to start cooking. He then asked Brick if he could make a delivery for him in town, and Brick told him he would be happy to. He asked Brick if he knew where Carolina Greenhouses was located, and Brick answered, "Yes sir, it's close to my house."

Raeford continued, "They bought a block of tickets for an Employee Appreciation Day for this coming Friday—admission and ride tickets. I would like for you to deliver them today so they can be given out early." Brick welcomed the assignment. It would give him a chance to stop by his house and pick up the book for Emily. Once he had the book, he would be able to drop it off at Emily's mom's workplace and at least have that favor accomplished.

Raeford turned back to Ray and said, "Ray, if you will, go talk to the vendors, and once you're done, find a place to dry out until it's time to pick up the food. Brick, you can come with me, and I'll get what you need to take with you. Once you have made the delivery, you can come back and help Ray with the luncheon." Ray, of course, knew exactly where he planned to wait out the rain while Brick made his delivery.

Brick accompanied Raeford to the office, and neither of them was able to avoid getting wet from the steady downpour even though they both had umbrellas. Raeford pulled together the tickets and a few prizes, telling Brick he hoped the prizes would further provide an incentive for the employees to attend. He then said, "We are going to need some strong attendance days to make up for today."

The greenhouses had twenty-two employees, so they had purchased a block of tickets—tickets not only for the employees but their families and dates as well. With such a large order, the greenhouses were given a discount on the tickets.

Raeford looked out his window, and the rain appeared to be coming down harder. He told Brick, "This is one of the downsides of having Mother Nature as a partner. You never know what you are going to get. She has a mind of her own." His thought process quickly changed, but he continued, "When you get to the greenhouses, ask for Mark Ellis. I will give him a call and tell him you are on the way. Hopefully, he will have a check for you to bring back."

Brick told Raeford he would like to do a small errand when he was in town; he needed to drop something off for a friend if that was okay. Raeford told him to take his time, but to try to get back before the luncheon started. Brick indicated that should not be a problem.

❧

Odom at The Fair

The fair was not the only thing being affected by the rain. Odom feared it would hinder the turnout for the protest, and this just added to his frustration. If he hoped to make a statement, he needed as many people as possible to not only protest but to see it as well.

Driving onto the fairgrounds, Beverly and Gail were the ones on the receiving end of Odom's anger. He knew he had no control over the weather, but that didn't keep him from complaining that the rain would not help anyone, and that the day would be a complete waste of time. Beverly tried to be positive, telling him that their efforts were worth the time. But he responded with his usual negativity, "The fair will leave in a few days, and we will be left with the same small congregation with nothing accomplished." Odom was tiring of Beverly's positive attitude. He wished she would get angry as well.

Beverly always tended to look at the bigger picture, and she tried again to assure Odom he was making a difference by saying, "Now Patrick, we've talked about this. You are making a difference, and I am sure people are noticing. You need to calm down and take credit for the work you have accomplished."

Odom responded, "It's just so frustrating. The paper won't give us any attention, and if they don't cover the movement, I'm afraid nothing will come from our work."

Beverly knew her words were not what Odom wanted to hear, however, she reminded him again of what Reverend Hinson had said; he needed to be patient, and things would work out.

The anger in Odom's voice seemed to be rising when he said, "That's easy for Hinson to say. He has a large church and a growing congregation, but we are small, and we hardly get noticed. Right now, few know about us and even fewer respect us. We need our voices heard. If I cannot convince anyone that what we are doing is right, we are just wasting our time and money." Beverly knew that when Odom got agitated it was better to let him stew as there was not much she could do to change his attitude.

Gail chimed in, hoping to sway Odom's opinion by telling him, "Consider this, if we protest in the rain, everyone will see how determined we are, and surely that would gain us some notoriety."

Odom blew her off, saying, "Yeah, it will say we don't have sense enough to come in out of the rain." Beverly told him there was no need to be rude; they were there to help and not to be criticized.

Beverly looked at Gail and mouthed the words, "Let it go."

Gail tried to change the conversation, asking if Jimmy Key would be joining them. Odom responded, "Yes, he's coming and hopefully bringing others with him."

Unfortunately, Gail's asking about Key seemed to only stir Odom up more as he talked about needing a large group of protesters to help make a statement, and her biggest concern was whether or not Key would be there. Beverly placed her hand on Odom's arm, telling him not to worry as things would work out. She sounded like Hinson, and Odom was not looking for pity; he needed action.

It wasn't long after pulling into the parking area before Odom spotted Key's car. He stopped and suggested that Beverly and Gail just wait in the car as there was no need for everyone to get soaked. He was walking toward Key's car when he heard Key call out to him. He was standing under an awning near the main gate.

It was nearly ten o'clock, and the gates would open soon. Key had a few others with him, which helped calm Odom's nerves. Key asked if Beverly and Gail had come, and Odom replied, "They're in the car. I told them there was no sense in them getting wet until they had too." Odom then saw Harland Jones and his wife, Patrice, standing behind Key with another couple he did not know. Key introduced them as the Mitchells, George and Becky.

The notion of new volunteers coming to help pleased Odom. He thanked everyone for coming, and Key told him he felt some others would be joining them once the gates opened. Considering the weather, Odom knew this small group was about all he could hope for.

Odom suggested that he and Key go to the car and get the signs as they may as well get started. They could all stay under the awning until the gates opened and then move to the exhibit hall. Key accompanied Odom to his car, and they pulled out several painted signs, Sin No More/Stop the Sin/Thy Shall Not/Shame, Shame, and so on. Odom and Beverly had created some, and others were sent by Hinson. A few were beginning to show the wear and tear of the three-day protests. Beverly and Gail helped with the signs, and all brought ponchos to wear for protection from the rain. With signs in hand, they went under the awning to join the others.

❦

Brick

The book Emily needed was right where Brick thought it would be. It was in his room under a pile of papers and a couple of notebooks. Most of the stuff had not been touched since he walked across the stage for his graduation. Next to the pile of papers was Emily's framed senior picture. He took a moment to admire her smile and reassuring eyes and once again thought about how screwed up he was when it came to girls.

Brick was at his house just long enough to get the book, and then he went straight to the greenhouses. He had no trouble finding the office. Once inside, a lady at the receptionist's desk welcomed him and asked if she could help him. Brick introduced himself, telling her he was from Howard's Amusements and that he had a delivery for Mr. Ellis.

She knew immediately why Brick was there and said, "Oh yes, Mark said someone would be coming by. Let me get him." She then offered Brick, still wet from the rain, a seat, saying she was sorry she did not have a towel for him. Brick thanked her and said it looked like the rain would be with them for a while. He took a seat and waited.

Brick had mixed feelings about the rain. He knew if it continued all day, the day would be a washout for the fair—affecting attendance and revenue. He also knew the rain might give him a chance to have that date with Mary Jane.

After a short wait, Mr. Ellis walked into the room, extended his hand and introduced himself. Brick shook his hand and told him he was with Howard's Amusements and had the tickets he ordered. He also showed Ellis the box of prizes Raeford sent along in hopes that the prizes would help with their Employee Appreciation Day.

Ellis looked as if he might have played football in his younger days. He was a large man and was thrilled with the incentives, saying,

"Well, isn't that nice. We can sure use them, but the truth is everyone here is already pretty excited about coming out on Friday." Ellis then turned to Terrie and said, "There should be an envelope with a check for Howard's. Do you, have it?" She picked up the envelope and handed it to him. He then took the time to write Thank You and his phone number on the outside of the envelope before handing it to Brick. They shook hands again, and Ellis said, "I appreciate your coming out in the rain to deliver everything. Please tell Mr. Raeford we are all looking forward to Friday, and if he needs anything else to give me a call."

Brick thanked him and looked over at the receptionist, saying, "I guess we'll see you both on Friday." They both smiled and said they would be there. The brief interaction only added to Brick's feeling of being a part of Howard's Amusements.

Brick's next stop was Dr. James's office. He had been there a few times during the summer when he would take Emily by to see her mom for one reason or another. It was a short drive, and once inside the office, Brick asked for Mrs. Dixon. He explained he had a book he needed to drop off for her daughter, Emily. He took a seat and waited. Brick knew he could leave the book, but he hoped seeing Mrs. Dixon would give him more credibility with Emily. Brick knew it could never hurt to show your girlfriend's mother that you're helpful. When Mrs. Dixon came to the waiting room, Brick greeted her with a smile and told her he had a book for Emily. She was charming as usual, telling Brick he could've waited until it stopped raining.

Brick smiled and said, "The way it's raining, I'm not sure when that would be possible." It was a nice humorous interaction for both. He told her it was not a problem; he was out anyway, running some errands for work. Brick was happy to learn Emily had called her earlier and told her that he might be coming by with the book.

Mrs. Dixon then said, "I don't know what happened to Emily's copy, but I'm sure she'll appreciate your sharing yours. Harold and I are going up to see her on Saturday, and we'll give it to her then."

Brick was pleased when Mrs. Dixon said, "Emily tells me you are working at the fair. What do they have you doing?"

Brick answered, "Yes ma'am, Ray Hill and I are working out there. Right now, we are doing different things—nothing specific. We've helped with the games and other stuff. It has been interesting work, and I've met some good people. We both felt it would be good to pick up some extra money before leaving for school."

She told him that sounded like a good idea but added that they needed to be careful. Brick assured her it was a safe job, and they were not doing anything unusual. With that, Brick excused himself and told her he needed to get back to work.

Before he could get away, Mrs. Dixon said, "It's nice to see you, Brick." He told her he was glad he got a chance to see her before leaving for college. She then asked when he would be going, and he told her he would be leaving the next Tuesday. She smiled and said, "Take care of yourself and good luck. I appreciate your bringing the book with by."

Once back at the fair, Brick immediately went to the office to drop off the check from Mr. Ellis. Betty Anne was alone when he arrived, and she took the envelope from Brick and thanked him. Brick told her he was going to the exhibit hall unless she had heard otherwise. She said, "No, I haven't. You will probably see Raeford there."

At the exhibit hall, Brick spotted the protesters outside the main entrance. They had positioned themselves in an area where everyone could see them. The small group was chanting, "End sin, stop the revue" repeatedly. Brick felt it strange that the group was outside the exhibit hall and not at the revue. It was as if they were protesting the senior luncheon. He didn't feel the group was getting much attention, as most of those going in and out of the exhibit hall were running, trying to avoid the rain. The group had umbrellas, which prevented their signs from being seen.

When Brick got inside, he caught up with Ray, and they began talking about the protest. Ray asked Brick if he saw the protesters on his way in, to which Brick replied, "Yeah, I saw them—looked like a bunch of wet nuts if you ask me." Ray laughed and agreed. Brick then asked if he felt they would be there all day.

Ray shrugged his shoulders and said, "Who knows? All I know is I wouldn't stand in this rain very long."

Brick asked if Ray's dad had said any more about the group. "No, I think he just wishes they would go away. So far, they haven't caused any problems, so there is little anyone can do."

Brick showed his disgust when he said to Ray, "If you ask me, they are just a bunch of assholes."

As they were discussing the protest, Raeford came up and said, "Boys, we need to get the food."

He then asked Brick if he was able to deliver the tickets and prizes, and Brick responded, "Yes sir, they're excited, and I think they'll have a lot of folks coming out. I took the check down to the office and gave it to Betty Anne." Raeford thanked him for making the delivery.

Raeford suggested the boys take a couple of the golf carts to pick up the food. He added there were a few tarps by the entrance that they may want to take with them to keep the food from getting wet. They found the golf carts parked on the back side of the exhibit hall, and they were happy to have them. Ray led the way, as he knew which vendors were preparing food for the luncheon. Due to the rain, not all the vendors had opened yet, so it wasn't hard for Brick to know where they would be stopping.

Their first stop was a hot dog stand where the owner had prepared what seemed to be more than enough hot dogs—some plain and others with chili and onions—all marked and separated in boxes. Next up were the corn dogs and a mustard dispenser. The process continued as Brick and Ray collected sausage dogs, ham biscuits. fried baloney sandwiches, bins of corn on the cob, and French fries. Desserts consisted of cotton candy, caramel apples, and a fried dough called elephant ears. It may not have been a meal suited for a king, but the Lions Club and Howard's Amusements certainly hoped it would create a desire for more. As they unloaded the food into the hall, Ray told Brick, "It will be interesting to see how much these folks eat; this is a ton of food." At eighteen, both boys felt the amount of food was overkill. They could only imagine what their grandparents would think of all the food.

Once the food was spread out, Brick and Ray stayed to help serve, and when the luncheon was over, they helped break down the tables and chairs. They both were surprised at how many attended, and it appeared to them that the weather had kept few folks at home.

During the luncheon, emceed by local radio personality Stuart Ross, it was announced that the 1969 Grandparent of the Year was Nanny Lee Osborne from Jonesboro. Her nomination spoke of how kind and supportive she was to everyone, especially her eleven grandchildren. She was affectionately known as Mama Lee to all the young people of Jonesboro. Brick and Ray knew her from church and were excited for her and her family. They were proud to be part of the community and Howard's Amusements.

There was a large amount of food left over. The appetites of the seniors certainly did not mirror those of the young people. Brick and Ray were able to eat their fill, and the remainder of the food was packaged and taken home by the Lions Club members who worked the luncheon.

Few seniors ventured out onto the midway due to the rain. Most stayed in the exhibit halls, reviewing the displays of cakes, pickles, and quilts that had been judged for ribbons. The overall attendance on the fairgrounds was way down due to the rain, which meant there would be little need for Brick and Ray.

The boys met up with Raeford at the office, and he told them they could take the remainder of the day off. Feeling disappointed, he said, "Hopefully, things will be better tomorrow. I'll need you both to come in around seven o'clock in the morning. Just try to enjoy the rest of the day." He then asked if they wanted the day's pay, or should he just add it to the next day's. Both suggested he hold on to it. They had already made as much in three days as they did for an entire week during the summer.

Ray suggested they drop by and see the girls before leaving. Hoping to catch Jill, he went to the barracks, knowing her booth had not opened, and he felt she would be resting. Brick, of course, stopped by Mary Jane's trailer. He was surprised to find her alone and reading. When she answered the door, she was wearing dark-rimmed glasses and had a book in her hand. She welcomed him inside, and the two stood in the living area as she explained she felt it was a good day to curl up with a book. Brick asked, "What are you reading?"

"Believe it or not, it's Hemingway's Death in the Afternoon," she answered.

At that moment Brick wished he had read more and could talk with her about the book. But instead, he simply said, "I don't know that one. What's it about?"

Mary Jane smiled as she held up the book, and said, "It's Hemingway, so you figure there will be gore, and he does like bullfighting. Hemingway on a rainy afternoon—I guess you're a little surprised, huh?"

Brick confessed, "I must admit; I am."

Mary Jane told him she enjoyed reading; it always provided a nice escape from work. She then asked if he was working or goofing off. Brick said, "I'm off due to the rain. Raeford gave Ray and me the rest of the day off, and I was hoping you might want to take in a movie and see what Sanford has to offer; that is, if you can get some time off."

Mary Jane replied in a hopeful tone, "Sounds like fun. I would like that very much, but I will have to let you know later if I can get the time off. If this rain continues, I'm pretty sure I can."

The thought of going on a date with Mary Jane excited Brick. He tried to maintain his composure when he said, "If I can pull you away from Hemingway, I would love to show you some of Sanford's hot spots for fun."

Mary Jane smiled and said, "That sounds wonderful. I can read another day. What time were you thinking?"

Brick said, "The movies start at seven o'clock, so whatever time is good for you."

Mary Jane was looking as beautiful as ever, and she told him she had not been to a movie in a long time. She suggested they go to the movie first and then afterward get something to eat. It all sounded great to Brick, telling her he would leave her with Hemingway and would plan on seeing her around six-thirty that evening.

Mary Jane gave Brick a big smile and said, "This all sounds so good. I sure need some time away from here, and I can't think of anyone better to be with than you. I will try my best to get off. Just the idea of getting away from those damn protesters is exciting. It would be a welcomed change for sure. Thank you."

Brick said, "I will be back later. Get prepared for an evening of excitement and a memorable time."

Mary Jane laughed, and said, "I sure will."

As he left the trailer, he was full of energy and anticipation. He was ready to leave, but he needed to find Ray. He found him seated in the barracks with Jill. There was a common area with a couple of chairs and a couch. When Ray noticed Brick, he said to Jill, "Well, it looks like my ride's here." He then asked Brick if he was ready to go.

"Yeah, at least for a couple of hours," Brick responded. Ray stood up and told Jill he hoped to see her later.

Brick felt Jill looked tired. It appeared to him that the barracks did not offer the best sleeping conditions, and he was thinking if Jill could also get some time off due to the rain, it would do her some good. Even though she looked somewhat disheveled, her beauty still shone through. He also knew Ray found her attractive and was enjoying her company as well. Brick waved to Jill and asked how things were going. She waved to him in return and gave him a smile—but no words.

As they left the barracks, Ray asked about Mary Jane. Brick said, "Well, if it continues to rain, it looks like tonight I'll be taking her on that date we have talked about if she can get the evening off. She wants to go to a movie. Maybe we will do a movie and then get a bite to eat at Morton's."

Ray said, "I'm planning to come back out tonight. Hoping to see what kind of trouble I can get into with Jill. Of course, if that doesn't work, I'll try to catch up with Misty; she has been flying under my radar. I'm definitely going to try to spend some time with one of them this evening. The rain just may be what we need to cement the week's adventure."

Brick smiled and said, "I like that—a man with options."

Ray commented, "I may even try to stay in the barracks, as I feel a little employee research may be in order. Of course, it would have to be okay with Raeford. It's for sure; approval of anything to do with the fair will come easier from Raeford than from Russell."

Late in the afternoon, the rain had turned to a drizzle, but enough damage had been done from the earlier downpours to keep the crowds away. For the most part, the day was a complete washout. A few of the shows did open but were doing little business. Pee Wee Payne had taken his place at the front of the nude review and began calling out the girls for the show. With the crowds so small, Mary Jane was able to arrange her schedule so she could work during the daytime performances and take the evening off.

Patrick Odom

The luncheon had ended with the protesters once again getting little attention. Although it was still raining, Odom took his small following back to the site of the revue, hoping to continue the protest. Not only had Odom's group gotten smaller, but the revue had not opened. This made the protest even less effective. The only thing Odom's group was accomplishing was getting wetter by the minute. The rain had left more employees walking the midway than patrons.

Late in the day, a few of the rides were wiped dry and started to run. The only shows operating were the ones with fixed attractions, such as the Batmobile and the Petting Zoo, and most of the business for those were people trying to get out of the rain. Even if it stopped raining, the grounds were going to be soaked, and that would certainly keep people away.

It was not long before Odom and Key were the only ones left from the group. Even when the revue did open, there were few people attending the shows. The small crowds only added to Odom's frustration. Another day had passed, and there was nothing to show for it; his actions had garnered little attention. Odom had become more verbally abusive to the customers who did venture into the show. This, of course, was a result of his anger and frustration. Originally, Odom had not planned on confronting the patrons, but he was tired and angry, leading him to try and intimidate anyone purchasing tickets. He would yell at them, proclaiming they were sinners falling under the influence of the devil. Odom's vocal attacks drew the ire of Payne who was collecting the money.

Payne decided to address Odom directly, "Listen man, you can protest all you want, but you better leave our customers alone."

In a strange way, Odom saw the warning as progress; he was finally getting somebody's attention. Payne had no idea that he was boosting Odom's morale and resolve. Odom began to believe the verbal protest may be taking root. For him, it was the first time someone had finally said something directly to him, and now he felt energized.

With business being so slow, Odom's verbal attacks stood out more, and it was unsettling to the girls. The assault of threats and words upset Sugar, so she decided to take the microphone from Payne and address Odom directly.

Sugar called on Odom and Key, telling both they should come to the show and experience it all. Sugar said, "Once you have enjoyed a show, you will begin seeing things differently. We are the best show on the midway, and both of you look as if you could use a little entertainment."

A few of the men who had gathered to attend the next show began laughing and even echoed Sugar's words, saying, "Yeah, why don't y'all join us? We'll save you a place."

Odom's joy of Payne's attention was now gone. The crowd and the girls were mocking him and Key. All the laughter only added to Odom's anger. It wasn't long before he lost his cool and began screaming at the men going into the show, "You are going to Hell, and I don't plan on being with you." His outbreak only brought more laughter as the patrons made their way into the tent. Before Sugar made her way into the tent, she again directed her talk to Odom and Key, telling them they did not know what they were missing. She then exited the stage, and Payne made his last call, telling everyone the show would start shortly.

Odom steamed with anger; not only had the barker ridiculed him, but a stripper had also joined in the abuse. Key, trying to find a way to calm Odom down, said to him, "Patrick, I'm telling you, if we could get more people here tomorrow, we can block the entrance by creating the human chain. That will show them we mean business."

Odom's anger was still building as he said to Key, "They will be the ones laughing once the shows are shut down."

It wasn't long before Key said, "I know you don't want to hear this, but I'm ready to go. My clothes are soaked down to my skin, and I'm tired of looking like a rain-soaked duck."

Odom knew Key was right; there was little reason to stay any longer. Their signs were starting to ruin, and their clothes were now drenched. Reluctantly, Odom agreed to leave but declared he would have the last laugh.

The Date

Brick was confident, considering what Raeford had said about the rain, that Mary Jane would be able to get the evening off. He was nervous about taking her on a real date as he was not sure how much she would like what he had planned. Brick had warned her that there were few options in Sanford for entertainment, but he was going to try his best to honor her request for a full Sanford experience.

By the time Brick made it back to the midway, there was little doubt the day had been a bust for business as only a few people were milling around. He found Mary Jane in her trailer and told her he hoped their date was still on. She was in a reflective mood, telling Brick about the encounter between Payne and the protesters. She gave him details into how Sugar had gotten into a confrontation with the preacher.

Mary Jane said, "I don't feel good about that guy; he seems so mad, almost unstable. If anything, it seems his anger is misplaced. I don't believe it's all about the show, but he is surely taking it out on us." Brick, in an attempt to lessen her fears, told her that the preacher's bark was worse than his bite. Mary Jane hoped he was right.

Mary Jane then told Brick she had seen Ray with Jill a little earlier, and, from what she saw, they both appeared to be having a good time. Brick smiled and said, "Yeah, he came in earlier. We decided to drive separately today so neither of us would have to wait on the other."

This bit of news seemed to please Mary Jane. She smiled and said, "So, I have you all to myself." Brick liked how she phrased the statement.

Brick, now grinning from ear to ear asked, "Does that mean I have you all to myself as well?"

Her smile said it all as she told him he sure did, and she was looking forward to a night on the town. She did a little dance and said, "Let's have some fun."

Brick liked the outfit Mary Jane was wearing. It was a one-piece shorts outfit that zipped in the front. With his mind in the gutter, he immediately thought how simple it would be to remove.

Mary Jane wanted to know what Brick had in mind for the evening. He said, "I'm not sure what's playing at the movies. We only have two theaters, and one of those is questionable, but it would be my pleasure to take you to a movie."

The two of them were walking outside the gates of the fair, and once they got beyond the entrance, Mary Jane laughed as she said, "So, this is what the outside world looks like." Brick reached for her hand, telling her it might not be New York, but it is not Howard's Amusements either.

Mary Jane smiled, saying, "And that's a good thing."

Brick walked with her to her side of the car and opened the door. She commented on how polite he was, adding she could not remember the last time someone had opened a door for her. He was happy she approved.

Brick wanted to know if it was okay with her that they go to the early movie at seven o'clock and afterward get something to eat. Even though Mary Jane was so happy to be away from the midway that she probably would have agreed to anything, she thought a movie and dinner would be perfect. They drove to the Wilrick Theater, which was just a short distance from the fairgrounds. The Disney movie, The Love Bug, was playing. Brick jokingly asked Mary Jane if she was in the mood to see a car come to life. She told him it all sounded good to her, noting any movie would be better than a rainy night at the fair.

Brick asked, "Yeah, but will the movie be better than curling up with Hemingway?"

Mary Jane slapped his arm and said, "Be nice. I'll have you know; I can enjoy both."

For Brick, the evening was starting out great. The short time he had spent with Mary Jane was quite the bonus for his work at the fair. Being with her seemed so natural. At that particular moment, Brick was not worried about the consequences of the evening. The night was going to be memorable, and he was planning to enjoy it to the fullest.

Before the movie started, Brick bought them popcorn and sodas. He was going for the real date experience. They had no trouble finding a seat as the fair was not the only thing being affected by the rain. The Love Bug was an offbeat comedy starring Dean Jones, whose life was down and out until his VW Beetle came to life and rescued him. It was a light-hearted comedy they both enjoyed. For Brick, the best part of the movie was being with Mary Jane. Clowning around at one point in the movie, Brick told her maybe he needed a car like Herbie to spice up his life. They both laughed, enjoying their time together.

As they walked back to the car, Brick once again spoke of how he needed a Herbie; but unfortunately, if he had a Herbie, it would probably die of boredom.

Mary Jane said, "I don't believe that for a second. Today you are working the fair, and before long you'll be off to college. I think you've got plenty to keep a car excited."

Again, Brick opened Mary Jane's door for her, and she commented on how nice he was, telling him, "You know, you make a girl feel really special." Brick loved the compliment and came close to blushing. She then surprised him when she said, "I'll bet your girlfriend likes your manners."

Brick was caught off-guard by the comment; they had not talked about any girlfriend. He did not know if she was being nice or if she was fishing for information. Not sure what to say, he responded, "Who said anything about a girlfriend?"

Mary Jane grinned and said, "Don't tell me you don't have a girlfriend—a good-looking guy like you on his way to college. I figure you have a girl somewhere; maybe she has already gone off to school, giving you plenty of time to spend at the fair and with me. Don't worry; I'm not going to tell anyone, but I'm glad she's not around. I've enjoyed our time together."

Brick didn't feel a need to delve into a deep discussion, so he simply said, "You win. I do have a friend who's away at school, but I promise you, it's a tenuous relationship at best."

Mary Jane responded, "Aren't they all? But anyway, that's good to hear. I wouldn't want you to get into any trouble because of me."

Brick had never in his life been as mesmerized by a girl. She was so easy to talk to; the more time they spent together, the more relaxed he became. As Mary Jane slid into her seat, she smiled and changed the subject by asking where they were off to next.

Brick said, "I hope you're hungry. I'm going to take you to the hottest spot in town, Morton's. You'll get the ultimate Sanford experience there."

Mary Jane laughed and said, "Well, that's what I'm looking for, so let's do it."

The girlfriend comment began to play on Brick's mind. In a strange way, he almost wished Emily would learn of his fling with Mary Jane. Maybe then she would see Brick differently, possibly even becoming a little jealous; however, Brick felt this was just wishful thinking. He wondered if Emily did find out about Mary Jane, would it be the end of their relationship? This had always been Brick's biggest fear. There were times he felt he was a prisoner in a one-sided relationship.

The short time he had spent with Mary Jane was different; she made him feel confident and positive. He felt his flirtations with Mary Jane provided a much-needed distraction from his worry of Emily moving on without him. At eighteen, Brick knew long-term relationships could be hard, and he feared Emily had no interest in one; evidently, by his actions, he didn't either.

Brick wished for better control over his feelings, but when it came to Emily, he was hopeless. He was a naive romantic—at times uncertain and rather sad. There was no doubt that others sensed how pitiful he was when it came to Emily; his friend Don told him this many times. Brick needed to be more self-assured. If Emily was going to care for him, it would happen. Being so needy was not helping either of them. Around others, Brick was as self-assured as any eighteen-year-old could be, but around Emily things were different. Maybe it was love or fear; no matter which it was, it created problems.

Brick tried to put Emily out of his mind. He was in the company of a beautiful girl, and they were having fun. Hoping to change his thoughts, Brick began telling Mary Jane the Sanford tradition of cruising' the block. He suggested that before they stop at Morton's, they cruise the block a few times. Mary Jane knew it was a tradition in every small town in America, and she was all in for the experience.

In Sanford, cruising' the block was a quick drive around the tennis courts, Morton's, and the Dairy Bar. The trip on a typical night would take less than five minutes, but on a busy night for teenagers, the trip could take much longer. The block was nearly empty and took hardly any time before Brick proposed they make another loop. He continued talking about the tradition, allowing Mary Jane to enjoy the full experience.

After a couple of laps around the block, Brick pulled his car into Morton's. One reason for Morton's popularity with the youth of Sanford was that it offered a front row seat to all the activities on the block. From the booths you could gaze out on the street and keep tabs on everyone cruising' at the time. Even for a slow night, there was enough activity to entertain Mary Jane. Brick recommended the cheeseburger and fries and, of course, a glass of sweet tea.

As they waited for the food, Mary Jane said, "You know Sanford's not much different from my hometown of Clover." She then laughed and added, "But you do have a movie theater. We had to go to Rock Hill if we wanted to see a movie." Brick went on to say, "The theaters may be the only difference, but Raleigh and Fayetteville are our destinations for excitement." They both agreed something all small towns shared was the need to create your own fun and entertainment.

While they were enjoying their food, Mary Jane told Brick she was having such a good time and loving it all—cruising' the block, the food, and the movie. After they had finished eating, Brick suggested they take a few more laps around the block. This time Mary Jane rolled her window down, hung her arm out, and waved to others. She was becoming part of the Sanford scene.

It was still early. Neither of them was ready to return to the fairgrounds, so Brick decided to show her some of the other spots around town. Mary Jane was thankful to be away from the fair and especially the protesters. Brick found a good radio station so they could listen to music as he showed her the town.

Mary Jane was so appreciative and said, "I've missed this—just riding around having fun. It's been a long time since I've had this much fun. It reminds me of the life I used to enjoy."

Brick took her on a tour of Sanford. He drove by the high school and even by his house, but of course, he did not stop.

Their night together so far was as innocent as a scene from a Jimmy Stewart movie. After some time, Brick drove down a secluded road not far from his house. Fire Tower Road had always been a favorite parking place for the kids in Sanford. It was an ideal spot for teenagers wanting to make out or do some drinking. As he drove down the winding road, Mary Jane smiled and began poking fun at him, asking if he was taking her parking. He tried to remain cool, stopped the car, and replied, "You did say you wanted the full Sanford experience, didn't you?"

Mary Jane smiled and answered, "I guess I did."

They sat in silence for a few minutes, taking in the clearing skies. A blanket of stars was beginning to be revealed against the dark, beautiful sky. Brick awkwardly moved across the seat and reached for Mary Jane. She smiled and welcomed his tender kiss. When the embrace broke, Mary Jane told him just how much she was enjoying the evening, telling him, "This is so nice; you have given me the Sanford experience." Mary Jane caressed Brick's hand taking it to her mouth, and lightly began kissing his fingers. Brick's heart began to race. Never had he experienced such a sensation. He didn't know what to do or say, so he leaned over and started kissing her again. The kiss was soft and seductive, and with each kiss Brick's excitement grew. The passion of the moment was unbridling. He was crossing over into a new sexual experience with a beautiful, sensual woman. Mary Jane began kissing Brick on his cheek and his neck, and his hands began to explore the marvels of her body. The next thing he knew, he was pulling the zipper down. Brick considered the zipper the last line of defense for what he hoped would be a wonderful experience. As he lowered the zipper, he could see Mary Jane's bra and panties. This was uncharted territory for Brick. He fumbled with the clasp on her bra, and once he had released her breasts, he paused for a second and gazed at her radiance. She was as beautiful as any girl he had ever been with.

Brick then began to explore her breasts, caressing each with care while studying her nipples with his fingers. The one-piece outfit soon fell off her shoulders and Brick started to kiss her soft bare shoulders and then moved his kisses down to her hardening nipples. The passion they shared was unlike anything he had ever experienced. He held her tightly as he explored her body with his lips and tongue. His excitement climbed to an unprecedented level when he felt Mary Jane's hand as she began inspecting his body. As he kissed her nipples and squeezed the soft flesh, he felt her hand on his thigh and then the movement of her hand going up his leg. She gently began to stroke his erection; for Brick, this was an incredible sensation. She laid back in the seat, giving Brick full access to her body. He pulled her outfit down enough to unveil her parted legs, allowing Brick to find his way into her panties. The excitement was overwhelming. Brick tried to free his erection. Once he had pulled his shorts down, Mary Jane took him in her hand and began stroking slowly at first and then picking up speed until Brick finally exploded. Brick held her in his arms, and for a moment he was unable to speak. The silence was broken when Mary Jane asked Brick if he was okay. Now out of breath, he smiled broadly and said, "I'm better than okay."

He then kissed her again. The kiss was long and passionate. When they stopped the embrace, Mary Jane began putting her clothes back on, telling Brick how wonderful the evening had been. Brick didn't think it was possible that she could have enjoyed the evening more than he did. They dressed in silence with both knowing it was time to get back to the fairgrounds. Before Brick could start the car, Mary Jane leaned over for another kiss and once again told him how special the night had been. His face showed just how much he had loved the evening.

❦

Odom Returns Home

O dom took a seat in the living room and began to mull over the day's events. He couldn't help but feel the day was a complete failure. The seniors at the luncheon showed no interest, and to top it off, he and Key were ridiculed outside the revue. Sitting silently in the recliner, he began to gaze at the ceiling. It looked as though he was seeking divine intervention. He feared nothing would come of his efforts if the weather didn't improve. Maybe Key's idea to block the entrance was what they needed to do. A little civil disobedience now sounded good to him, but he knew it would require more followers than those who had shown up so far. Desperation was beginning to take hold, and Odom was becoming more unhinged.

Odom began reading the evening paper, and there were many articles about the fair. He learned about the beauty contest and the senior day events, but there was no mention of the protest. In addition to his usual anger and frustration, he was mentally exhausted. He simply could not understand why people were so tolerant of sin. His disappointment was twofold: The rally was having little impact on the revue, and neither he nor the church was gaining any publicity. Something had to change. The Vietnam War had produced great protests, and the civil rights movement had produced great demonstrations, and both received national coverage. Why couldn't his outrage not even get mentioned in the Sanford Herald?

Odom decided to call the paper once again to register a complaint, and this time he decided not to identify himself. He just wanted to register a complaint about the lack of coverage regarding the protests, feeling they were important enough to merit coverage. He would tell the reporter that not only were the protests important, but they were also needed. He planned to tell the paper how the protesters were trying to create awareness—awareness of an issue that should be reported to the public. The shows were promoting an evil that was affecting everyone in town. Odom decided he would try to put the protests in the same category as the other events at the fair, and they were being covered. Picking up the phone, Odom tried to remain calm as he placed the call.

The phone rang for what seemed like an eternity, and Odom became more agitated. Someone finally answered, and he lost his composure right away when asked his name and purpose of the call.

Odom, spewing with anger, said, "Never mind my name. I'm telling you, the toleration of sin in this town must come to an end. If the paper refuses to cover the story, I will find someone who will."

Unfortunately, for Odom, the man answering the phone had no idea who Odom was or why he was calling. He was in the Circulation Department and generally fielded calls for papers not delivered. His perceived ignorance only increased Odom's fury and resolve. The conversation made Odom even more defiant, and he was going to get the attention of the communities one way or another. Everyone would soon learn of the sin and degradation on display, and it would no longer be tolerated.

Odom was now becoming a victim of his own anger, losing all rational thoughts. He decided to look for other ways to protest. He left the house and went to the small carport adjacent to his house. There he located a gas can and a few bottles. He had an idea. He had witnessed the fury of Molotov cocktails and the destruction they could bring while he was living in Virginia. He felt the bottles and gas could be used to make a couple of the cocktails, and he was certain the firebombs would generate attention. If he decided to bomb the shows, then others would finally begin listening to his message and would certainly take notice.

❧

Return to The Fairgrounds

When Brick and Mary Jane returned to the fairgrounds, the gates had closed for the night even though a few people were still riding some rides on the midway. Fortunately, the clearing skies gave everyone hope for a good Thursday. Brick was in a euphoric state as they walked toward the trailers. He tried his best to act calm, but it didn't come easy. When they reached the trailer, Mary Jane once again told him how much fun she had and how nice the evening had been. Brick, still feeling excited about everything, could not find the words to express his feelings. He simply said, "Maybe we can do it again."

Mary Jane replied, "I'd like that, but we both know another night away from the fair is highly unlikely."

Brick kissed her goodnight, and she told him again that she hoped their night out would not get him into any trouble with his girlfriend. This disappointed Brick as she didn't need to continually bring up his girlfriend. Why would she do that? Brick did not want to think about Emily, and yet Mary Jane mentioned her once again.

Brick told her, "No worries. To be honest, I'm not sure she would even care."

Mary Jane smiled and said, "You feel that way now, but when Sunday gets here, and I'm off to another town, and you're off to college, the relationship you claim not to be thinking about will become more important to you. All I'm saying is that I don't want you to later regret the time we've spent together."

She then kissed Brick very passionately, creating turmoil in Brick's mind. Why was she giving him so many double messages? He was confused—but happily confused.

Mary Jane then told him she needed to get some rest and asked if she would see him the next day. Brick answered, "Of course, you will." He then kissed her again and said goodnight. As he turned to leave, she grabbed his arm and convincingly told him once more that it had been a long time since she had spent any time with a guy. She then thanked him again for the special evening, opened the door to her trailer, and told him goodnight.

Although Brick was disappointed with Mary Jane constantly bringing up his girlfriend, it failed to take anything away from the thrill he felt about the evening and their time together. The heavy petting was fabulous, but he also enjoyed the movie and dinner. She was fun to be with, and Brick knew he could easily fall for her. Take away the sexual exploration, which admittedly would be hard to do, and the date was no different than others he had enjoyed. It could have been a typical Sanford date night.

In the parking lot, Brick instinctively looked around for Ray's car. He had not seen him and didn't see his car. He hoped Ray had enjoyed his evening as much as he had. Brick pulled out of the fairgrounds, content with his memories, and drove home.

❧

Day Four

The rain had finally stopped when Odom noticed Key pulling into the driveway. Odom motioned for Key to join him in the carport. Odom showed signs he had selp little the night before and he began explaining why. I've spent most of the night agonizing over the failure of the protests. Evidently Odom had made an impression on Key when he heard Key if there was anything he could do to help. Odom could tell Key was trying his best to be upbeat even telling him "The sun is out, and today will be a banner day for our protest."

Odom knew the day should be better, and he said to Key, "Yeah, I think a lot more people will be coming in today and that's why I've decided to take the protest to a new level." Odom's tone had changed and he now came across more relaxed and self-assured, both of which appeared to pleased Key.

Odom then was questionned by Key as he asked. "What are you thinking, Patrick?"

As Odom spoke Key quickly learned the source of Odom's calm. He informed him he had decided to create a little havoc at the revue by using a couple of Molotov cocktails to disrupt the show. This bit of news was disturbing to Key, and he feared what might happen if things were to turn violent.

Key did not want to participate in a violent protest, and Odom sensed his hesitation. With Odom not wanting to lose Key's involment in the protest, he assured him the bombs would only be used as a last resort. He then added that if the protests continued to flounder, he may have little choice but to turn to the Molotov cocktails. Then everyone would finally take notice.

Key felt Odom may have already decided to use the firebombs. The tone and resolve Odom was using made Key believe it was not a matter of whether Odom would use the bombs—but when. Key tried to remain calm. Not wishing to show any fear as Odom talked of the potential attack, he questioned if Odom had thought the attack through. Using the firebombs could hurt people and destroy property. One couldn't burn down an attraction and not expect problems.

Odom, hoping to convince Odom of his plan, said, "No one is going to get hurt, but if I have to burn the place down, I'm going to do just that. Our efforts will then be recognized."

Key responded, "Damn, Patrick! That's not a good idea. You can't be sure no one will get hurt."

Odom again declared, "I don't plan on hurting anyone, but something needs to happen."

Key looked at him and said, "And breaking the law is your way of getting something done? This is serious, Patrick."

Odom told him he was not breaking the law; he was leading a protest. Key reminded him it was supposed to be a peaceful protest, and the use of firebombs was anything but peaceful and that such action would not serve him or the church well. It appeared that Odom was not listening when Key told him that using homemade firebombs was not the answer, and there had to be a better way.

Odom didn't want to hear normal reasoning. He was no longer thinking rationally as he wanted to see results—and the sooner the better. What had started out as a peaceful protest was now turning dangerous.

Odom stood his ground and firmly said to Key, "Listen, you don't have to come, but if I need to, I'm going to use these bombs. I want people to hear my message. We have tried marching, and we have tried sitting in the rain, and all that got us was wet and ridiculed. No more! We started these protests to make a difference, and, by God, I'm going to make a difference—with or without you."

Key shook his head as he said, "Patrick, you know I'm with you, but I hope you realize how serious this is. If it comes to using the bombs, you will get some attention, but it might get you the attention you didn't bargain for. You may find yourself in serious trouble."

Odom told him he was not worried about the consequences. He wanted to make a statement—a statement that showed the seriousness of the movement and would finally be recognized and understood.

Key, still trying to change Odom's mind, said, "All I can say is, if you use the bombs, people will get one hell of a message, and you will probably end up in jail. I just don't think that is what you want or need."

Odom said, "Look at this way; it's time to fight sin with sin—an eye for an eye. I realize that it is not a Christian act, but it is the action I'm willing to take. Hopefully, you will be with me." Key was not sure what to say but told him if it came to that, he would stand by him.

Apparently, Odom was planning on creating several firebombs, causing Key to question the need for such firepower. Odom told him he wanted to be sure to have enough if needed.

Key knew that using the bombs was wrong, but sadly, he had always been a follower, and he realized there was little need in arguing with Odom at this time. Key also knew Odom was right as none of their actions had worked so far. Reluctantly, Key succumbed to the pressure and accepted Odom's plan. Key asked how Odom planned on using the Molotov cocktails. The question energized Odom. He was pleased that Key was now talking about using the firebombs and no longer was trying to dissuade him.

Odom told Key, "I feel like we should go out to the fairgrounds as usual and set up for the protest. We'll wait for the crowds to arrive and the revue to open. Once the girls come out and begin enticing the crowds to promote ticket sales, we fight fire with fire."

Key wondered how Odom planned to get the bombs into the fair. It wasn't like he could walk in with a box of homemade fireworks.

Odom said, "I think I can conceal them in the stack of signs we've been bringing in every day. No one has questioned us about the signs. Once we have them on the grounds, we can decide the best time for the attack."

Key told Odom he hoped he did not think the police would sit idly by as he destroyed property and threatened lives. Bombing the show was a crime, and there would be consequences not only for him, but he would also be implicating Beverly and Gail with the attack. Again, Odom reminded Key he didn't need to be a part of his scheme and neither did the ladies, but one way or another, if he needed to use the bombs, he was going to.

Key said, "Listen, Patrick, I'll support you, but I don't want any of us to end up in jail. I sure as hell don't want that for Beverly or Gail." Odom told him he didn't plan on anyone going to jail, but if that's what it would take to get the shows shut down, it would be a small sacrifice. Key knew Odom wasn't being reasonable, but he also knew this plot could work. Who would convict a preacher for trying to stamp out sin?

Beverly joined Odom and Key under the carport. She feared Odom might be up to something, knowing how troubled he had been. She asked what they were talking about. Odom spoke up first and said, "We're talking about the protests, trying to figure out a way to get some publicity." Beverly spotted the bottles and gas can and asked Odom what he planned to do with them. He tried to brush her off by saying, "Don't worry, I have a plan."

After telling Beverly his plan, she told him he was talking like a crazy person. His rhetoric was not from the man she married, and it certainly wasn't from the minister of The Revival Revolutionary Church; this was crazy talk. She added in dismay, "Patrick, you can't take those things to the fair. That's stupid! Someone will get hurt—not to mention arrested."

Odom had heard the same from Key, and he was tired of their lack of support. He said, "Listen, you know perfectly well I don't want to hurt anyone, but I've got to do something. I need people to start understanding that these so-called sideshows are promoting sin and destroying families."

Beverly quickly pointed out, "If you bomb the shows, the only family that will be ruined is our church family. Violence is not the answer. Such an act is not in your best interest or that of the church."

As usual, Beverly's words did not make Odom happy, but he knew she had a point. He told her he knew she was right, but the week was almost over, and they had little to show for all the work they had done on the protest. Beverly tried to convince him otherwise, asking him to please think about the damage the bombs could do, not only to the revue but the church as well. She added, "The sun is shining. It is going to be a beautiful day, and the crowds will be the largest yet. We can make a difference without resorting to violence. Odom reluctantly agreed not to take the bombs in. He would give the protests another day to work, but if things didn't improve, he would consider bringing them in on Friday.

Beverly understood that Patrick was feeling pressured, and he wanted something to happen. But for now, she had at least talked him into delaying use of the bombs. She prayed that maybe the day would be different, turning Patrick away from the use of violence.

Key said, "Patrick, maybe this day will be the start of something good. Let's see what happens today before we worry about tomorrow."

Beverly knew she would not be able to hold off Patrick for long if things didn't change. She had learned early on in their relationship that it was nearly impossible to change Odom's mind once he had decided to do something.

⚜

Thursday for Brick and Ray

Anticipating a need to be free from one another, Brick and Ray drove in separately on Thursday. Although they were in different cars, they arrived around the same time for the seven o'clock start time. As soon as they saw each other, Ray asked Brick about his date with Mary Jane. Brick happily shared, "It was good; she received the full Sanford experience, including a visit to Fire Tower Road."

Ray slapped Brick on the back and said, "Well, no wonder you look so excited to be at work."

Brick responded, "Oh yeah! We took in a movie, then Morton's and Fire Tower Road, and hopefully today will be even better." He then asked Ray about his night.

"I was with Jill, and we had a nice time. Ray said with a smile. We did what we could at the fair, mostly enjoying the rides. It was a little wet, but it was all free. I tried to convince her I should stay with her in the barracks, but she was not buying it. It was still fun though."

Brick chuckled and said, "So, guess you hope today offers up more chances with Jill as well." Ray told him he was certainly hoping the night may end with different results. They both had discovered being a fair employee did have its advantages.

When they reached the office and saw Raeford, they learned that the day could be a long one, but the thoughts of a bright sunny day put everyone in a better mood. Raeford, with his usual positive attitude, said, "We need to make a push to catch up on all the business we lost yesterday. The crowds should be the largest yet and, hopefully, will only get bigger this weekend. If we are as busy as I am anticipating, both of you can count on making some good money." The boys felt they had been making good money, but it still sounded good to them.

Raeford explained that once they had checked the tickets and completed the day's distribution, he needed them to concentrate on getting some of the standing water out of the way. There were puddles of water nearly everywhere you looked. Wednesday's rain had surely left its mark. Raeford felt that once the crowds arrived, it would be a lot easier to keep them there if they did not have to trudge through mud and standing water.

With such limited business from the previous day, they were able to complete the ticket count and distribution quickly. When they had finished, Raeford instructed them to go down to the utility shed near the livestock exhibit and ask for a man named Cole. Cole was pretty much the handyman of Howard's Amusements, and Raeford told them he should have something they could use to help remove the water.

Raeford said, "Just tell Cole I sent you down to help out. He is not much of a talker, but he can get you going. Start where you want to and work your way around the midway. Unfortunately, we have a real mess, and it is going to take some time to get rid of it. You will most likely have to go back and do it a second time. You'll need your gloves; they should still be in the bin where you left them." Raeford then informed them he planned to get a couple of loads of sand delivered to help dry things out, and he was hoping all of their work would make a difference. He then left and told the boys he would catch up with them later about the sand.

Again, Brick was so impressed with the efforts Raeford put into his work. He was now looking to make sure anyone attending the fair would only be marginally affected by the standing water. He was always trying to make the fair a success. Brick had worked with others outside the carnie spectrum who were not nearly as dedicated to their job as Raeford.

Brick and Ray picked up their gloves and made their way to the utility shed to find Cole. They resisted stopping by to see the ladies. It was early, and there was much to get done. They were forced to walk through a lot of water and mud; there was definitely a need for the sand and water tools.

For the first time, the boys realized there was a certain amount of manual labor that went along with their new jobs, but being able to work together was a bonus. Both wished they had brought a change of clothes, or had at least worn different shoes, as it looked like the work could be messy. Ray joked that if they got too dirty, they might have to shower in the barracks.

The boys saw a man out front of the utility shed who right away gave the impression that he wasn't very motivated to work, but they knew it was Larry Cole by the name on his shirt. Other than that, it would have been tough to tell. Cole indeed was not one for small talk— or any talk for that matter. Brick and Ray introduced themselves, and Cole seemed to pay them no mind. Ray spoke first, saying, "Raeford asked us to check in with you and get some rakes, hoes, or something, so that we can remove the standing water."

Cole just stared at the boys. Then he finally spoke, indicating they would find them in the shed. When it looked like he had nothing else to say, he advised them to use the rakes with the broad sweep, saying they could remove the water better with them. Ray thanked him for the advice. By the time they located the rakes, Cole had already left. Ray smiled and said, "Like Raeford said, not much for conversation. I guess it's up to us to formulate a plan. We have mud to move."

They decided to start at the entrance and make their way around the main loop of the midway. Fortunately, they found the entrance area in relatively good condition, considering the amount of rain that had fallen. This was due primarily to a large amount of crush and run laid down before the fair opened.

It was the areas not covered by the crush and run that needed the most attention. This was a learning process for the boys as they had never done anything close to the work they were doing, and they were not sure they were even making a difference. They tried different techniques for removing the puddles and giving the mud a chance to dry out. Fortunately, the sun was out, and there was a small breeze blowing that also helped with the drying.

They had been slowly moving around the midway for about an hour when they heard a dump truck making its way down the drive. It was a truckload of sand, and Raeford was telling the driver where to make small deposits of the sand. Raeford spotted Brick and Ray and told them to get some shovels and a couple of wheelbarrows from the shed and to start moving the sand around to the wetter spots. Before reaching the hut, they spotted Cole and another guy coming toward them, directing another truck with a load of sand. Brick asked Cole where they would find the wheelbarrows, and Cole merely pointed to where they could be found.

Cole then said, "When you get the wheelbarrows and your shovels, meet me at the truck." Ray looked at Brick, saying, "Damn! did we do all that raking for nothing?"

Brick, a little annoyed, replied, "I sure as hell hope not, but at least we're getting paid."

Both trucks were distributing the sand in various spots throughout the grounds, which lessened the need to move the sand with the wheelbarrows. One of the vehicles had about a half load of sand remaining when Raeford asked if they had seen any areas needing special attention. Brick and Ray agreed that the area around the Tilt-a-Whirl seemed wetter than most and could use some work. Raeford knew the area was somewhat lower than the surrounding areas, and he told them they had some concerns when constructing the ride on Sunday. Raeford hopped in the truck and told them to meet him there.

Neither boy was thrilled with the idea of moving sand and water, and Ray commented that he was beginning to learn there was a lot more to fair work than just hanging out with the pretty ladies. Brick simply replied, "You think?"

They had worked for nearly two-and-a-half hours when the gates were preparing to open. Fortunately, they had finished scattering the sand by the time the gates opened. With the raking and spreading of the sand, both boys felt they had done a decent job with negating the problems of the standing water. It was not ideal, but the grounds were ten times better than when they started.

With the number of folks coming through the gates, it appeared Raeford was right on target; Thursday was shaping up to be a busy day. He told the boys earlier in the week that many considered Thursday the real start-up day for the fair as it was then that the money started to roll in. He stuck by that and said, "Thursday through Saturday we should do more than double the business we have done so far this week."

Raeford told Brick and Ray he was going to need them to run a couple of the rides. In jest he told them they might as well get the entire Howard's experience, adding that once the ride checked out for safety, they could begin operating them. He also assured the boys it would not take long to learn how the rides operated.

Brick was assigned to run the Round-Up and even though he had ridden it several times, he had never paid any attention to how it operated. Ray's assignment was the Mad Mouse. By design or not, these turned out to be two of the busier rides. It did not take them long to realize they would have little time for socializing. Raeford was right; the actual running of the rides was easy enough. The main concern was keeping track of how long the ride should last. They needed to move the patrons through quickly, and yet, try to ensure they had a pleasurable experience. In the entertainment business, time is indeed money.

At the Round-Up, Brick met Laura, an older lady who showed him how to operate the ride and gave him some tips on how to keep it moving. Laura looked rather unimpressive, but at least she offered to help with a smile.

Laura was another example of how looks can be deceiving. He found her to be very pleasant and helpful. She was very outgoing and shared she had been with the fair for several years, telling him there was little that surprised her anymore; she felt she had seen it all. Having not met him before, she was curious and wanted to know Brick's story, asking when he had joined up. She didn't mind asking questions, and Brick thought it was funny when she asked if he was running from or to something.

Brick explained, "It's not quite that dramatic. I just wanted to experience the work here and meet some new people before heading off to school. I guess it was more out of curiosity than anything else."

Laura laughed and said she had heard that before. She didn't mind telling him that the more he experienced, the more he would want to experience, and before he could realize it, fair life would get into his blood. Years later he may be asking himself what happened. Laura told Brick that he should enjoy his time, but he needed to understand that the life of a carnie could be addicting.

Brick asked her if she was endorsing the work or warning him. Laura smiled and said, "Don't get me wrong; I love working here. It is part of my life, but I've seen more than a few come for a week and end up losing a year or more to the life of the midway."

Brick smiled and thanked her for the warning. He then told her he was only there for the week, so maybe he would be safe.

Laura then said, "I've been traveling with Howard's Amusements for close to ten years, and before Howards I worked with a traveling circus called the Stable Brothers' Shows."

Brick asked about the circus—another area of curiosity for him. She told him it was a one-ring circus and went on to say, "I was required to do all sorts of different jobs, and I just got too old for it." Brick, trying to be friendly, said she didn't seem that old. Laura told him that it was nice of him to say, but her bones told her differently.

She began telling Brick of her duties at the circus: "I've been a clown, a horseback rider, and an erotic belly dancer. You name it; I've done it. With the Stable Brothers, I enjoyed the hours. It wasn't as demanding as it is here, but the work was harder. At the circus, you have scheduled performances. Here, you go to work once the gates open and work until they close. Stables went out of business back in '58, and my life as a clown came to an end. I was able to latch on to Howard's and have been with them since. I would have never thought I would still be doing this, but now it's in my blood. So, be careful, or before you know it, you will live your entire life on the road in small towns across the U.S. In my twenty plus years, I have seen it all and done most of it as well. I have two children, both raised in the business, and they are now living the carnival life."

Brick wondered if they were with Howard's as well. She responded, "No, both my kids are with a traveling show in Europe. They got hired right out of school and have never looked back. We keep in touch the best we can, but the lifestyle is in their blood much like their mother. I say again, be careful. You never know what this business will do to you."

Laura's looks failed to do her justice when Brick met her. He wasn't sure what to expect, but what he found was a friendly, protective lady.

Maybe her maternal instincts were taking over as her children could not have been much older than him.

Laura was anxious for Brick to learn how to operate the ride and shared with him a few tricks to help him keep track of everything. He learned that, unfortunately, the Round-Up had no timer, requiring it to be operated manually. To ensure everyone got a full ride, Laura used a sand hourglass timer. The timer took a little over four minutes to empty, giving everyone a satisfying experience. Brick felt it was a simple, yet effective, means of keeping things on track, and he indicated how impressed he was with her make-do system.

Laura said, "Well, like I said, I've been doing this for a long time, and let me assure you that in the beginning I needed a system that worked. I may not need to use it now, but there are still times it comes in handy."

Brick wondered if she ever had any problems forgetting the timer or failing to use it. Laura laughingly told Brick about getting distracted in Virginia when everyone on the Round-Up enjoyed an extended ride. She could hardly control her laughter as she said, "Nearly all those poor bastards on the ride got sick. And believe me, you don't want them to get sick."

Brick cautiously said, "I am afraid to ask, but what happens when someone does get sick?" Laura told him the ride must continue to run, and someone would need to clean up the mess. She then asked if he had any idea who that would be. He reluctantly replied, "I guess I do."

Laura then pointed out some cleaning supplies that were under the counter at the operator's stand. She said, "Hopefully, you won't need them," adding, "It's the downside of operating a ride." She then told Brick that there were always those who wanted to prove their manhood, so she suggested that he try to dissuade any drunks from riding as alcohol and the Round-Up did not mix well.

Laura continued, "Generally, I'm fairly good at remembering to time things out correctly. It gets ingrained in your head. You will find it easier to let people get in their seats first, and then collect the tickets and check the security belts at the same time. I'll stick around until you get the hang of things. First off, you collect the tickets and check the belts, and I'll run the ride."

It did not take long for Brick to have the routine down pat. Although he was aware of the drop box, Laura pointed it out, telling him it helps to track the day's business. Brick told her how he had been assisting Raeford with the count, and it seemed to be a good system.

Laura said, "You may be ahead of the curve then. Raeford has been at this for a long time, and he's a pro at getting things done. He runs a tight ship and does not stand for any nonsense. That's something I've always liked about him."

Brick assured Laura he could handle things but asked if she would leave the hourglass. She smiled and told him about the hourglass travels with the Round-Up. Before leaving, Laura told him the Round-Up was very popular, and he should expect to be busy most of the day. She indicated she would return later to give him a break. Once she was gone, Brick could not help but think about riders getting sick, and he just hoped it would not happen on his watch. Brick was able to manage both collecting the tickets and running the ride with little trouble.

The change in the weather certainly brought out the crowds, and as Raeford predicted, buisness was booming. All the sand and work they had done earlier was paying off as well. The grounds were getting dryer by the hour.

Brick caught on to running the Round-Up pretty quick; after all, it was not rocket science. The time passed quickly, giving him little time to think of anything else. He had been running the ride for a few hours and was surprised no one he knew had stopped by to see him. When Laura returned later in the day, he told her business had been good, and he was proud to announce no one had gotten sick or complained.

Laura was pleased and said, "Great! Why don't you take a break? I'm sure you could use one. I can handle it for a while."

Brick was happy for the time off. His first stop was to visit Ray while he was running the Mad Mouse. Ray was alone and hoped it would not be long before he could get a break. Brick told him if he got free in the next thirty minutes, he could find him over at Brenda's food stand as he needed to get something to eat.

Before going to Brenda's, Brick decided to drop by the revue, hoping to see Mary Jane. The push for business was on, and the revue had opened earlier than usual. Payne was out front and told Brick that the ladies were in the back getting ready for the next show. Brick stuck his head inside the tent to look for Mary Jane, but Payne told him to be quick as he was about to start the introductions. Brick decided not to push his luck and chose to back out of the tent, allowing Payne to begin his announcements.

He waited for Mary Jane's debut, and once she walked on the outside stage, he had mixed emotions. It was strange seeing her up on the stage, considering the night they had enjoyed together. Maybe he was feeling a little protective of her and even a bit jealous of those lusting for her. He made his way closer to the stage. When Mary Jane noticed him, she smiled and motioned for him to come toward her. She met Brick at the door and motioned for Payne to let him in. Payne smiled. Brick was confident Payne's thoughts were not clean, but then neither were Brick's.

Brick did notice the protesters were in their regular spot, but thankfully they were not verbally abusing anyone attending the show. Instead, the group waved their signs and shouted, "God will forgive, but will your family?". Brick was not sure what they were trying to say.

Brick waited on the side of the stage, hoping to speak to Mary Jane before she performed. She motioned for him to come up to the dressing room. Some of the men who had claimed their spot at the front saw Brick walk onto the stage and a few began to howl, "Hey! I want to come back there too!" Mary Jane smiled to the howling crowd, took Brick's hand, and led him into the makeshift dressing room. Here Brick saw the other girls preparing for their time on stage. Fortunately, they were all smiles as he walked in.

The experience was surreal to Brick. He was backstage with the other girls, all nearly nude, and not one of them appeared the least bit modest about their appearance. Brick smiled, thinking he must have made it. He was indeed a true carnie. One thing was certain; being backstage with the beauties was a hell of a lot better than operating the Round-Up.

Brick told Mary Jane he had been running a ride since the gates opened, but earlier he and Ray were shoveling sand and moving water to dry things out for the day's activities. Mary Jane asked him how the crowds were and if he met Laura.

Brick answered, "Yeah, she seems to be a nice lady." Mary Jane then wanted to know if she said anything about the protesters." Brick told her they just talked about operating the ride—little else. He questioned why she was asking.

Mary Jane, with a little worry in her voice, said, "I was just wondering. Earlier today she told Misty she had a bad feeling about the protesters. She fears there may be trouble, especially with that loud-mouthed, fat guy. She asked us to be careful. It may just be her thoughts, but from what I know about Laura, her intuitions are usually right."

Brick asked if they had had any problems, and Mary Jane replied, "None so far, but we have just opened for business."

Brick tried to ease her concerns by telling her from what he had seen, it looked like their numbers were down. He added, "Let's hope this whole mess ends soon, and they will go back to where they came from."

Mary Jane said she hoped he was right, but so far, the leader appeared to be determined to get his way and doesn't appear to be the type to give up easily. She then added, "I pray they don't get crazy."

It was getting close to showtime, and Brick knew he needed to get going. He told her he needed to get some food, but he hoped to see a show later. Mary Jane smiled and gave him a soft kiss, saying that sounded good to her. She squeezed Brick's hand and told him she would see him later.

By the time Brick reached Brenda's, Ray was already enjoying a corndog and a soda. Ray knew the answer, but he smiled and said, "Let me guess, you've been to the revue. Or should I ask, how is Mary Jane?" Brick told Ray the revue had opened, and it looked like the rides weren't the only thing enjoying a banner day.

Ray said, "Banner Day all around. I've run so many people through the Mad Mouse that I feel like I'm beginning to go mad." He then wondered how Brick's Day had been.

Both boys discussed the ins and outs of running two of the more popular rides on the midway. One thing was for sure; neither of them were bored with their jobs. They were, though, a little surprised that neither of them had seen anyone they knew. Brick ordered his food and began telling Ray just how much he had enjoyed the week thus far. Ray agreed and added that meeting the ladies certainly did not hurt.

Brick told Ray about meeting Laura, telling him how she had been with Howard's for over ten years and even had her children working with her at one time. He went on to say, "Laura says to be careful as this lifestyle can get in your blood, and before you know it, you are a carnie."

Ray laughed as he said, "That seems to be a warning shared by many." He told Brick it had been a great week, but he was certain he would not have any trouble walking away when it was over.

Brick agreed and said he would miss the people but certainly not the roundup, adding, "I'm not sure I could think of a better way to prepare for college."

They enjoyed a laugh as they sat there and ate.

❧

Odom at The Fair

O dom's group of protesters began to diminish, and Beverly feared what Odom might do. If things failed to pick up, she knew Odom may resort to using the Molotov cocktails. Odom was far from satisfied with the efforts put forth by his group; he could see little impact from the protest. Beverly had hoped the day would be better, but unfortunately, there was little difference from the other days, and there was no indication things would change. Although Patrick was, for the time being, containing his anger, Beverly knew how easy he could pivot from the man she loved to the frustrated, angry man she feared.

Patrick was a proud man with little patience. Beverly felt the protest had turned into a personal vendetta for Patrick, making him talk and possibly act irrationally. She thought if she could only hold him off for two more days (until the fair left town) that she and Patrick could return to the life they had made for themselves. As Beverly held up her sign proclaiming the evils of the show, she feared Patrick may be moved to do something destructive.

Odom had thought the protest would successfully elevate him and the church to the notoriety he desperately craved; however, with each passing day, a successful demonstration was becoming elusive and now appeared unattainable; a dream that continued to evade him. His sense of failure added to his feeling of desperation.

Odom needed more to come of the protest. He thought of the time and money already invested in the movement and how they had rendered no good. He was frustrated with himself and the citizens of Lee County. How could he grow his church if no one knew they existed? Odom was beginning to believe his followers and their efforts were now becoming a sideshow to the sideshows.

Beverly was trying her best to appease Odom. She told him once again that she felt more people were beginning to take notice. With the sun out and the large number of people attending, everyone should view the day as the official beginning of the protest. Beverly saw progress in how many people were learning about the protest as well as the church.

Beverly had decided to implement a petition seeking signatures in support of shutting down the revue. Sadly, Odom was becoming so blinded by his anger that he saw little value in her efforts. He told her he did not feel a handful of signatures would have an impact. Beverly saw the petition as progress, and she decided she and Gail would go out onto the midway and gather even more names. Beverly told Odom she and Gail would share the church's message while garnering support with the petition. This part of her idea appealed to Odom. Maybe Beverly was on to something. Going out on the midway, more patrons would see her and learn of the protest.

Beverly carried a clipboard with the petition, and Gail took a sign that read, No More Revue/Stop the Sin. The two of them would work on gathering signatures of those supporting the cause while generating more attention for the protest. She hoped their work would keep Odom from using the firebombs while also calming his anger.

With Beverly and Gail walking the midway, Odom and Key were left alone at the protest. No one from the media had stopped by, and the customers who did walk past just gawked at them, saying little and showing even less interest. Odom was convinced success was not coming, and it was his sense of frustration that made him say to Key, "It's time we make a plan of attack." Odom's choice of words disappointed Key. He was hoping Odom had reconsidered his plan of using the Molotov cocktails to bomb the revue, but Key also knew how important the protest was to Odom and understood his desire to create awareness.

Key asked, "You still want to go through with it, don't you?"

Odom firmly replied, "I do, and I think I know how we can do it without the ladies being involved."

Odom began to share his plan with Key, "Tomorrow, we'll bring the bombs in early before anyone else arrives. I will hide them in that stack of supplies for the protest. Then later in the day, I will send Beverly and Gail out to gather signatures, and we can attack the show while they are away."

Although he supported Odom, Key was hesitant, so he said to Odom, "You know if you use the bombs, people will get hurt, and you could burn the whole thing down."

Odom reiterated, "Listen, the show needs to stop, and at this point the bombs may be our only recourse."

Key noticed a change in Odom. He no longer was talking about the church but more about victory over the revue. Key, still trying to change Odom's mind, said, "Patrick, if you do it while the ladies are on the grounds, they could still be implicated. You need to think about that."

Odom just replied, "Don't worry. No one's going to bother them."

Odom was concerned about the layout of the show. He told Key they needed to find out how the show operated inside the tent, so he suggested Key take in one of the shows. By doing this, Key could tell Odom how the stage was laid out and where the customers would be. Key had no interest in going inside as he was sincerely trying to change his ways and felt attending the show would show digression back to a life he was trying to put behind him. He questioned how he could protest the show one moment and attend it the next. To Key, the idea was a mistake.

Rather determined, Odom said again, "I want you to go to the show, check out the stage, and map out the area where the men stand. I'm telling you, I don't want to hurt anyone, and if you could get the lay of the land, that would give me a better idea where to throw the bombs."

Key, with a sound of desperation, said, "It just doesn't feel right, Patrick. What if somebody recognizes me?"

"You don't need to worry about anyone recognizing you," Odom said. "Hell, no one has paid us enough attention to recognize us, but if you are that concerned about being recognized, put on a disguise; wear a cowboy hat, or something that helps conceal your face."

Key worried what Gail would think, so Odom told him he could go in after Gail and Beverly had gone home for the day. Although Key was against going into the show, he finally gave in. Key didn't want anyone to be hurt, and maybe he could convince Odom to change his mind once he learned what was behind the curtains.

A Day of Rides

B rick spent most of his day running the Round-Up, and he learned more about the ride than he cared to know. The ride relied primarily on centrifugal force to produce fear and excitement. Spinning at such a high rate of speed was not only exhilarating; it could also produce some disgusting finishes. Luckily for Brick, the riders on this day were able to handle the speed and movement with no clean-up needed from mishaps. As he manned the twirling cylinder and listened to the screams of excitement, his thoughts were on Mary Jane.

He daydreamed about making love to her later that evening. He played out an entire fantasy in his mind—from her sweet smell to the taste of her breast. He was ready for his daydreams to cross over into reality. Mary Jane had unlocked his sexual desires with her beauty and seductive flirtation. He now wanted to experience it all again—her love, her attention—everything she had to offer.

Brick was a typical teenage boy whose hormones were ruling his thoughts. In Mary Jane's case, she had introduced Brick to a new chapter in his imagination. If things proceeded as he envisioned it for tonight, maybe his desires would be fulfilled.

With closing time approaching, Brick was ready for the long day to be behind him. He had been at the fairgrounds for nearly sixteen hours and was feeling it. Even though it had been a long day, Brick still had the energy to be excited about what the night may hold for him and Mary Jane.

Laura came by to help Brick with shutting down the ride. He learned closing it down was little different from starting it. The two of them made the safety checks of the belts as well as ensuring everything was clean for the next day. When the lights were switched off and the ride became quiet, it was finally time to leave. Brick hoped once he took the tickets to the office, his work night would be over.

After turning in the tickets, Brick had no problem finding Mary Jane. Her evening had ended, and she was standing outside her trailer talking with Lucy. Mary Jane gave Brick a friendly wave and began walking toward him. He sensed something was wrong as she wasn't smiling or looking like her usual jovial self. When he reached her, Brick quickly recognized she was preoccupied with something and even seemed distant. It didn't take long for his feelings to be confirmed when she told him she was not feeling well. She was happy the day was over and expressed how she needed time away from the revue.

It was evident Mary Jane was upset, and Brick could not figure out why. Earlier in the day, everything appeared okay, but now she was different—not as outgoing or talkative. His insecurities were beginning to resurface; he tended to blame himself for everything. He began to fear he may have done something to upset her.

Brick was relieved to learn he was not the source of her changed demeanor. He learned she was distressed by the protesters and their actions. They had upset her, and she was somewhat unnerved by their talk.

Mary Jane told Brick she no longer knew what to think, adding, "That preacher, the one leading the protests, is nothing but trouble. He is disruptive and has everyone on edge. Tonight, he was louder and more abusive."

The protests were beginning to affect everyone associated with the revue, and Mary Jane found them especially threatening. The preacher's actions were not only impacting Mary Jane; they were now affecting Brick. The girls had become fearful of what may happen since this group of protesters was unlike any they had encountered before. Brick thought, That damn son of a bitch is messing up everything. Fortunately, he was smart enough not to vocalize his displeasure to Mary Jane, knowing it could show that he was more concerned with his fantasy than with her safety. She began telling Brick how it was less intrusive when the protests were quiet, but now they had turned verbally abusive, and she was feeling threatened.

Mary Jane said, "I'm afraid this group may do more than yell and wave signs. The leader seemed dead set on making trouble." As she shared her fears, tears began to fall, and she started to cry. Brick had never known her to be vulnerable. She was now questioning her feelings. Was she doomed to go to hell as the preacher often screamed? Brick had no answer. He had been consumed with his lust and desire, but that was now turning into disappointment.

Brick wasn't interested in looking at any moral implications of the show. He was far from a choir boy himself, although he did attend church regularly and participated in most of the church's activities. It had little to do with right or wrong; it served more as a social outlet. Nevertheless, even if one could question his faith, he still believed there was more sinning going on in the world than that occurring at the Lee County fair.

Brick tried to reassure Mary Jane that the protesters were merely outliers and didn't represent most of society, but his words seemed to ring shallow. Mary Jane was fearful of a man who claimed to be doing God's work as this was not her understanding of God. She was frightened and said, "I can't help but feel something bad is going to happen. We have had protesters before, but these people seem particularly hateful and dangerous. The leader has hatred in his eyes and waves of anger in his voice; it is something I've never seen before. They even have a petition going around asking for us to be shut down. I'm afraid the mood of the fair may turn against the show." She feared if the petition was successful, it may empower the preacher to continue his verbal assaults, seeing the signatures as a license to disrupt. Mary Jane continued, "I hate hearing his taunts saying we are all walking a path to hell. He said we need redemption. It's all so frightening."

Brick tried to find a way to relieve her concerns and show his support, telling her he felt the preacher was looking for attention. He went on to say, "If anyone needs redemption, it's that damn preacher! The way he is attacking innocent people and trying to scare everyone with his talk is wicked."

The sad truth was that Brick had no idea what to think of the preacher and the protests. He wanted to calm Mary Jane down in hopes of living out his night of sexual fantasy.

Mary Jane wiped the tears from her eyes. She knew Brick was right. The actions of the preacher were a far cry from that of a Christian, but the words still stung. She also knew her lifestyle over the last year had not honored her faith. She told Brick, "Maybe I'm overreacting, but the other protest groups were more in control, giving out flyers and holding signs—never going as far as to attack those working or attending."

Brick called the preacher an old redneck who didn't know what he was doing. With a chuckle, he suggested the girls give the fat one a private show and maybe that would change his tune. As soon as he said it, Brick knew it was a mistake. He was nervous and unsure of what to say or do, but that statement was definitely wrong. Mary Jane failed to see the humor in his assertion, telling him the situation was far more serious than he was taking it. He began scrambling for words.

He apologetically said, "I'm sorry, I know it's frightening. I was trying to help take your mind off of the protests. I know it will be hard to do but try not to let that redneck get you down. You are stronger than the preacher! They will not be successful if the revue doesn't give in to them." Brick often used the term redneck to describe anyone he didn't agree with, and this indeed was one of those times.

Brick didn't want to give up on the night, so he awkwardly tried to kiss Mary Jane. He was disappointed that his efforts were met with resistance as she was not in the mood for affection. The protests and the constant yelling were getting to her, and there was little Brick could do to keep her from being upset. Rejecting his advances, Mary Jane told him she was sorry, but she felt she needed some time to herself as it had been a long day; she was tired and worn down and needed to get some sleep.

Brick tried to hide his hurt feelings, now knowing the night wasn't going to turn out as he had hoped. His disappointment must have been evident when he asked if he would see her the next day.

Mary Jane possibly recognized his insecurities, so she took his hand and said, "You better; I've gotten used to seeing you, and I like it." It was then that she gave him a goodnight kiss—a kiss that would rival any he had experienced before. Her touch and her moist lips only added to Brick's excitement, but she pulled away and said goodnight. Brick told her goodnight and began walking to his car. He had not seen Ray for a few hours and wondered if he was still on the grounds.

The entire day, while raking the sand and moving the water and operating the Round-Up, Brick had thought of Mary Jane and what he hoped the night would offer. He now realized his desires would have to wait.

On the outside of the gates, Brick walked past the preacher and another man in conversation. He wished he had the nerve to confront the two men and tell them to leave the revue alone. Instead, he just calmly walked past them. He played an entire confrontation out in his mind about how the revue was a legitimate business, and the girls had a right to make a living. Unfortunately, he knew even if he dared to confront the men, his words would do little good. Brick was disappointed and angry but still unwilling to do anything about it.

Brick overheard the larger of the men (the one he assumed was the ringleader) saying, "Tomorrow will be different, and people will finally take notice." He thought, Hadn't they already made enough trouble? He continued listening, and he heard the big one declaring, "I promise you, tomorrow the people of Sanford will finally see our resolve and learn we cannot and will not tolerate such sin." Brick just shook his head and wondered what made this overweight wanna-be preacher feel that he was the protector of others' morals.

Brick hoped he was right in his thinking that the preacher was just a crazed, misguided redneck. He refused to put much stock into the protesters. What bothered Brick the most was the fear Mary Jane was feeling. He knew her fear brought on by the protesters had sidelined his hopes for a special evening. That crazy bastard had already spoiled one night for Brick, and he certainly didn't want it to happen again. Brick questioned why. Why couldn't they leave everyone alone? Why did they choose this year to protest? This was the one year he was experiencing the carnie life from the inside. He was gaining an education on the life of a carnie, and the church was trying to close the school. Sadly, Brick knew his anger was misguided and more selfishness than worry.

Brick didn't see Ray's car and thought maybe he had suffered the same fate. Both had come to work with high hopes of an exciting night, but it appeared they both would have to wait for another day. He hoped the next day would bring new opportunities and better results.

Once again Brick began to think of Emily, now unable to separate his feelings for her from those he was feeling for Mary Jane. If only Emily had shown more interest in him and their relationship in the past, maybe this relationship with Mary Jane would not have developed. He couldn't blame Emily for his actions though; he certainly wasn't acting like someone who had a special girlfriend.

Brick was now feeling every bit of being eighteen, and the insecurities he had for both girls only added to his confusion. The sad truth was that Brick would be devastated if Emily ever found out about Mary Jane. He viewed Mary Jane as a mysterious and sensual older woman with life experiences he could only imagine until now. She was the undefined fruit of relationships. Although he had no real choice with either, he saw Emily the more desirable. He had fallen for her beauty and personality from the first time they spoke in school. Emily's innocence gave her the girl-next-door quality.

Once in his car, Brick turned the volume up on his radio, hoping the music would help drown out his conflicting thoughts. "These Eyes" by The Guess Who began to play. Maybe it was fate or just a coincidence, but either way the song rang true. Brick had more questions than answers when it came to girls.

Key and The Show

The success Beverly and Gail was having with the petition excited Beverly. Together they had collected close to a hundred names, all with support for shutting down the revue. Unfortunately, she was still fearful that her efforts would fail to ease Patrick's mind. She knew he was still contemplating the use of the firebombs, but she hoped he would at least recognize the value of the petition and begin to calm down. To Beverly, the petition indicated the protests were making a difference.

When she returned from the midway, she shared with Patrick how successful their efforts had been. She was pleased to tell him that some who had signed the petition suggested sending it to the local churches to create a grassroots movement to have the revue removed before next year's fair. Beverly thought this was a great idea and told him if he shared the petition with other churches that maybe he could begin gaining the respect he desired.

Beverly was happy that Patrick appeared to be encouraged with the petition, and he even thanked her. He then suggested she go out and collect more names the next day. He even said it seemed like a good idea to take the petition to the other churches. Beverly found hope in Patrick's response; maybe his attitude was changing. He appeared more reasonable and didn't mention his makeshift bombs. She could only pray that the petition was beginning to change Patrick's way of thinking.

Beverly considered the day a success even without any attention from the paper. If only the newspaper would do a feature on Patrick and his protest, he would surely find peace with himself and his actions.

Not long after Beverly and Gail returned, Bill and Maxine Porter, a couple from the congregation, stopped by and asked if there was anything they needed as they were leaving for the evening. Odom saw this as an opportunity to get Beverly and Gail away from the protest, so he suggested that they give Beverly and Gail a ride home. He told the ladies he would be home shortly, noting the protest was winding down for the day. He and Key had already decided to stay until closing. Odom told Beverly he wouldn't be late, noting the next day was going to be the busiest day yet. At first, she resisted but finally agreed after Patrick assured her, he wasn't going to do anything stupid.

Odom gave Beverly and Gail plenty of time to leave the fairgrounds. When he was sure they were gone, he became more vocal with his attack on the revue. His words were mean-spirited, creating more anger in the patrons and the workers. He was turning the peaceful protest into a distraction no one desired to be a part of. One of the couples protesting, the Millers, stayed for a short time, but Odom's verbal assault made them beg off. They told Odom they hoped to see him the next day, but they needed to get home. Odom was unaware that his actions were not increasing his following but instead were causing him to lose the support of his congregation.

Once everyone else had gone, and Odom was certain Beverly and Gail had made it home, Odom suggested Key walk around a little and then attend one of the shows. Key still had no desire to go into the tent and hoped he could put it off. He told Odom he was going to get something to eat and would consider taking in a show. He left the protest, bought a corn dog, and even tried his hand at the basketball throw. He was avoiding the show as long as possible.

At one of the games, Key placed two quarters on his birth month of April, and it came up a winner. His prize was a large stuffed mouse. Key was happy it was something he could give Gail, and he thought he may also be able to use it in some fashion to protect his identity if he did attend a show at the revue.

While Key had been participating in the protests, he had begun to see the merits of shutting down the revue. He believed something needed to be done but was hesitant to agree with Odom that bombing the shows was the answer. If the revue was going to close, it should be the result of orderly protests—not a violent attack.

Key had his share of negatives in his life, but now being part of the movement to close the shows had stirred his pride and caused him to view the wrong in the world differently. Maybe it was the chants or the signs; whatever it was, he had been changed by the protest and had developed a sincere distaste for the shows. Although he was against the shows and the sinful activity they represented, he still believed it was wrong to use the explosives to make a point. He didn't want people to be hurt, and the bombing would inevitably result in injuries and destruction. But he was a good soldier for Odom and would follow his wishes over his own personal objections.

Once it was obvious that Key was alone at the protest, he decided to attend a show at the revue. Carrying the large mouse, Key made his way to the counter and placed his two dollars down while resisting eye contact with anyone.

After he paid for his admission, Key went through the curtains, and there, just as he suspected, he entered a large open space for spectators with a small, wooden, elevated stage for the performers. The stage was an extension of a flatbed trailer with curtains separating the girl's dressing room from the patrons. There were steps leading to the stage with a No Trespassing sign in place. The simplicity of the layout surprised Key. He wasn't sure what to expect but was surprised there were no chairs; everyone was required to stand. Those who had preceded Key were standing around the stage—some even leaning on the platform. The men could eye the dancers, and in some cases try to touch them. Being one of the last ones in, Key had to stand away from the already crowded stage, and he hoped no one would recognize him as one of the protesters.

Key's curiosity began to grow as the first dancer appeared. He had not paid much attention to the introductions, but once the dancing started, he began to feel mixed emotions. He felt concern for the dancers, questioning their safety as the group of unruly men began to clamber to see and touch them, but he also felt a sense of arousal and intrigue as the dancers performed. It was clear that many of the men attending the show were under the influence of alcohol, creating more apprehension for Key. He wasn't there to police the show; he was there to learn how the show operated and where a well-placed Molotov cocktail would have the most impact. However, he couldn't help but worry about the dancers.

Key could have exited the show once he saw the layout, but he was not as strong as he claimed to be. The dancers enticed him, and as each appeared on stage, he felt as if he was drawn into a web of sin and seduction. He was ashamed and disgusted, but yet he was excited. The dancers moved in such a sensual manner that he began to question his resolve. Was he any better than the men who demanded the dancers make their way to their portion of the stage? These men hoped to touch the ladies as if they were at a petting zoo, and the show created an uneasy feeling for Key. Fortunately, for him the performance was short and ended quickly. When the dancers started encouraging everyone to return for more excitement, Key knew the show was over. He hurried out of the tent, hoping he would not to be spotted.

Rather than returning to Odom, Key decided to walk the midway. He needed more time to think and process his feelings. He was uncomfortable with his desire for the dancers, and he began to feel guilty. The uneasiness was nearly overwhelming. The dancers were seductive, and their glistening bodies had awakened his desire for sins of the flesh. Rather than accepting his weakness, Key needed to blame others for his sinful thoughts. He saw the dancers as mere pawns of evil, provoking unnatural desires with their tantalizing dances. Key's irrational thoughts were making him more entrenched to support Odom and his desire to bring the shows to a halt.

Friday at The Fair

Friday morning Beverly was full of hope that the day would be different. She believed in Patrick and the movement but also feared he may have lost sight of the main goal. Patrick's obsession with the protest had become unhealthy, and Beverly was afraid he may still consider a violent attack. She was aware of how his anger and frustration had led him to believe the community might favor the revue over the church. Beverly continued to take on the role of Miss Optimistic, reassuring Patrick he was making a difference, and people were learning of the protest and the church. She made it a point to remind him of the good he was doing and that he needed to see the benefits of the protests—and the petition. Although Odom was pleased with the petition, he didn't see how it would help grow the church.

Beverly had become more concerned about what Patrick could possibly do. She said to him, "Patrick, you're not planning on using those homemade Molotov cocktails, are you?"

Odom hated lying to her but felt he had no choice, telling her, "No, I'm not planning on using them. I'm hoping the day will be our best yet, and there will be no need for such violence."

The way he phrased his words, "… no need for such violence," concerned Beverly, but she resisted asking him any more questions. She knew Patrick sensed time was running out, and that only added to her concern over what he may do next. Beverly accepted the notion that she needed to continue to support Patrick and hoped he would get through the week with no violence.

Beverly asked what she and Gail could do. For Odom, this was perfect timing. Knowing he wouldn't be able to bring in the Molotov cocktails if she was with him, Odom seized the opportunity to tell her she and Gail should ride in with Key. He explained he hoped to make a couple of stops before going to the fairgrounds, telling her, "I want to go by the radio station one more time, and I want to stop by The Sanford Herald to try to get them to do something as well. I'll take the petition that you and Gail worked on and show it to them. Maybe they will see the strength of the protests and will be willing to finally cover our efforts."

Odom felt his plan had eased some of Beverly's fears. Regrettably, she failed to see his motivation for having her ride with Key. Odom was looking for a way to sneak the bombs in without her knowing. Odom hated deceiving her as she had always supported him in every effort, he made to grow the church, but this time he felt he had no choice; he couldn't allow her to stop the attack. Odom now believed his calling was stronger than the need for honesty with Beverly.

Although Beverly was encouraged, she still felt uneasy about Patrick and what he might do. At this time, all she could do was hope and pray that Odom would sense how much she believed in him and would not go through with his plan to attack the show. Before leaving, Beverly told Patrick she loved him and then added, "Patrick, I hope you realize you are making a difference. We have a lot to build on; we can be successful, but we can't do it if you are in jail."

Patrick hated hearing her words. It was as if she knew what he was going to do. Even though he knew she was right, he felt he had no other options, and he responded, "No one's going to jail—certainly not for a few words of protest."

He promised once again not to do anything that would bring shame to the church or their home. Beverly felt his words rang shallow, but she prayed he meant them.

Beverly soon left with the others, and Odom assured everyone he would see them shortly. Now alone, Odom began constructing the Molotov cocktails. He knew time was running out on his protest, but he was also aware using the bombs would be the act of a desperate man. His emotions were troublesome. If he did use the explosives, people would finally take notice and no longer would he be viewed as a sideshow or a joke, but such an attack would also be a betrayal of Beverly's love for him. He could only hope that Beverly would find it in her heart to forgive him. It was now time to get everyone's attention, and, if that involved violence, then so be it.

Odom did go by the radio station WEYE located in a Jonesboro shopping center. The receptionist was polite and thanked him for stopping by. He showed her the petition, explained the protest, and asked for the radio station to offer some coverage. She told him she would bring it to the attention of the station manager, and she took Odom's name and phone number so he could call Odom later. Odom felt it was a waste of time, not convinced she would even tell anyone, but at least he was honest with Beverly for this part of his story.

Odom decided not to go by the Herald office as he had been so frustrated with their lack of attention that he feared stopping by would only add to his anger.

When he arrived at the fair, the grounds were abuzz. He unloaded the extra signs and the Molotov cocktails, using a large cardboard box as a container to hide the explosives. When he reached the protest site, he put the box away from everyone, explaining it contained additional supplies, markers, and tape, etc., if needed to make more signs. Odom failed to mention the Molotov cocktails, preferring not to alarm or implicate anyone in the attack. He would not use the bombs until everyone else had left for the evening. It was his fight, and he would take full responsibility.

After he put the box down and joined the protesters, he felt a new sense of calm; he was at peace with the decision to use the bombs. He knew once the fires hit the tent that the news coverage and attention would become a reality for him and the church. It wouldn't be long now before everyone would learn of the Reverend Patrick Odom and The Revival Revolutionary Church.

The small group of protesters had taken their usual place outside the revue, chanting "Hi Ho, Hi Ho, the revue must go," and Beverly and Gail were already walking the midway trying to get more signatures.

Odom was aware of Key's knowledge of what was in the box but tried to remain calm. He told Key, out of sight, out of mind. But knew this would not apply to the box and its contents.

Trying to remain upbeat, Odom thanked everyone for being there. He then took his place with the other protesters and led them in a short prayer for guidance and support.

Friday for The Boys

Brick and Ray arrived at the fair, as usual, at seven o'clock on Friday morning. Both, knowing their week would soon be ending, couldn't help but think how it would be to tell their new friends goodbye. They also hoped they would have experienced more stories worth telling. Each of them was looking for more romance and adventure before the week officially came to an end.

The boys made their way to the office, and Raeford asked his standard question, "How's it going?" Both were ready for the week to be over, but they still told Raeford how much they had enjoyed working.

Brick added, "It's been a good week. I just wish those damn protesters would stop; they seem to be upsetting a lot of folks, especially the dancers."

Raeford shook his head and said, "Unfortunately, like I said before, we see more and more of these protests. I'm afraid things are changing, and I don't feel shows like the revue will be around much longer. I hate to say it, but the shows may soon be a memory—a historical chapter of the traveling carnival."

The boys were saddened by Raeford's bleak outlook for the shows, so Brick questioned Raeford, "You believe the protesters are that strong?"

Raeford responded, "Yeah, I'm afraid it's more than a protest. It's a movement that's gaining a lot of traction. So far, nothing has come of it except for frazzled nerves, but I fear others will take notice before long, and things will start changing."

Brick wanted to hear Raeford's thoughts on this group of protesters. "I don't really know what to make of this group," Raeford shared. "The leader seems particularly motivated, and he's nastier than the others we've encountered. Until now, the protests have been more peaceful—just carrying signs and marching. Some gave out flyers, but rarely did the protesters become verbally abusive. Personally, I feel he's a real son of a bitch and appears a little unstable, and that's always scary. I've asked to meet with him, and, so far, he has shown no interest in meeting. It's almost like he wants more than the shows shutting down."

Ray told Raeford he heard his father on the phone asking the police to check into the protesters, hoping to be able to quiet them down. Raeford said, "Yeah, I talked with your dad; he's a good man, and we both feel a stronger police presence is needed. This group is hard to figure out. Hopefully, we can get through the week with no incidents. I don't feel they will do much more than what they have already done, but Russell and I both agree it's best to be proactive."

Brick said, "Well, the guy doesn't appear to be much of a Christian with his words and fear tactics." Ray had to smile as Brick talked about Christian actions, especially considering how the two of them were hoping their week would turn out.

When Brick and Ray finished with the tickets, they received their assignments for the day. Raeford was expecting a large crowd again and told the boys they would be operating rides again. Although they had only been working for five days, both were beginning to tire of the work—but not the people. The work was starting to get old, and with the long hours, it was turning into a job more than an adventure. They both were ready for college. They found the job exciting, but now they were beginning to think of college and what it may hold for them. One thing, however, that remained alive with the boys was the thought of having a send-off from the fair that included more time with their new lady friends.

Both returned to the rides they had been operating on Thursday with the hopes it would not be for the entire day. Raeford indicated it might only be for the morning, but they would have to see how the day played out.

For Brick, the morning had been relatively slow at the Round-Up. For the most part, the crowds were made up of parents with young children or older adults, and none of them were interested in the Round-Up.

His morning improved when he was surprised by a visit from Mary Jane. Dressed in shorts and an oversized long-sleeve shirt, he found her as desirable as ever. Her mere presence brightened his day. Brick wasn't sure how to react after the disappointment he felt the previous night, but he smiled and tried to be upbeat as he said, "This is a nice surprise. How are you this morning?"

Mary Jane returned a quick smile but then said, "I've been better. The protesters have already set up, and we haven't even opened. They are still causing problems and making everyone uneasy."

Brick responded, "Don't let those bastards get to you; that's what they want."

Mary Jane continued, "I know, but they seem hell-bent on disruption. The leader is as abusive as ever. It's frightening! I feel as if he is following our every move, and he has such a menacing look; it's just damn creepy. I feel all of us are about to freak out."

Again, Brick wished he could confront the protesters. They were scaring people, and for what? The shows would be gone and forgotten in a day or two.

The two of them talked for a few minutes until Mary Jane said she needed to get back to her place but hoped to see him later. She then surprised Brick when she said, "I feel I may owe you an apology for last night."

With that simple statement, Brick was back on cloud nine. He wasn't sure what he had hoped to hear, but those words were nothing but encouraging. He told her he would definitely come by later, and she didn't need to apologize; after all, he understood how upset she was by the protesters.

Before she walked away, she gave him a hug and kissed him on the cheek. The kiss was confirmation to Brick that she did care for him, and he hoped the day would be better. After she was gone, Brick turned his attention back to the ride, and his excitement of being part of the fair had returned.

Ray was taking a break from the Mad Mouse, and he came by to see Brick. So far, the morning had been slow for both. Pete Smalls, who worked the Tilt-a-Whirl beside Brick, said he could handle both rides for a while and suggested he take a break with Ray. Brick told him he wouldn't be long and that maybe he could reciprocate when he returned.

They went to the Burger Wagon to get something to eat and to talk. Ray told him Jill wanted him to come by after work as she was going to be staying in one of the trailers, and they could be alone for a while. Brick couldn't tell if Ray was excited by the offer—or scared.

Both boys were feeling a sense of uncertainty when it came to their short-term romances. Since Donna was off at school, Jill offered quite a temptation for Ray. They both knew if either of their girlfriends found out how they had been fooling around that there would be hell to pay. For Brick, this may have been wishful thinking, but it indeed was the case for Ray. His situation with Donna was more defined than Brick's was with Emily. Everyone knew Ray and Donna as a couple, but no one, especially Brick, knew what type of relationship he and Emily shared.

Now that both had been working the whole week, their conversations were either about the girls or finishing up their jobs. Ray told Brick he was ready for school and Brick high-fived, saying, "Maybe it's time to learn something else. I've learned plenty this week, some things good and some not so good, but I'm ready to move on." Both smiled, knowing one thing for sure, they had stories to tell.

When they finished their snacks, both returned to their respective rides. Raeford came by later in the day and asked Brick how things were going and if he would mind staying at the Round-Up. Although this was not what Brick wanted to hear, he told Raeford he would be glad to. He even added that he had gotten used to running the ride, and with the crowds picking up, he knew he would be busy.

Busy or not, Brick continued to fantasize about Mary Jane and what he hoped the evening had in store for him, but he was still a bit nervous. He certainly wanted to be with her, but his usual lack of self-confidence could spoil the evening. Brick felt he had little to offer her but knew she had plenty to offer him.

Friday was turning out to be a hectic day. Brick felt the crowds were much larger than any of the prior days. Brick and Pete were kept busy running their rides. Fortunately, both were able to offer the other short breaks, swapping off running the rides. Brick was happy that the time was moving quickly as it prevented him from worrying about what the evening might bring. He did see a few friends—most hoping for a free ride. He was able to give some rides, but it all depended on how busy he was at the time they came by. He felt there was little harm in doing so, especially if no one was waiting in line. He ran the ride as if he had been working the fair all summer, and only a few would know he hadn't. The variety of people who enjoyed the ride surprised Brick; young and old, there were plenty of both. On this day, everyone seemed to be enjoying the attractions on the midway.

⚜

Friday for Odom

O dom continued his verbal assault on the revue. Although he tried to be disruptive, only a few seemed to notice. Occasionally, a customer would yell back at him, but those few instances were generally fueled by alcohol. Odom found energy when confronted by the drunks; at least someone was hearing him. Fortunately, no physical altercations occurred, and there was no need for police interventions. Odom mentioned to Key that there seemed to be more police walking the grounds than usual but felt it was due to the bigger crowds and had nothing to do with the protest.

As the day progressed, Odom became more empowered hyped up by his desire to use the homemade bombs. Rather than see the downside of using explosives, more and more, to Odom, it felt like it was the right thing to do. He was convinced now more than ever that using the explosives would result in the shows shutting down and the rise of The Revival Revolutionary Church. He believed that soon he would be hailed as a hero of the religious community. He was not only prepared to use the devices, but he was also anxious for the attack.

At nightfall, the crowds had grown to the largest yet, and Odom knew the time to use the bombs was nearing. Fortunately, he was rational enough to know he would need Beverly and Gail to leave before he could use the bombs. Even believing he was right, he didn't want to implicate them. Although his promise to Beverly not to use the bombs was shallow, he still felt a need to protect her from the violence.

Later in the evening, Odom complimented Beverly on the work she had done and told her she deserved some time away from the protest. Beverly was hesitant to leave, but she was tired; it had been a busy and stressful day. Odom assured her he would not do anything rash and that he and Key would stay only a few more hours. Beverly was too tired to offer any more resistance, so she gave him a gentle kiss and said, "Please be careful. You know I love you."

Odom felt it strange that she was asking him to be careful. Was it possible she had seen through his lies and knew what he was planning? He couldn't worry about that now. His mind was made up that he would go through with the attack. In his crazed mind, there was no other way to get his message across; he would bring the revue down one way or another. He believed it was not only necessary, but it was the right thing to do; he would be doing the Lord's work. Odom would shut down the sin factories in the name of the Lord, taking a stand and triumphing over the sin on display at the revue.

Odom waited nearly an hour after Beverly and Gail left. There were no other protesters remaining—just him and Key. He informed Key it was time to strike. Key remained hesitant to use the bombs, fearing the destructive results from such an attack. Key had been to jail before and certainly didn't want to go back. He also knew there was a high probability people would be hurt. Once again, he asked, "Patrick, do you really think this is necessary?"

Odom took offense to the question and replied, "Of course, it is. We are doing the Lord's work. The sin needs to stop, and it is our calling to serve the Lord."

Key made one last effort to change Odom's mind, but it was to no avail. Odom became angry once again, feeling Key failed to understand the need for such an attack. He told Key he could leave if he wanted to, but he was going to use the bombs—with or without him. He then pointed out to Key that the fire would bring down the revue as they had planned. Odom was determined that the citizens of Sanford would soon learn of The Revival Revolutionary Church and that the church would not tolerate the revue and its sinful activity.

Key felt Odom was talking like a crazy man and was not being rational. He began to look for an opportunity to leave, hoping maybe if Odom were left alone, he would change his mind. He looked nervously at Odom and said, "Listen, before you do anything, let me check the grounds. The last thing you need is for an innocent church member to be implicated in the attack. I'll make sure no one from the church is around."

Odom didn't object although he had a feeling Key had turned yellow on him. He felt Key was looking for a way out and was using the church members as an excuse. He felt Key would not return. Odom had told him to do what he felt was necessary as he had made it clear that the bombs would be used. Odom would not be stopped—not by Key or anyone else.

After Key left and the dancers were standing out front for the introductions, Odom decided it was time. He waited until the line of men had purchased their tickets and were behind the curtains where everyone was out of sight. For Odom, it was the time of reckoning. Even with it being late in the evening, there were plenty of people moving about the midway. With Payne gone and the dancers and patrons behind the curtains, the outside of the revue was left unattended.

Odom brought the box up to where he would be able to throw the bottles for the best results. Two of the bottles were sealed with rags. He pulled the rags out of the mouth of the bottles and began soaking them with gas, and once each rag was saturated, he stuffed them back into the bottles and prepared to light them with his lighter.

Odom quickly put his plan into action. Lighting the first rag, the flames leaped from the bottle. It was then that Odom hurled the fiery bottle toward the tent. When the first bomb left his hand, Odom had a rush of adrenalin and immediately lit the second. As he was lighting the second bottle, the first explosion rocked the outdoor stage, and flames leaped up to the entrance. Odom threw the second bomb toward the outdoor platform, and it began spreading flames. He could hear people screaming, and he was overtaken with fear. He knew he had made a mistake, but it was too late. The fire was spreading, and people were beginning to rush to the scene. There was no turning back. The damage was done.

With the flames' intensity growing, Odom was thinking, What have I done? The revue quickly became a flaming pit, and he turned to run. In the hysteria that was gripping the area, he ran through the gathering crowd. He was no longer enamored with the attack; he was a frightened sinner. His defiance had created fear along with destruction, and he ran. It was too late for repentance as the damage was beginning to spread.

Before the actual attack, Odom had plans to stand tall and address the crowds as the flames took over the revue, but no, he was not that strong. He was frightened, and all he could think about was getting away. Odom fled the burning site as fast as he could, but there was no escaping his destruction. He had become a victim of his anger and greed; it had overtaken him, turning him into an irrational criminal. He now feared his actions would lead to his downfall. No longer standing proud, he was panicking and trying to escape the evil he had created. His only hope of escape would be the confusion the fire had created.

Key heard the fire erupt and realized Odom had followed through with his plan. He now feared he would be recognized as one of Odom's followers and would be picked up by the police. Key knew he could not return to the site. He had to find a way to get away from the fairgrounds before anyone could place him with the attack.

Brick Hears The Attack

B rick heard an eerie sound; it was as if air had been sucked out of a room. Then the skies were filled with smoke, and he could hear people screaming. Brick thought it must have been an accident at one of the rides. He couldn't imagine the revue being bombed.

The smell of the fire was everywhere. Brick could not see the flames, but the smoke was climbing into the night air, and the cries of those near the fire gave him the feeling that someone may have been hurt. Chaos was everywhere, and Brick intuitively stopped the ride and began getting everyone off. No one complained about the abbreviated ride; everyone wanted to know what had happened.

Panic and fear were beginning to take over the midway. As Brick worked to get the riders off, he heard someone scream that there had been an explosion at one of the shows and a tent was on fire. He had a knot in the pit of his stomach as he feared it was the revue. He couldn't help but think that the crazy son-of-a-bitch preacher had done something. Brick was now panicking and feared something may have happened to the girls, especially Mary Jane. With things in such an uproar, no one was thinking of riding the Round-Up, and Brick decided to leave his post and run to the site of the fire.

As he ran toward the fire, he prayed that everyone was all right, but he feared for the worst. Brick wasn't the only person running toward the fire. Others had left their stations and were running to help. The attack had led to disarray throughout the grounds. When Brick reached the revue, the tent was engulfed in flames, and he could hear the cries of many. Several people were stunned by the explosion, and others were receiving help from volunteers. The scene was surreal. Men were laying on the ground, some with charred- smoked clothing. The area was in total chaos. Everywhere Brick looked, he could see the damage caused by the fire.

Frantically, Brick began looking for Mary Jane. He feared she may have been hurt by the explosion. He finally spotted her standing alone outside the fiery tent. She had tears rolling down her face, which was now covered with dirt and stained by the smoke. She appeared to be okay, even though she was half-clothed and noticeably shaken by the attack.

The flames rising from the destruction were intense, leaving many looking for help. Others were looking for answers to what had happened and who was responsible.

When Brick reached Mary Jane, he instinctively put his arms around her, and she fell into his embrace. At that moment, all Brick heard was the sound of Mary Jane crying. He tried to console her but found no words. He continued to hold her tight, hoping she would feel his support and love. Finally, Brick spoke, asking if she was all right. Through her tears she said, "I'm not sure. I was in the back of the tent, and an enormous blast knocked me to the ground. I was able to get up and run outside." She was shaking as Brick held on to her. Her smell was now that of smoke and burnt canvas. Brick couldn't see any physical wounds but could not imagine what might be going on with her mentally after such a shock.

Crying, Mary Jane began to ask about the others, questioning Brick if he had seen any of the other girls. She feared for Misty and Lucy as they had been the closest to the blast. Her emotions became raw with fear and she began to speak rapidly, questioning if everyone had gotten out and if anyone was hurt. She wasn't waiting for answers—just rambling with questions—continually asking about the others. Brick was unable to offer much information and was unsuccessful in calming her down. She was not herself.

Brick could see others were being treated everywhere he looked— some crying, others bleeding. Before long, Tammy came over—shaken and tearful. She first asked Mary Jane how she was doing and then wanted to know if she had seen any of the others.

Brick felt the area now resembled something you may see in the movies—not where you lived. The attack had left everyone in disbelief.

Brick held on to Mary Jane as she continued to tremble. With tears in her eyes, she now was asking why anyone would do such a thing.

Brick knew who was responsible. It had to have been the protesters. He asked Mary Jane if she had any idea what happened. Mary Jane's voice rose to a scream: "It was that man—that preacher! He did this; I know it was him! He's the one that set the fire! He's the one responsible for this terror!" Now, nearly hysterical, she continued to cry. As she cried, she told Brick, "No Christian would do this. That preacher is the evil one. He's crazy and needs to be punished. We dance to entertain, and he attacks to hurt others. He is the immoral one." Brick let her talk as there was not much he could do to calm her.

After several minutes, Brick noticed Ray coming their way. As he approached, he looked at Brick and said, "What the hell, man?"

Brick angrily responded, "I'm not sure, but I bet it was that son-of-a-bitch preacher. He must have used a firebomb to destroy the show."

Mary Jane quickly said, "Of course, it was that damn preacher! He did this! Who else would do such a thing?"

Ray, like Brick, was angry and worried. He asked if they had seen any of the others. Ray left before Brick could respond. He hoped to find out more, but he also wanted to see if Jill was okay.

An employee of Howard's soon came over with a blanket for Mary Jane. Once she wrapped herself up, she began to gain some composure. Her tears returned, though, when she heard sirens. Ambulances, fire trucks, and other law enforcement vehicles were coming onto the grounds.

The violence and resulting damage had unnerved many.

Brick only knew Mary Jane as a strong, independent woman, but now she was as vulnerable as a small child. As he held her, he realized how much he cared for her, and her vulnerability made her even more desirable. She was no different from any other girl; she had her ups and downs, disappointments, and fears. He now knew that Mary Jane was much more than a dancer; there was another side of her. She was now hurting and scared. Brick wondered if one could fall in love in only a few days.

Still not knowing what to say or do, Brick told her things would be okay; help was on the way, and they would catch the son of a bitch responsible. He emphasized she was safe now, and no one could hurt her or her friends.

Brick began leading her to one of the ambulances. It was there that he noticed Raeford assessing the damage as he moved through the crowd. He soon made his way to Brick and Mary Jane, asking if they were all right. Before anyone could answer, he insisted Mary Jane get checked out. An attendant began to ask her questions, and he checked her for injuries. She was surprised to learn of a small cut on her leg. Mary Jane insisted she was okay and began asking about the others. At that moment, Mary Jane spotted Misty on a stretcher outside one of the ambulances. She immediately ran to her.

Misty was conscious but seemed to be in a great deal of pain. With tears flowing, she said, "It looks like the preacher won after all."

Mary Jane defiantly said, "Oh no he didn't! He didn't win! Don't say that! We are stronger than him! He did not win!"

Tammy and Sugar saw Mary Jane with Misty and ran over to be with them. All four girls seemed to be in shock. As they cried, their anger was evident. It was wrong what the protesters had done. People had been hurt and property destroyed. An investigator from the sheriff's department soon came over and began asking the girls some questions.

As they prepared Misty to be taken to the hospital, Mary Jane clutched her hand and told her she loved her. Misty was placed in the ambulance, and the doors closed. The ambulance slowly moved off the grounds, and Mary Jane once again began to cry.

For most, the attack was something few had ever experienced, and this was especially true for Brick. The attack and resulting fire now left him with no idea what to expect. He was, however, impressed with the concern shown by everyone associated with Howard's Amusement. As he had been learning all week, those working the fair were family, and sadly, it was now a hurting family. Everyone's response to the attack showed the strength and love shared through a personal bond. Brick was seeing firsthand the importance of support for one another. He was also gaining a lesson on the impact of emotions. He now realized that no matter what someone does in life, they are not immune to feelings.

Maybe a result of the attack was how Mary Jane's actions had shown Brick she was much more than a dancer; she was a friend and a sister to the other girls, and she was a caring and loving person. Brick was gaining a major lesson in life, primarily that first impressions can be wrong. It was now reaffirmed that no matter what direction one's life takes, they still deserve respect.

As he witnessed the care being given, Brick became conscious of the thoughts he had been harboring for Mary Jane and the others. His adolescent, petty fantasies were just that; what mattered was how people treat one another. The attack gave Brick an education about people and life. No longer could he look at those working with a carnival as a curiosity. They were people who lived, worked, and were now suffering as anyone would be doing under such circumstances.

Brick also came to realize that his feelings for Mary Jane were greater than his sexual desires. He saw her as a friend in pain and in need of comfort and support. The protests had been bad enough, but it had now turned to violence, creating a dangerous and unsettling environment. People were attacked and their lives threatened. What led the preacher to be so violent and disruptive remained a question, but Brick knew the act of the preacher was not God's will. He believed the preacher failed to look beyond his prejudices and chose to act as the judge, jury, and executioner. The church teaches forgiveness and acceptance— not intolerance and anger. Brick may have been naïve, but he knew the preacher's actions were wrong.

Brick's parents and the church had raised him to care for people— not hurt them. He had been shielded from violence, never witnessing those he cared for being attacked, especially in such a cowardly fashion. Brick now realized he was part of the Howard's Amusements family, and he too was concerned for his fellow family members. In the short time he had known the workers of Howard's, he learned they could be friends and confidants, and that was especially true of Mary Jane.

Brick was now feeling anger, confusion, and passion. He was angry at the protesters, confused as to why anyone would do such a thing, and passionate about his feelings for the others. Brick knew that going into the next week his life would be changing with college, but there was no preparation for the change he was experiencing at this time.

Odom After The Attack

O nce Odom had let the bombs go, he ran from the scene. As he ran, he could hear people in pursuit yelling for him to stop, but he kept running. Odom (overweight and out of shape) had little chance of outrunning anyone. It wasn't long before a group of men caught up with him and wrestled him to the ground. He was held down by the force and weight of the men. Out of breath and frightened, Odom laid on the ground trembling. The fight he once had was now gone. Feeling the pressure of the men holding him down, he knew there woud be no escaping. He was powerless—not able to move or fight. His defiance was gone; he was a beaten man.

Lying under the weight of his capturers, Odom began to realize all he had worked for was gone; he was the villain—not the revue. With his face pressed against the ground, he could see the flames rising to the sky, and he could hear the screams. He would finally get the recognition he so desired, but at what cost? Odom began to feel remorse and started questioning his actions, but it was too late.

Odom was not the only one questioning the attack. He soon felt the presence of an angry group of bystanders surrounding him and shouting, "Why?" Why had Odom done it? With tempers raging, Odom was scared the group would turn their anger into a physical attack as he lay defenseless on the ground.

Odom got the attention he desired, but in doing so, he had created mass hysteria. He could hear voices identifying him as that crazy preacher—the one who had been protesting all week. He was called everything from a madman to a coward. Odom attacked innocent people and chose to run. Many questioned who he was—certainly not a God-fearing man but a low-life coward. The angry voices were soon replaced by the sirens of the police and fire trucks, and he was still unable to move. The weight of those holding him down was nothing compared to the burden of the guilt he was now feeling as he listened to the crying of those around him and watched the night air fill with smoke.

The police arrived quickly and pulled Odom to his feet. He stood in silence as they read him his rights and began searching him for weapons. The police asked his name and a series of other questions. Out of breath and still having difficulty breathing, Odom had few answers for the police. He was now alone, and he was scared.

Odom, feeling the brunt of his actions, began to panic. His defeated emotion was replaced with rage, and he began to strike out at the police. He screamed, "Why are you asking me these questions? I was doing God's work—the work you should have done the day the fair opened!" He was belligerent and now lashing out. He wanted to know why he was the only one being questioned and handcuffed. Odom kept screaming, "You don't reward God's people this way!" He became illrational, pleading to the onlookers. Didn't they realize he was serving the Lord? Why was he being singled out? "One day you will understand, and you will thank me."

Odom's declarations fell on deaf ears; no support was coming his way. He began scanning the crowd, now three to four deep, circling him. He saw no one from the church. He recognized no one. He was alone and now had to face the consequences of his actions. Odom was exhausted from his verbal outbreaks, and his defiance was short-lived. His mood returned to that of a defeated man. He now grasped the sad reality that after such an attack, he would never gain acceptance by the local clergy. He was nothing more than a common criminal, and he was left with only questions about what he had done and what it meant for his future.

As Odom was being escorted to a police car, he saw an ambulance pulling onto the fairgrounds, and he watched it begin to navigate its way through the people and rides. Seeing the ambulance intensified his fear. Had he hurt someone? This was not supposed to happen. He was only looking to make a public statement. He was taking a stand against the sinful activities of the revue. It was for the good of the city, and no one needed to get hurt. He had tried to lead the community in a movement that would peacefully end such immoral girly shows. Instead, it turned violent, and he was responsible for people possibly being hurt.

The police officers who took Odom to the car said nothing, and he was left alone with his thoughts. Placed in the back of the squad car, several police officers remained outside and began to talk—one wondering if he had acted alone. The group of officers began to speculate too on whether he had accomplices.

Odom started to think about the others who had been with him during the protest. He had chosen to act alone, and he alone was solely responsible. He was an emotional wreck. His anger accentuated the fear he felt. If only the paper had reported on the protests, such a violent act would not have been necessary. Odom felt lost; he was being arrested and would soon be taken to jail. This was not the ending he had visualized. What would become of him and his church? As he waited, he was left with more questions than answers.

When the police drove Odom off the grounds, he was able to see some of the chaos created from the attack. He saw many flashing lights—those of police cars, fire trucks and ambulances. The attack on the revue was getting plenty of attention now. He had made his statement all right but at a tremendous cost. As the car was pulling away from the fairgrounds, Odom wondered if the revue would finally close. He envisioned that it might but so would The Revival Revolutionary Church. No winners would come out of this attack— just losers—and Odom was the biggest. He could only wonder what his future would be like.

⚜

Brick and Mary Jane

As the fire was being extinguished and those injured were being treated, Brick sat with Mary Jane on a small staircase leading into the haunted house. Brick kept his arm around her, saying little. The scene of destruction left many to wonder what was to become of the show and the fair.

With tears still in her eyes, Mary Jane asked Brick, "Now what?" Brick wasn't sure if "Now what?" was a question or statement. He wanted to give her comfort, but he had no answer for "Now what?"

After thinking for a minute, he responded, "Hopefully, everyone will be okay, things will get back to normal, and the attack will soon be a bad memory." But Brick knew this would not be the case; the innocence of the fair was gone. He questioned how the revue could ever return after such a violent act.

Mary Jane dropped her head to his shoulder and said, "I'm not talking about the fair. I'm talking about me and my life. I have no idea what I will do or what's next for me."

Brick squeezed her a little tighter and told her not to worry about that right now as she should concentrate on getting better; there would be time later to discuss what's next.

It wasn't long before Raeford came by with some information. He said, "Thank God, no one appears to be seriously injured, but they are taking Misty and Lucy to the hospital for further evaluation. They'll probably be there for a while. Four customers were injured as well and taken to the hospital. It may not seem like it now, but I feel we were mighty damn lucky. This could have been so much worse."

Raeford's report failed to comfort Mary Jane, who was now emotionally spent. Raeford asked Brick if he would stay with Mary Jane for a while, feeling someone needed to be with her. Brick responded, "I'm not going anywhere." Hearing Brick's word's made Mary Jane smile. She thanked him and returned his hug.

They had been sitting for nearly an hour, and the crowds were beginning to thin out. The fire was extinguished, and the police were talking to several witnesses when Mary Jane asked Brick, "Can we go to my trailer? I need to clean myself up; maybe a shower will help me feel better." Before they left, Brick found Raeford to let him know he was taking Mary Jane to her trailer and to see if he needed anything.

Raeford replied, "Not right now, but I'm sure I'll need you in the morning. You should try to get some rest. I'll have someone close down your ride, and I'll see you later."

When they reached the trailer, Mary Jane asked Brick if he could stay the night as she didn't want to be alone. He smiled, telling her, "I'm here for you." Through her tears, she managed to come up with a small, but genuine, smile and thanked Brick for being there for her. He knew this was what he had been hoping for all this time but not under these circumstances.

They were seated in the living area of the trailer when she asked Brick if he would like something to drink: "I'm afraid all I have is Coke if that's okay."

Brick replied, "A Coke would be great."

She pulled out the drinks and with sadness in her voice said, "I guess Misty won't be home tonight. I wish I could see her." Brick told her he would take her to the hospital the next morning.

Mary Jane, still wrapped in the blanket, was covered with dirt and grime from the attack but needed a few minutes to unwind before going to shower. They sat for a short time in silence, and Brick could not help but believe she was contemplating her own answer to "Now what?"

Brick wasn't certain why Mary Jane chose this moment to tell him her story; maybe the exhaustion and fear she had felt were causing her to do some personal reflection. The reason didn't matter. She began to tell him her story. She started sharing a little of her background and how she came about working with Howard's Amusements: "I would've never believed my life would turn out this way. About this time last year, I was sitting in my dorm room at the University of South Carolina, preparing for my first year of college when I had an unexpected visit from my parents. They came to Columbia to tell me in person the news no one wants to hear. They were there to tell me Dale had been killed in Vietnam."

Tears again appeared in her eyes as she continued, "Dale was more than a boyfriend. He was the love of my life; he was my everything. We were going to create a life together. He wanted to complete his time in the Army before he went to college, but he never got the chance. He was going to be an engineer, and I was going to be a nurse. We were going to marry after he got out of the Army. We often talked about the day we would be together, raise our children, and grow old together. But he never returned from that damn war. He was killed in a helicopter crash in that Godforsaken land. His death changed everything. That damn war destroyed everything—all our hopes and dreams. I not only lost my soul mate; I lost my direction."

Brick was surprised to hear her story. Up until now she had shared close to nothing about her life. Although he had hoped to learn more about Mary Jane, this was not what he was expecting. She was now sharing a story of sorrow, leaving him to wonder where she found the strength to live. He was shocked by what she had told him. Death was an emotion he knew very little about. He had only known her for a few days, and she was now confiding in him about her life of disappointment. As Mary Jane shared her story of pain and distress, Brick began to see life differently. He now had a better understanding of life and how quickly it can change.

Mary Jane continued, "After Dale's funeral, I felt so alone. All I wanted to do was run. I resisted help. I was numb. That's how I ended up here. I had little direction, no money, and less hope. I was lost, and I wanted to escape. I chose to join the fair and travel from town to town with no attachments and little time for regrets. Working with Howard's allowed me to avoid my feelings. No one knew my story, and that's how I wanted it to be. Tonight's attack brought it all back: the sadness, my disappointment, and uncertainties I had been living with. That damn preacher destroyed more than the tent; he destroyed my escape."

Brick tried again to be supportive, telling her, "Listen, I may have just gotten to know you, but in the past few days, I've seen a lady not running or escaping; I've seen a lady who knows how to live. That son-of-a-bitch preacher didn't know you. He didn't know any of you. He was wrong, and he will pay for his sins. You don't need an escape plan. You have so much to offer others, and you are stronger than that man and the attack. We may have just met, but during the time we've been together, I've learned how special you are, and no attack or angry preacher will ever change that. I have seen the care and the love you have for others. You had it before the attack, and you certainly have it now."

Mary Jane was flattered with his kind words. She thanked him and then added, "I don't know what to do. My best friend is in the hospital, and the show is ruined. The little direction I did have is now gone. Ever since Dale's death, I've feared the unknown, and now, once again, it's staring me in the face."

Brick affectionally said, "You are not the show; you are more than the revue." His words even surprised him. The attack had affected him as well. His view of life was changing; he had received a lesson on pain and fear. The attack impacted everyone—Brick included. That preacher was the evil one—not the dancers or those attending the shows. The preacher was the one who attacked them, and he was wrong.

After a few minutes, Mary Jane stood up and said she needed a shower, and she thanked Brick for his kindness. Brick decided to escort her to the barracks and the shower, asking if there was anything she needed. She painfully replied, "No, I just want to wash the night off." He could tell she needed time alone to process everything that had happened. When they reached the barracks, Brick told her he would wait for her outside.

While she was in the shower, Brick called home to tell his parents he was okay and to share with them the news of the attack. He told them there had been protesters outside the revue all week, and the protest turned violent that evening. He wanted them to know he was fine and went into a little detail, telling them the show was attacked by firebombs, and the resulting fire had destroyed the tent. He added things were chaotic as a few people were transported to the hospital, and they had asked him to stay the evening to help wherever he could. He told his mother he would talk to her the next morning and not to worry.

❧

Odom to Jail

The officers took Odom to the local detention center where he was charged with suspicion of arson and the endangerment of others. The booking was quick, and he was informed his charges would most likely be upgraded once the investigation was complete.

Odom was processed and fingerprinted before an officer escorted him into a small holding cell off the main lobby at the jail. Few words were exchanged as the jailer placed Odom into the confined space. The cell was little more than an eight-by-eight-foot room with a sink and toilet in the back and an uninviting cot with a plastic covered mattress—nothing else. The officer then took Odom's personal items, including his belt and shoelaces, in order to prevent him from self-harm.

Once alone in the confined space, Odom had plenty of time to think about what he had done as well as what may become of him. The Molotov cocktails had hit their target with accuracy, leaving the revue in a fiery mess. The fire had caused damage not only to property but to people as well. Innocent people had been harmed in the attack, and he feared the penalties he would be facing. Odom knew he was in serious trouble.

The homemade firebombs Odom used brought destruction and pain, and he was now left with the reality that he was responsible for it all. There was no avoiding the fact that he was in the wrong, and there was nothing he could do to change that. His only option was to face the consequences of his behavior.

Odom took a seat on the cot in the dimly lit cell and began thinking of Beverly and how she would react to the news of the attack. He had dishonored her by breaking his promise to not use the bombs, and it was her reaction he feared most. Odom prayed she would find the courage to come to the jail to visit him. He wanted to see her and needed to talk with her, but he worried he may have destroyed not only the love she felt for him but their marriage also.

Odom then began thinking of Hinson, and he wondered how he would react to the news. He was confident the fire had created enough damage to the revue that it would not be able to continue operating for some time. Wasn't closing the revue what Hinson wanted? After all, Hinson was the one who wanted to make a statement against the sinful activity promoted by the revue. Odom had accomplished both— making a statement and closing the show. Odom knew he would need Hinson's assistance, and in his mind, he questioned if any would be forthcoming. He feared Hinson would try to distance himself from the attack and run—just as Key had done.

Now becoming angry with Hinson, Odom's emotional roller coaster began to turn to anger once again. He felt as if there would be no help coming from Hinson in his time of need. The protest, after all, was Hinson's idea, and if he had been more supportive, maybe the fiery conclusion could have been avoided. Odom now wondered if Hinson would even acknowledge that he was one of his followers in the war against the girly shows. Odom felt Hinson had some responsibility as he was the one who orchestrated the protest. Even though Odom had allowed his emotions to overtake him, Hinson still should take some responsibility. The protest was to be the start of a new Revival Revolutionary Church, increasing membership and its community status. But here was Odom; he was all alone in a tiny cell with no congregation and no public support—alone while facing fears and an uncertain future.

Odom finally came to the realization he would be the one punished—not Hinson, not Key, not any of the other protesters. He was fully responsible for the attack, and he alone would have to deal with the penalty. He started thinking about the last few days and what had precipitated his vengeful actions. He was searching for answers as to why the protests had failed.

In the beginning, he had no interest in destroying property and certainly didn't want to hurt anyone. All he wanted to do was make a statement and create a movement—a movement others would be proud to join. Was there anything he could have done differently? If only the media had paid them some attention, none of this would have been necessary. But he acted out of anger and frustration, and he was left wishing he had taken better control of his emotions. Unfortunately, his desire for publicity led him astray.

Odom's main objective was to grow the church, seeing the movement at the beginning as a path to do just that. Unfortunately, the movement became personal, and Odom's desire for success outweighed any rational thoughts he had. His hope of creating a large church was misplaced; he had gone from preacher to criminal in just a few days.

Back at The Fair

As Brick noticed Mary Jane had finished her shower and he sensed she was pleased to see him waiting for her. Brick smiled and asked her if she was feeling better. She replied, "I do, thank you, and thanks for waiting for me." There was a peaceful sound in her voice as she approached him. She was wrapped in a white, cotton robe and carrying her clothes, no longer covered with reminders of the attack. Brick once again was drawn to her radiant beauty. It was as if the shower had not only cleansed her body but her soul as well.

When they returned to the trailer and before either could sit down, Mary Jane took Brick's hand and led him to her bedroom. They exchanged no words as she became the aggressor and passionately kissed him. She allowed her robe to open, and when the tie fell to the side, her beautiful body was exposed. Brick now understood she was making herself available to him; he was being invited into a world he had only visited in his fantasies. The fresh, clean smell of her body was as welcoming as her beauty; it filled the room with an intoxicating aroma just adding to Brick's desire.

Brick became hypnotized by her every movement. Slowly, she began to unbutton his shirt. His excitement was hard to control; he quickly started to help her, but she kissed him and insisted she would do it, telling him, "Let me."

Shortly, his shirt was tossed aside, and she then loosened his belt to remove his pants. The robe then fell to the side and the two of them were standing nude before each other—two naked bodies awaiting a connection. Brick's heart raced even harder; he had never experienced anything as exciting as this shared moment. It was as if the heavens had opened up, welcoming him inside. His desire and love for her became one; it was unbelievable.

Although Brick's fantasies were coming to life, he was uncertain as to what would happen next. He placed his arms around her and as they kissed their bodies fell to the white sheets covering the bed. Brick's lust for her was replaced with unbridled passion, and they soon began to make love. His desire was unleashed, empowered not by his actions but rather by the love he felt for Mary Jane.

As they laid in bed near exhaustion, Brick told Mary Jane he might be falling in love with her. Those were the first words spoken, and it shocked him when he said them. What did he know about love? Yet, he said them with such conviction. Was he falling in love with her, or was it an attempt to describe the experience? Brick found himself even more confused. Mary Jane didn't respond; maybe she didn't hear him. Was it possible he hadn't said the words but had just thought them? There was much confusion in his head and yet such euphoria.

Until now, Brick's lovemaking had been confined to dreams and reckless teenage sexual exploits. He had never experienced such passion, leaving him nothing to compare with what he was feeling. He felt he had moved into manhood. There would be no returning to his high school fantasies now that he had made love to a beautiful woman—a woman who needed him, a woman who was vulnerable, and a woman who saw him as her refuge.

If Mary Jane did hear Brick's words, she gave no indication. Maybe the words were more passion taking hold of Brick than genuine love; either way, she never responded, and Brick never repeated to them again. At that moment, Brick took Mary Jane into his arms and kissed her lightly. The two of them then fell into a deep sleep.

❦

Odom Waits in Jail

The time Odom was spending in the tiny cell was starting to wear him down. There was no one around who could answer some of the questions that were haunting him. Did anyone get hurt? Was the revue destroyed? Would the fair have to shut down? More questions than answers left Odom unable to sleep. The lack of information, the lack of sleep, and no answers to his questions were now affecting his thinking. He felt it had been hours since he had been booked and placed in the cell, and now his frustration over not knowing anything was making him crazy.

Another point of irritation for Odom was the fact no one had yet come to his defense. No one, not even the police, had bothered to talk with him. With no information, he could only assume the worst. His agitation rose with each passing hour. Why was he still in jail? No doubt, word of the attack had spread. Why had no one from the church come to his aid? Did he not have any supporters? Thus far, nothing was happening.

He now questioned Beverly's response. Why had she not visited? He assumed she had learned of his arrest. He had the right to make a phone call. Did he need to call her? He knew why he hadn't called her; it was his fear of rejection. After all, he had lied to her and broke her trust.

The isolation was too much to handle. He was agitated, angry, and fearful; he could only see himself as a failure.

Where was Key? Did he just run? Would he come to the jail to check on him? What Odom did not know was that Key had returned to the scene of the attack. Key wanted to see firsthand the damage created by Odom and the bombs. At first, he feared he might be stopped and questioned, but his curiosity outweighed his fears.

With all the commotion, no one paid any attention to Key. He was happy that he wasn't recognized as one of the protesters. He fit right in with the rest of the curious patrons. Key was immediately impressed with the number of news people surrounding the smoldering ruins of the revue; there were television, radio, and print media from all over. Key felt it sad that the protest failed to bring the kind of attention Odom had hoped for, but now his violent act was being covered extensively. The reports would be negative for Odom and his church.

Odom's actions would put Sanford on the front page of papers across the state. Now arrested and sitting in jail Odom could not realize how much publicity he was now getting the news reports were identifying The Revival Revolutionary Church and its preacher, Patrick Odom, as those responsible. The damage from the attack was more than Odom could have imagined. The fire had destroyed the stage area, leaving the tent in a smoldering pile. Odom had gotten his wish, and there was no way the revue could reopen in Sanford.

Now identified as a crime scene, the tent area was being taped off. Key felt it was sad that Odom would not be able to rejoice in his success; he had closed the show and brought attention to his movement. But no, Odom would remain in jail for some time.

While Key was studying the damage, he noticed police officers collecting the signs that had been left behind. When Odom chose to run, he left all the evidence the police would need to convict him. Seeing the police going over the protest site caused Key to fear he may be recognized as one of the protesters, so he decided to leave the scene as he didn't want to take a chance at being implicated in the attack. As he was leaving, he walked past law enforcement officers and firefighters. He heard them talking about the attack being the biggest catastrophe to hit Sanford in quite some time.

Key knew Odom would want to know about the publicity the attack was receiving. He thought about going to the jail to check on Odom and to report that there was no way the show would now be able to continue, however, he quickly began to rethink this idea. He was afraid if he went to the detention center, he may be identified as a suspect. Using his better judgment, he made the decision to stay away; he would just wait it out. Maybe he could see Odom later after things had calmed down, but for now he chose to remain silent, feeling it would be better to keep out of sight.

Saturday Morning

The bright sunlight streaming through the window awoke Brick. Lying beside Mary Jane, he began replaying the events of the previous evening; the horror and the pleasure both played in his head. Although his fantasies had become a reality, he had to wonder at what price for him, Mary Jane, and Howard's Amusements. He grew restless, wanting to know more about the attack and what the day would hold. First, Brick needed to know if the fair would open as usual, and he then wondered about the others hurt. He quietly rose to put his clothes on.

Mary Jane was stirred by his actions. She was barely awake as she turned to him with a smile and said, "Good morning."

Brick was still excited about the evening they shared and told her good morning. Unfortunately, he was feeling some guilt about everything that had happened between the two of them and what it said about his feelings for Emily. His mind was full of unanswered questions—some about Mary Jane, some about Emily, and many about what his future held. Brick also questioned why he felt he could live out his fantasy with Mary Jane and feel guilty. Had he taken advantage of Mary Jane when she was most vulnerable? And Emily— what did this say about him and his feelings for her?

Brick, needing some time away to think about everything, said to Mary Jane, "Why don't you go back to sleep, and I'll try to find out what's going on today. I'll see if I can get any information about Misty and Lucy, and I'll be back shortly."

Mary Jane softly responded, "Thank you." She rolled over so she wouldn't face the sunlight and tried to go back to sleep.

Brick wasn't sure what to expect. He was questioning if the fair would even open, and if it did, would he need to work? As he began walking from the trailer, he sensed things were still up in the air about whether they would open or just move on. Everyone was concerned, not knowing if they should start packing up and traveling to Tarboro. It seemed most wanted to stay and finish out the run, but all that was yet to be decided. Brick felt if they did open, it would be a message to those protesting that they may have won the night—but not the week.

When Brick reached the midway, he saw many police officers—even more as he got closer to the scene of the fire. The yellow police tape was now marking the area as a crime scene.

Historically, Saturday would be the fair's busiest day, but with the attack and its destruction, no one knew what the day would hold. Brick spotted Laura near one of the rides and asked if she knew anything about the plans for the day. She replied, "No word yet on whether we will open or not. It is still undecided, but if we do I feel it will only be with police approval."

She then asked how he was holding up. Brick told her he just didn't know what to think; it was such a cowardly act, and there was no need for it. He then told her he was going to the office to see if he could catch up with Raeford. Laura said, "I'm not sure you will find him there. He's been at the scene of the fire most of the night. I'm just hoping he lets us know soon one way or the other about today."

Before Brick reached the office, he heard Ray calling out to him and asking, "Have you heard whether we are going to open or not?" Brick told him he had just gotten up and had no information.

Both boys seemed somewhat disheveled from an eventful evening. They were happy to see each other, but neither knew what to say or think. Both had been affected by the attack and were struggling with their thoughts of the protests and the people who worked the fair. Ray told Brick he stayed in the barracks overnight, not one of the trailers, adding it was so late when things settled down that he wasn't going to go home. Jill was pretty shook-up by the attack and didn't want to be alone.

Betty Anne was in the office and happy to see them. She was working as usual, but it was apparent she was disturbed by everything that had happened. Unfortunately, she had very little information to share. Betty Anne indicated the decision to open was still up in the air.

She echoed what Laura had said, Raeford had been up most of the night working with the police. From what she understood, a decision would be made later, depending on the recommendations of the police. She asked if they had talked with anyone.

Brick responded, "I spoke with Laura, and she was okay. She had no information though. I did hear others talking while I was walking around, and some were questioning if the fair should move on from Sanford, and others were hoping to open—a lot of speculation and few answers."

Ray remarked that it was rather quiet outside, and he felt everyone was still processing everything. Neither Brick nor Ray gave any details of their evening.

After a few minutes, Betty Anne suggested they go to the site of the revue. She felt Raeford would be back there soon as he had gone to get something to eat. As they were leaving, she again shared that this attack was the first they had ever witnessed. There had been protests before, but none had ever turned violent.

Brick asked how Misty and Lucy were doing. Betty Anne told them she understood they were still in the hospital, but she didn't think their injuries were serious; they were keeping them more as a precaution. She had no information on the others who were hurt during the attack.

Brick shook his head as he said, "That damn preacher—what the hell was he thinking?"

Betty Anne responded, "That's just it. I don't believe he was thinking. Maybe you can find out more from Raeford."

Brick and Ray took time to look over the destruction at the site of the revue. The fire had been extinguished, but the damage it created was a sad reminder of the attack. The canvas tarps once used to market the revue laid on the ground—charred and ruined. The colorful pictures of dancing girls were left smoldering. The fire must have spread rapidly; the stage was destroyed with little being left of any value. The scene was horrific, but both knew it could have been much worse.

The revue wasn't the only thing ruined by the fire. The attack had killed the innocence of the fair for many—especially for Brick and Ray. No one was comfortable with what had taken place, and many were left speechless and sad.

Brick and Ray spotted Raeford talking with a police officer near the center of the attraction. He noticed the boys and motioned them over. Raeford looked as if he had been up most of the night.

Raeford asked if they were doing okay, but before they could answer, he told them he hoped they were planning on working. They could tell that Raeford had a lot on his mind. Ray then asked if the fair would be opening. Raeford replied, "That's what we were discussing, but either way I'm going to need you boys to work. I know some would like to put all this behind them and move on to Tarboro. I'm going to leave it up to them, but if they want to pack up and leave, they will need your help. I'm hoping most will stay, and we'll be able to open with the help of the police department." He knew there would be tension and some uneasiness but hoped things could resume in some fashion.

Ray told him he had stayed in the barracks, and everyone seemed to be on edge. Raeford acknowledged the attack created a lot of fear and then added, "I'm just hoping everyone realizes this occurrence was an isolated incident. The protesters were there to wreak havoc on one sideshow, and now that show is closed. Since an arrest has been made, I don't feel we'll have any more protests or violence."

Brick asked about Misty and Lucy. Raeford told them he hoped to go to the hospital and check on them as soon as possible, and he would also try to find out something about the men who were hurt. He then said, "I'm hoping to bring Misty and Lucy back with me. In my twenty plus years, I've never seen anything like this; that idiot could have killed somebody. Thank God he didn't. It could have been horrific."

Raeford then asked Ray if he had spoken to his father. "I called him last night, and he was trying to monitor things from home. He said he would be here as soon as he could this morning."

Brick and Ray were asked to go back to the office and help Betty Anne with the ticket count and distribution even if no one was certain the fair would be opening. Brick felt Raeford's compassion when he asked them, "When you make the delivery, tell everyone we are planning on opening unless they hear otherwise. It's important that we prepare, and I hope there's a need. If anybody asks about shutting down and moving on, tell them that's fine; it's their decision. In light of what happened, I'm not going to strong-arm anyone to stay open."

Before leaving the scene, Brick and Ray took another look at the damage. Both were still in disbelief that such a thing could happen in their hometown. They hoped the fair would open, but they knew, even if it did, the fire would have a lasting effect on everyone.

Both boys resisted talking about their previous night with the girls. They were genuinely concerned about their friends and not interested in telling any war stories.

Betty Anne was pleased to learn Raeford wanted the show to go on. It was her feeling that opening back up would be a strong message to everyone that Howard's Amusements would not be intimidated. With much conviction, she said, "The protesters have caused enough damage. We can't just roll over and let them win. I don't get the feeling that anyone wants to run. Howard's Amusements stands for a lot more than that preacher realized. He was wrong, and we need to prove it by staying open."

Even with the evening's chaos, most of the rides and games had turned in their tickets. With Betty Anne's help, they were able to account for the previous day's activities, and Brick and Ray distributed the tickets for Saturday with little trouble. The attack had undoubtedly altered the mood of those working. There was no question the firebombing had frayed many nerves. Fortunately, most of the operators were happy to learn they would possibly be opening, but they also feared the attack would negatively affect attendance.

It was about thirty minutes before opening time when Brick heard Raeford make an announcement over the loud speaker. He thanked everyone for their patience and then announced they would be opening. The gates would open at the regular time, and the fair would go on as planned. With the announcement, applause broke out across the fairgrounds.

Raeford reminded everyone to continue being on the lookout for anything that looked suspicious, but it was the feelings of the police and fair management that the attack was an isolated event that targeted the revue. He then said they were very lucky no one was seriously injured, and he then gave an update on Misty and Lucy. They would be released from the hospital later that morning and would be returning soon. Again, there was applause.

Raeford then asked everyone to bow their heads in prayer, and he prayed for safety and tolerance. Brick was impressed that Raeford had chosen to pray. He proved to Brick once again that Howard's Amusements was indeed a large family with everyone caring for one another.

Once Brick and Ray heard the announcement, they went looking for Raeford, hoping to learn what their assignments would be for the day. Raeford was pleased to learn everyone would be staying open, and no one was planning on shutting down or leaving early. Raeford said, "I'm not sure how busy we will be. It could be a banner day with attendees as well as curiosity seekers, or it could be a flop due to folks feeling the need to stay away. I guess we will just have to wait and see what happens."

With the ticket distribution completed, he told the boys to check with some of the attractions and see if anyone needed anything, and then they could take some time off. Raeford said, "I know you boys are tired. Come back to the office around two o'clock this afternoon, and I should have a better idea of what may need to be done." Raeford was exhausted, and he still needed to go to the hospital.

Both welcomed the opportunity for some free time. They wanted to check on the girls, but they also needed to clean up a little. For them, what had started as a fun adventure had taken a serious turn, giving both much to consider. They had learned about themselves, but they had also received a lesson on human nature, and a few of their discoveries were not a welcomed feat.

Beverly's Visit

W hen morning arrived, Odom was still alone in his cell. No one had bothered to talk with him during the night, leaving plenty of time for him to ponder his actions. Not having any information made it even more difficult. Still covered in grime and dirt, he felt dirty and ashamed. He was a beaten and defeated man and could only question what lay ahead for him.

It was long after the sun came up that the jailer brought him something to eat. Odom didn't need food; he needed answers, and he needed someone to talk with. He was frightened and alone. Odom tried to speak with the jailer, but he had little to say—only leaving the tray of food and then exiting the cell. Unable to eat, he fell to his knees, and there he began to pray. He asked the Lord for forgiveness and direction. What could he do? It may have been the first time he had ever genuinely prayed. He began to reflect on all his sermons and realized how hypocritical he had been. If he ever needed divine intervention, it was now. After Odom stopped praying, he began pacing in the small cell.

Where was Beverly? Why wouldn't she see him? Did she even know he was in jail? How about Key? Why hadn't he come? After all, Key had been a part of the plan. He knew the bombs were going to be used to bring down the revue. Key had some responsibility in this. Why hadn't he been to the jail?

As he paced, Odom began talking to himself, voicing his fears, anxiety, and the need to speak with someone. He still had no answers when a police officer by the name of Wagner finally came to his cell. He told Odom they believed he didn't act alone, and they were searching for others, adding it would be in his best interest if he would share all he knew about the attack and identify anyone else involved.

Odom, though angry and frustrated, knew he had acted alone. Sure, there were others who took part in the protest, but the attack was his responsibility. He didn't want to implicate Beverly or Gail, and he saw little need for anyone else to suffer. It would be hard enough for Beverly without pulling her into the attack. There seemed little reason for Odom to deny his actions, and he decided to confess, telling Officer Wagner he had acted alone. None of the other protesters had any knowledge of his plan to use the firebombs.

The policeman said, "Suit yourself. It's totally up to you, but we know you had others with you."

Odom responded, "There were others with me at the protest, but they had nothing to do with the attack." Odom had little hope, but he now knew he must take full responsibility. He was the one who had made a mess of things, and there was little he could do now to change his future.

Finally, after what seemed like an eternity, the jailer came to get Odom and told him he had a visitor but did not give him the visitor's name. An officer escorted Odom to a visitation area. There, he saw Beverly, and the two of them immediately rushed to each other. Beverly was relieved Odom wasn't hurt. Still, her anger was so intense that she almost instantly screamed, "Why, Patrick, why?" Odom had no answer; he had abandoned her and their church.

Beverly began to cry, asking what in the world they were going to do now. Regrettably, there were no answers that would have quieted her anger. Through her tears, she asked, "Patrick, what's going to happen with everything we have worked so hard for?" Odom began telling her how sorry he was and how he realized now the mistakes he had made. Their future was in the hands of the authorities, leaving both feeling helpless and scared.

Although Odom had begun the ministry with questionable motives and little calling, he was now turning to the Lord for help. He needed direction and strength in handling the mess he had made. Beverly had always been a firm believer in God, and she also believed in Odom, but now she wasn't sure what to think. With tears filling her eyes, she cried, telling Odom, "The church may have been small, but it was growing. People believed in you, but how could anyone believe in you now?" Beverly again asked, "How could you do such a thing, Patrick? You promised…you promised me you wouldn't do this!"

Odom shook his head, saying, "I felt like I had no choice. No one cared about the protests. They weren't working. The shows went on as if we weren't even there."

Beverly was defiant with her anger when she said, "I cared, and those who followed you cared. You are the one who didn't believe in you. You were wrong, Patrick!"

Odom lowered his head and began to cry, telling her she was right; he had allowed his temper and greed to take control of him. He could barely speak as he said, "I know I made a mistake; I allowed my anger to overtake me and destroy our mission. I lost sight of what was right and what was wrong. I am so sorry."

Beverly began wiping his tears, telling him, "Patrick, you hurt people; you destroyed property; you let others down. People didn't need to be hurt. The attack was wrong, Patrick; you were wrong! How can you face your congregation after doing such a thing? You need to pray—and pray some more—for forgiveness."

Patrick had not given much thought to the church or the congregation. He was more concerned about Beverly. He needed her love and support more than he needed the church. He knew if he was going to survive this self-inflicted turmoil, he would need her beside him. Odom knew she was right; the harm the fire caused would mark him forever. He now questioned if he could ever repair his life. His unhealthy desire for acceptance and fame had destroyed him.

Odom was a broken man. He started begging Beverly for forgiveness, telling her how much he loved her and how much he needed her. He told her that while he was alone in the cell, he started to see a lot of things about himself he wasn't happy with.

Odom understood the evil he had done and was ready to accept responsibility for his actions. He knew amends needed to be made to her and those he had hurt. He pleaded, "I promise I can change, Beverly, but I need for you to please give me another chance. Beverly, without a doubt, the attack affected me more than I thought it would. I vow to you that I will become a better person and a better Christian. Please give me a chance to prove myself to you." Beverly was witnessing a broken, vulnerable man begging for help.

Beverly was lost in her thoughts, wondering how he could have been so stupid. Did he really think he could burn down an attraction and walk away without being punished? She tried to conceal her tears, but whenever she attempted to speak, she would begin to cry again. Beverly loved Patrick for who he was and not for what he hoped to be, but to Odom, it never seemed to be enough.

After a few minutes of silence, Beverly gained her composure enough to ask him if there was anyone, he needed her to call or if there was anything she should be doing. Odom, who once felt he could control the world, was now a sad shell of an individual. His guilt was apparent as he said, "Beverly, I feel hopeless. I don't know what to do." Odom could not hold back the tears, and he reached for her hand, saying, "You don't deserve to be tangled up in the web of destruction I have created." She took him in her arms, holding him as if he were a defenseless child. She told him she would be there, and together they would get through it. Odom knew it wouldn't be easy, but Beverly just held on to him and repeated her words, "We will get through it."

Back at The Fair

When Brick returned to Mary Jane, she was up, dressed, and appeared relaxed. Greeting Brick with a kiss, she said, "I'm glad you're back. I was afraid I might have scared you off last night." Brick smiled and told her there was no way that would happen. Mary Jane gave him an affectionate hug and told him thanks. Brick felt there was no need for any kind of thanks. He was doing what he wanted to do—and that was being with her.

Brick thought how nice it was to see that her smile had now replaced her tears, but he was somewhat puzzled with her demeanor after such a traumatic night; she seemed more relaxed and self-assured. Mary Jane was no longer the scared girl he had held during the night. Brick knew he had been changed by the evening he spent with her, but he now wondered about Mary Jane and her reaction to everything. He felt more like an adult and no longer a teenager with adolescent thoughts. It now seemed to him that Mary Jane had changed as well.

With a look of calmness on her face, Mary Jane said, "I need to tell you something. I've been doing a lot of thinking since I woke up this morning. The bombing of the show last night was terrible, but it was also enlightening. After you left this morning, I started doing a personal inventory. For the last few hours, I've been thinking about my life and my future. I want to thank you for the love and caring you showed me, especially last night. It's been a long time since I've felt such passion and love. You exposed me to the fact there is more to life than what I've been living.

"When Dale died, I lost so much. Not only did I lose him, but I also lost my way. I walked away from school and started running—running from the pain and the loneliness. You could say, I was numb to life. The girl you watched dancing every night wasn't really me. I'm not sure who it was, but it wasn't me. Before Dale's death, I had hopes and dreams just like everyone else. I felt I had things to offer, but when he died, I saw no need to go on. I was struggling with his death, myself, and my life. Joining Howard's Amusements allowed me to be anonymous; I didn't have to be anything or anybody. I could just exist. Traveling to strange towns and seeing nameless people gave me a chance to avoid my demons—spend one week here, one week there, and move on. I never took the time to process my feelings; I was running. This week has been different though; maybe that preacher was a blessing. Once the attack occurred, it was as if an emotional dam had burst. I was finally able to cry and mourn not only Dale's death but also the death of my hopes."

Brick sat there stunned, not knowing how to respond. He finally found the courage to say, "Mary Jane, I hope you know, you are a much better person than you're giving yourself credit for. It was you who made me feel welcome, and it was you who gave me the confidence to do things I had only dreamed of."

Mary Jane reached out for Brick, telling him, "That's sweet, but you don't know me. This last year, all I've done is avoid life. I have been running from all things personal, especially my emotions. I've been void of direction. I have been going through the motions, but I wasn't living. Then you and that crazy preacher entered my life."

Brick smiled as he said, "The preacher and me, huh! Not so sure that is a compliment."

Mary Jane gently slapped his arm and said, "Listen, I'm serious! You and that preacher taught me a lot this week. Both of you impacted my life but in different ways, of course. It was your kindness and his attack that led me to think about my life—something I haven't done for nearly a year. I haven't wanted to take any risks or believe in anything, but that began to change this week.

"When we met, you helped me discover that girl I used to be. You were sweet and sincere. I don't remember the last time I've allowed anyone to enter my space, but you came into my life, and I began to change. I don't know what it was; maybe it was the attention you gave me. All I know is it was different, and it reminded me of what I had at one time. I have not always been a carnie stripper. I was a girlfriend, a daughter, and a friend, but all of that seemed to vanish when Dale died. It was as if I died with him. I stopped living; I just existed. I felt I didn't deserve to be happy. How could I be happy? Dale was dead.

"Then you came into my life. First, it was your innocence that made me smile. I was attracted to that boy filled with wonder and desire. You showed me respect; you showed me friendship; then, last night you showed me love and passion. I haven't felt that way for a long time. It was a reawakening for me. You accepted me as a friend and a lover. From you, I learned that people still care, and maybe I should care as well."

Brick affectionately responded, "I can't say anything about who you were or who you used to be. All I know is that in the last few days, I have enjoyed every minute I spent with you. Your laughter and your love made each of my days a little brighter."

Mary Jane smiled, saying, "Thank you."

Brick then asked, "But how did the preacher help?"

Mary Jane told him the actions of that crazy preacher also helped open her eyes, and she went on to say, "He scared the hell out of me, and his attack showed me that I still could care for friends and others. I learned that there is still some fight left in me. It's almost funny to think about it; the passion I felt for you and the fear and sorrow he created made it clear that I am still alive, and I need to act like it. It may be crazy to think this way, but in a sense you both helped bring me back to reality. I guess the biggest thing I learned last night was that life should be lived and not taken for granted. This past year, I've avoided friends and family. I have lived in a self-constructed bubble, allowing no one in; and, if I did allow someone into my life, it was on my terms—not based on mutual need or respect. It's been a tough year, and the fire last night showed me I was wrong, and that I do need others."

Brick considered Mary Jane's words and began to realize too that even with the night being tragic, it was also beautiful. He too had learned from the experience. Maybe for the first time in his eighteen years, he was beginning to "be" an adult. Could it be he too had learned something from the crazy preacher?

Epilogue

It was no surprise that the revue failed to open following the attack. The damage resulting from the fire left little to salvage. The structural loss was one thing, but the mental anguish had lasting effects.

The emotional pain endured by the dancers was far greater than the damage to the tent. Misty and Lucy only spent one night in the hospital, but it would be weeks before anyone was ready to return to the stage. Everyone associated with the revue feared the possibility an attack could happen again and at what cost to them—both mentally and physically? All were left questioning their future.

Jill never joined the dancers on stage as Brick and Ray had hoped, but she did reach out to the girls after the attack. She saw Ray as a special friend and a much-needed distraction from her personal doubts, and he had given her the desire to develop new friendships. Once the fair packed up and moved from Sanford, she realized she now had a family with Howard's. She felt the love and support from those who had suffered through the attack.

Odom failed to realize his success in bringing down the show. Although temporary, his actions would keep the revue from reopening for several weeks. It would be early October before Howard's Amusements would feature the revue again, and that would not be until they traveled to Dobson, North Carolina, for the Surry County fair. When it did open, it was with tighter security and a new look—and without Mary Jane Morris. To many, the attack served as an accelerant to Raeford's prediction that the shows would soon disappear, becoming part of carnival lure and history—no longer being a staple at the county fairs.

For Mary Jane, the day of the bombing would turn out to be her last day with Howard's. It took the destruction of the revue to close a dark chapter in her life. She made the decision to stop running from her sorrow and returned to her home in Clover, South Carolina. Fortunately, her parents had not given up on her, and she was welcomed back with open arms. With the help of others, she realized the need to accept life as it was—not what she had planned. In the last year, she had suppressed her feelings following the death of her fiancé. It had impacted her more than she realized, but she had now gained a better understanding of what she needed to do to move forward. The pain would only become more manageable with her recognizing and dealing with it. The experiences she had while working at the revue and with Howard's gave her insight into not only who she was but also who she hoped to be.

One of the more valuable lessons she took from the entire experience was the need to accept vulnerability. She needed to own her feelings so she could begin to grow as a person. She also realized she was not living the life Dale would have wanted her to; he would be disappointed that she had lost her way without him. Dale loved her, and he loved her approach to living. He often told her how her take on life, full of energy and curiosity, was what he loved most about her. The attack had awakened her old self, and she now realized it was time to take on life again.

Mary Jane's awakening led her to the reality of her weakness. It was clear that pain had found her, but joy was something she needed to find for herself. It was time she started accepting the ups and downs of life. She made the decision to honor Dale and the love they shared by being the person he knew and loved. No longer would she avoid her feelings; she would celebrate them: the good, the bad, and the indifferent.

Brick and Ray returned to work on Saturday and helped with the show moving on to Tarboro. That one week with the fair gave them a new perspective also. From love to hate and from fear to bravery, both had a new understanding of life. The two of them learned many life lessons about others, as well as themselves. It was an education neither had expected, but both cherished.

Two days after finishing up their time with Howard's, Brick and Ray arrived on the campus of Elon College. They were now different individuals. Their experiences at the fair affected each of them differently.

For Brick, the time he spent with Mary Jane revealed confidence he had not known before. His experiences that week failed to diminish his love for Emily, but it did change how he viewed their relationship. He no longer would allow the relationship to be defined by fear and uncertainty. He now believed he had more to offer and was ready for the experiences that awaited him at Elon. If the relationship with Emily was going to survive and develop into a mature relationship, it would be because of who he was—not the person he thought he should be. Maybe witnessing the pain brought on by the bombing gave Brick the understanding he needed to be true to himself. Brick had learned a valuable lesson; he could love, and he could grow—with or without Emily in his life.

Ray was happy that he made the decision to join Brick on this adventure. His experiences that week, although similar to Brick's, did little to change his approach to life. He had always been full of self-confidence, and his time with Jill only added to that. He did appreciate the time he spent with her, but he knew from the beginning that it would never be more than a week's fling, if that. His relationship with Donna was solid and possibly prevented him from doing something he would later regret.

The week proved to be beneficial for both Brick and Ray. They had learned more about the real world than they had through any class or textbook. Both knew before accepting the job with Howard's that the challenges of college and adulthood were just beginning, but thanks to their week there, they now had previously untapped potential to face those challenges, and it felt good. They realized that one week with the fair did not give them a pass for future problems, but at least now they knew they could move on from adversity. No matter what came their way, they felt they had a fighting chance to handle the situation. They both looked at the week with Howard's as stepping up to the first rung of the ladder to adulthood.

The Saturday after the attack proved to be a hectic day once the gates opened. If anybody stayed away due to the attack, it was not noticeable. Various reasons were given for the tremendous turnout. Those who felt optimistic about the fair and what it meant believed it was a show of support. Others felt that maybe it was because of curiosity seekers wanting to see what had happened. Whatever the reason, it was a banner day, and it appeared everyone was having fun. There would be few distractions other than the usual ones created by too much alcohol. On this day, no protesters were around to disrupt the fun everyone was having. It reflected the way Raeford had always felt the fair should be—fun and entertaining. To him, the best part of the day was seeing people enjoying themselves—playing games, eating fair food, and riding the rides. The Lee County fair again was a place for family fun and excitement.

The damage from the fire was clearly visible, and the area was roped off from those wishing to get a closer look. The site, now an eyesore, caused few distractions. The damage to the tent could easily be replaced, but the cost of the attack on the emotions of the dancers was another story. Had Odom and his church won? Maybe so. They had at least won this battle.

Raeford felt pride in how everyone came together—the entertainers, the workers, and now the patrons. All were in support of an American tradition like no other—the county fair. The fair and Howard's Amusement would continue to live on with or without the revue.

It was nearly a week before Odom was arraigned and given bond so that he could return home to await trial. The charges of arson and endangerment of life remained. He avoided being charged with attempted murder, although some in the judicial system pushed for this charge. With the attack, Odom gained the publicity he desired, and there were those in the community who came to his defense. Even though his actions were selfish, they did create an awareness of the morality of the shows.

Jimmy Key and Gail greeted Odom and Beverly when they arrived at home. Key had failed Odom, and he was not sure how Odom would react to his being there. Words were few, and they did not bring up the past. Although there were some hard feelings on both sides, they were able to forgive and rebuild their friendship.

The local religious community voiced their support for him and his church, but all were thankful no one was seriously injured from the attack. The ministerial community began understanding Odom's passion and his mission. Although his actions were misplaced, they now believed there was a need for change. Hinson and a small group of his followers from Wayne County came to the first service Odom preached after he was released from jail. It was the biggest crowd ever assembled at The Revival Revolutionary Church.

Back in the pulpit, Odom asked for forgiveness. He had learned a valuable lesson. No longer an impatient showman, he was a changed man; he was becoming a man of faith. His time in jail and the realization of Beverly's true love now gave him hope. If prison were in his future, he would accept it and try his best to find new ways to serve the Lord. He understood the wrong he had done, and he now had a genuine understanding of biblical responsibility.

The bombings had thrust Sanford and Lee County into the headlines of the state's news. The attack shone a light on the town and the revue. Although the attention would be short-lived, it served as another indication that the summer of '69 would be one to remember for years to come.

Printed in the United States
by Baker & Taylor Publisher Services